AHEAD FULL

AHEAD FULL
THE KURTHERIAN GAMBIT™ BOOK 19

MICHAEL ANDERLE

DISRUPTIVE IMAGINATION

DON'T MISS OUR NEW RELEASES

Join the LMBPN email list to be notified of new releases and special promotions (which happen often) by following this link:

http://lmbpn.com/email/

This book is a work of fiction. All of the characters, organizations, and events portrayed in this novel are either products of the author's imagination or are used fictitiously. Sometimes both.

Copyright © 2017 Michael T. Anderle
Cover by Gene Mollica and Sasha Almazan
https://www.gsstockphoto.com/
Internal Artwork © 2017 Michael T. Anderle Drawn by Eric Quigley

LMBPN Publishing supports the right to free expression and the value of copyright. The purpose of copyright is to encourage writers and artists to produce the creative works that enrich our culture.

The distribution of this book without permission is a theft of the author's intellectual property. If you would like permission to use material from the book (other than for review purposes), please contact support@lmbpn.com. Thank you for your support of the author's rights.

LMBPN Publishing
PMB 196, 2540 South Maryland Pkwy
Las Vegas, NV 89109

Version 2.2 March 2023
eBook ISBN: 978-1-64971-586-9
Print ISBN: 978-1-64202-084-7

The Kurtherian Gambit (and what happens within / characters / situations / worlds) are copyright © 2015-2023 by Michael T. Anderle and LMBPN Publishing.

THE AHEAD FULL TEAM

Beta Editor / Readers

Bree Buras (Aussie Awesomeness)
Timothy Cox (The Myth)
Tom Dickerson (The man)
S Forbes (oh yeah!)
Dorene Johnson (US Navy (Ret) & DD)
Dorothy Lloyd (Teach you to ask...Teacher!)
Diane Velasquez (Chinchilla lady & DD)

JIT Beta Readers

Kelly ODonnell
Micky Cocker
James Caplan
Larry Omans
Paul Westman
Keith Verret
Kimberly Boyer
John Findlay

Tim Bischoff
Sarah Weir
Mike Pendergrass
John Raisor
Alex Wilson

Thanks to our JIT Readers for this Version

Dave Hicks
Diane L. Smith
Deb Mader
Rachel Beckford
Peter Manis
Kerry Mortimer
James Caplan
Timothy Cox (the myth)

If I missed anyone, please let me know!

Original Editors
Stephen Russell
Lynne Stiegler

This version edited by
Lynne Stiegler

Thank you to the following Special Consultants for AHEAD FULL

Jeff Morris - US Army - Asst Professor Cyber-Warfare, Nuclear Munitions (Active)

*To Family, Friends and
Those Who Love
To Read.
May We All Enjoy Grace
To Live The Life We Are
Called.*

BABA YAGA

ART BY ANDREW DOBELL

LEATH MILITARY

THE KURTHERIAN (tm) GAMBIT

CHAPTER ONE

<u>The QBS *Princess Alexandria*, in Transit</u>

Franath D'Tzaa, a D'tereth vid reporter, touched the recording symbol after reviewing her notes.

"Hello. My name is Franath D'Tzaa. I'm aboard the QBS *Princess Alexandria*, a Nacht Fleet battleship and presently the flagship of Empress Bethany Anne, who is returning with her team from Nodrizen's World.

"What follows is a continuation of the interview we aired yesterday. In this section I ask the Empress about the Leath and how that relationship has worked for the Etheric Empire over the last few decades. And here she is."

"Empress, the Etheric Empire has been involved in different arguments—some would say battles or wars—with the Leath for many decades now. Would you tell us why, in your opinion, these two powerful spacefaring races do not get along?"

The Empress leaned back in her chair, her initial smile fading. "Certainly. It has everything to do with the Kurtherians, who claim to be their gods." She looked at the reporter. "You have seen our videos, correct?"

"Who hasn't?" Franath replied. "Every few years there has

been a battle on some world or another between the Empire and the Leath. Afterwards they spin their story, and your people provide video proof that they're wrong. Unless someone was present for the altercation, it would be impossible to tell what is truth."

"I believe quite a few of your audience know the history of the Kurtherians," Bethany Anne replied. "There were twelve tribes, or clans, who believed they were ready to Ascend. They also believed they should help other alien species Ascend. Unfortunately, seven of the twelve went down a darker road, and their efforts to assist other races has somehow become twisted. Each of the seven clans support their races differently. Some, like the late Yollin king, used his advanced abilities to drive the native Yollins from power. From what we understand, the Kurtherians from the Phraim-'Eh clan who rule Leath are working to move them up the Ascension path."

Bethany Anne stopped a moment, pursing her lips in thought. "Well, *their* version of the Ascension path, anyway. There are many thoughts on that," she clarified. "However, supposition is that for the Leath to gain the next level in their enlightenment, they must defeat the Etheric Empire."

Franath looked down at her notes, then back up at the Empress, who was waiting patiently for her. The reporter finally spoke. "I'm sorry, but I can't find where this has been mentioned before."

"I understand," Bethany Anne nodded. "This is supposition by a Kurtherian consultant…"

"'Consultant?'" Franath jumped on Bethany Anne's statement. "I've never heard that term."

"And I'm not going to explain it to you," Bethany Anne countered, "so don't even ask."

Franath bit her tongue. If she screwed up this interview, she would never get another chance with the enigmatic leader of the Etheric Empire, and probably wouldn't leave with her interview material intact either. She was completely aware of others who had left with video the Etheric Empire didn't wish to air, only to find the video damaged by the time the person was in a position to attempt to make a copy.

"Is this a business?" Franath finally asked, trying to find a way to score the contact. "Do they have additional resources I can verify?"

Bethany Anne sent to TOM, *Do you have additional resources?*

I don't know how to answer your question, Bethany Anne. Are you suggesting I out myself?

Sure, TOM. It's as easy as saying 'TOM, come out of the closet'... or in this case, 'Come out of the human, TOM.' TOM, come out of the human!'

Ha...ha. Believe it or not, being inside you hasn't always been bitches and dreams.

What the hell, TOM? Bitches and dreams?

There was a momentary pause before TOM answered, **Peaches and cream?**

Ha! Bethany Anne barked a laugh in their mental discussion. *That is the funniest shit you have said all week.*

Ba-dum crash! I'll be here all week. And next week and the month following and probably the next decade until we can go looking for a mysterious race of creatures who can pull me out of you.

Don't worry, my friend. Bethany Anne turned her attention back to the reporter. *I haven't forgotten that.*

Bethany Anne spoke to Franath. "I imagine this consultant could answer questions. However, he is, as you might imagine, not fond of having others know much about him or his location." Bethany Anne crossed her legs, then leaned forward in her chair and winked at Franath. "I'll give you a contact routing through the galactic mail."

Franath wondered what was wrong with the Empress' eye.

Bethany Anne leaned back in her chair. "To return to the

topic at hand, we have based our strategy on what the Kurtherian 'gods' behind the Leath are doing. This is why we have played a longer game."

"It has been," Franath agreed, "some time since your last altercation. However, at this point both sides are again enhancing their militaries. In fact," Franath glanced down at some notes, "this has caused fourteen different spacefaring races to embark upon their own military buildup." Franath looked Bethany Anne in the eyes. "Do you have any thoughts about this?"

"About which part?" Bethany Anne asked, a glimmer of humor in her eyes. "That we haven't fought in a while, that others are willing to support their own ability not to be pushed around, or something completely different?"

Franath considered her options, then asked. "The fact that other groups are building up their militaries."

"I think it is a good thing."

Franath waited a moment before realizing Bethany Anne wasn't going to add to her comment. "Why?"

"As I mentioned, if you can put up a good defense then other races pause before trying to take you over."

Franath continued, "Are there any negatives to other races doing this?"

"Of course," Bethany Anne responded. "Those with large militaries start looking either inside or outside to see what they can do with that military. A despotic regime could take power and use the military to subjugate their own people, or a particularly aggressive group could come to power and decide to push their luck by attacking others."

"Is this the reason the Etheric Empire keeps fighting the Leath? Or, at least, this is what you are proposing is the reason?"

"Yes." Bethany Anne kept her answer short, waiting for the likely follow-up.

"And why is that?" Franath continued.

Bingo, Bethany Anne thought. *I love to answer this.*

Bethany Anne looked into the camera, allowing the barest bit of red to infuse her eyes. "Because I really, really hate bullies."

The video clip ended and the reporter finished her piece with, "This is Franath D'Tzaa signing off. I will provide another clip tomorrow from my interview with one of the most intriguing beings of our galaxy."

Planet Leath

Hours later, the Leath Prime One Intelligence officer watched the interview in the comfort of his own living space. He had paid personally for the intelligence so it didn't go through the Leath infrastructure, and at the moment he wasn't sure if he had just damned himself or possibly liberated his people.

He re-watched the video one last time, trying to commit the information to memory. Then he shook his head. Getting up from his seat, he made his way to an old desk on the lowest level in his home. He opened a drawer and extracted an old tablet he had used in his youth before he could afford better tools.

He turned the unit on, surprised to see that it had been charged recently enough to still have power. He would have thought it had lost its charge over the many years since he had last powered it up.

He plugged in the password and was surprised to see a note appear.

"Hello, Jerrleck. This is you, from earlier in your life. If I am correct, you have had your memories modified by the Seven."

Jerrleck stopped, realizing immediately that if he continued, whatever he learned could possibly be accessed by the Seven. He wasn't sure how deeply they read minds, but he was positive they scanned his topmost thoughts.

He dared to read another line.

"If you read any farther, realize what I say below may possibly be discovered by the Seven." Jerrleck smiled. At least the younger him and present him were both intelligent Leath.

"If you are still reading," the note continued, "I have had plenty of time to realize what must have happened to our people, to me and consequently to you. Think about just how many Leath have been killed in our war against the Etheric Federation, and how many more will die if we continue this attempt to Ascend our people under the direction of the Seven."

Jerrleck considered the truth of this statement. Only a few years ago he'd helped one of his best friends mourn their only daughter.

All because the Leath had been told to take over a world the Leath had no business or interest in ruling. He had done the numbers…

Jerrleck's eyes opened and other information started pouring into his mind. He stood up and walked to the opposite wall in the windowless room. Feeling down a line, he found a small indentation and pushed it.

The wall opened.

Jerrleck stopped a moment, knowing this was his point of no return. He wasn't sure just how long ago he had been mindwiped, but it was apparent that he had. He put the tablet down and walked back up the steps to the main level. It took him only a short amount of time to secure his residence against intrusion and return to the bottom level.

Now it was time to see what his younger self had been into, and what he could do with it now that he was older and hopefully wiser.

An hour later he was in a state of shock. His mind was confused, but in his heart the path was clear.

He needed to revive a rebellion that had been put on hold until he became aware of it. The last leader had been taken away in the middle of the night.

He should know—he had pulled her from her bed and taken her to the Seven himself.

He looked at the monitor in this hidden room and ran a finger across the image on the screen. "Dur'loch, my love," he whispered. *"This will be for you."*

QBBS *Meredith Reynolds*

The children huddled together—human, Yollin, Torcellen. Their frightened eyes darted around the massive space. The *bump, ba-bump, ba-bump* of their hearts seemed loud in their ears.

Their friends and the other young ones around them could definitely hear how scared they were, right?

Red lights illuminated the giant cave. In this area the asteroid's rock walls hadn't been smoothed. They were still rough.

Just as they had been when the ship was created so many decades before.

They had come in here, laughing together after their last fright, becoming closer as they weathered the challenges of this night.

However, this was the final room, and *she* was here.

The kids could feel it, and the fear was starting to get to them. Many grabbed the hands or appendages of the kid next to them. Those who had weathered the experience so far and kept up a strong front in the other rooms couldn't keep the fear from their eyes now.

"My name," the darkness hissed, its voice guttural, like stones rubbing against each other.

"Is Baba…*Yaga*…"

The lights were extinguished and the children screamed.

Seconds later—a time which seemed like an eternity—the massive lights came back on, the cave blazing white as the kids looked around, trying to find the lady with the voice.

"*There she is!*" a young male Yollin yelled, his mandibles open as he pointed toward the ceiling high above them.

And there she was indeed.

Her red eyes flashed at them, and her white hair hung loose over her shoulders as her black skin gleamed in the light. Every child there saw how long her claws were.

"Happy *Halllooweeeeennnn!*" She grinned, and they could see that her teeth had all been sharpened to points.

"*AHHH!*" Many girls (and more than a few guys) yelled when she disappeared from the walkway above.

The kids were glancing around, worrying she was coming down, when the exit doors opened. They recognized Empress' Bitches John and Scott. "Don't run!" John commanded, and the kids stopped.

"You know the drill!" Scott called. "You are all in the Etheric Academy. You will be orderly as you leave the Empress' Haunted House!"

How did I do? Bethany Anne's voice echoed in both her friends' heads.

I'd say a few will probably need a change of underwear, Scott sent back.

Some are wondering if that was really you or just a good hologram, John added as he listened to the kids' conversations. Their voices were excited as they chatted while waiting to exit the final room in the Haunted House.

No crying, though, Scott added. *I think maybe ten is the minimum age of those we should allow to come into this room of the Haunted House.*

I didn't ramp the fear up nearly as much as I did for that first batch, she replied. **I think I was trying to go for too much effect the first time.**

John watched as the kids raced to meet their parents at the end of the hall. Their excitement at seeing the avatar of the

Empress' displeasure, even if many were saying she was just a hologram, was evident in their expressions and loud chatter.

I think you might have started a tradition, John told her. *I hope you won't regret this.*

I'll get a hologram project going, she replied. ***I can use that same technology to display Bethany Anne from a distance. It will be good for us to have a backup plan to prove I'm around.***

And do it where? Scott asked. He walked over to two arguing human boys. The larger one pulled his hand back, only to have it enveloped in another hand. When the boy pulled it didn't budge, and he looked up to see that the problem was Scott.

The boy swallowed as Scott glared down at him. "Do you want," Scott asked, "to have a personal discussion with Baba Yaga?" Scott looked around the large cave. "This is part of where she lurks."

"Uhh…" The boy, his eyes flitting around the hallway, looked uncertain. "I thought she was a fake."

From above, a cackle could be heard. Those kids still in the room looked up to see a black-skinned woman, white hair floating in the wind and eyes red, looking down at them. "Do I look like a fake to you?" she hissed.

Scott had to catch the boy before he hit the ground when he fainted.

YES! Bethany Anne cackled in their minds. ***I've still got it! Bullies ain't got nothing on the Baba Yaga.***

Scott shook his head as he lifted the young boy into his arms and turned toward the door. "And how am I supposed to know which set of parents he belongs to?"

"Oh, I know," the other boy told Scott.

"Yeah?" Scott asked as they walked toward the door.

"Sure," the young boy replied. "He's my older brother."

CHAPTER TWO

Planet H'lageh, Two Jumps from Yollin Sector

The bar was very nice; even modern-looking to Christina's eyes. The H'lageh world wasn't very large. In fact, it only had four major cities, plus the Holy City and the occasional *very* small scientific outpost.

All these areas were situated on ground that rose above the darkness, the lower areas of the planet where the heavier gases had settled, and no light penetrated.

This planet was, Christina thought, *nice and tidy.* She had been on other planets, many larger than Yoll itself, which were covered in cities built anyplace that wasn't too wet or too steep.

Or in the case of Yrrmock, too volcanic.

This particular city probably had about two million inhabitants and her most recent boyfriend—or alien friend, whatever—hailed from this city. Christina had decided to ask about swinging by to transact business, since they were jumping through the Gate anyway…

Unfortunately, Prometheus, their ship's EI, had pulled her contact's name from the information he had plundered from the memory module of the robot entity Beethlock. A follow-up communication with Beethlock was simple, since he had been inserted into Bad Company's hierarchy after a failed attempt to take out Bad Company's primaries. His new role was nominally called "Keep your mouth shut and do what we tell you or suffer."

He was very supportive about locating additional information on Christina's latest interest. That person hadn't checked out, though, and Prometheus had notified Christina of the information.

She'd had an equally quick conversation with Prometheus, requesting that he *not* tell her mom…or her dad.

Especially her dad.

Now she was waiting patiently for Allahnzo to show up. He was a Torcellen, which was why Christina had never bothered to check his background herself.

Torcellens, by and large, didn't like violence. Given that, who would think one of them would get into the rough-and-tumble business of crime?

Certainly not her.

"You think he is going to show?" her Yollin uncle R'yhek asked while placing his now-empty drink back on the table.

Christina briefly thought back to how she had convinced R'yhek to join Bad Company years and years ago.

"If he doesn't," she answered, "I'll find his absent ass and carry him back up here so I can throw him out the window."

R'yhek glanced out said window, from which there was a drop of about four hundred or so feet to the ground below. The building they were in wasn't the tallest in the city, but it was close. "I don't think he will have anything polite to say to you after that drop," he commented, looking across the small table at Christina.

"I wouldn't want him to speak to me again in that case."

"That will do it," R'yhek agreed. "He can't speak if he is dead."

"There would not be a need to warn him to stay away from

me then, right?" Christina asked, her eyebrow arched the same way R'yhek had seen the Empress' do from time to time.

"I think you are trying too hard to be like the Empress, young Lowell," R'yhek answered, lifting his glass to tell the waiter that he wanted another drink. "They brew a good Pepsi here."

"Tastes more like New Coke to me." Christina took another sip of her cola and swished it around her mouth. "Yup, New Coke."

"Whaaaat?" R'yhek looked aghast. He opened his mandibles wide, then lifted the glass to his nose and sniffed. "Smells different, but taste is closer to Pepsi than Coke."

"It's a thing from old Earth," she answered. "At one time, according to Uncle Scott, Coke was getting its ass kicked by Pepsi in something called the Pepsi Challenge. So, Coca-Cola, in their ignorant wisdom, decided to fuck with the recipe. They tried to create a taste similar to Pepsi."

"How did it go?" the Yollin asked, intrigued with an event on a planet so far away he couldn't write enough zeros after the first number.

She smirked. "They took it off the market once the fans rose up with pitchforks and matches to get their Original Recipe back. From the standpoint of introducing a new product, it failed miserably. From the standpoint of energizing the true believers, it was amazing." Christina thought for a moment. "I imagine we can blame the Empress for this."

"What?" R'yhek looked at the glass of cola the waiter had just brought. "Why?"

"She thought the whole Pepsi thing was funny, until she realized that when she is off on one of her walkabouts she can't get Coke a lot of the time."

R'yhek smirked. He loved the Empress, but it *was* rather funny the royal lady couldn't find Coke because of a snafu in her plan to distribute Pepsi in areas that weren't supporting her.

He saw Christina's head move and looked up to see that

Allahnzo had arrived, accompanied by two goons. Oh, they dressed better than normal goons, but most Torcellens didn't keep Skaine mercs around them unless they were into mischief.

The odds were much better that an individual Torcellen would be into crime than that two Skaines were doing something legal.

R'yhek noticed that everyone else in the bar was moving to the walls. Allahnzo wasn't getting any closer. Apparently, he knew about human females' feelings when they felt shafted.

"Toss me out the window?" Allahnzo asked conversationally.

"Oops," Christina spoke aloud, "You have me on microphone?"

Allahnzo glanced at the Skaine to his left. "Apparently it is for my own good." The Skaine smirked and nodded. Allahnzo returned his eyes to Christina. "You are not quite the docile little business mogul's daughter I thought you were."

"Nor are you the proper Torcellen I was expecting," Christina admitted. "I'll admit I allowed your white hair to sway me a little." Her eyes flashed yellow so fast Allahnzo wasn't sure if they had changed or he had just caught a reflection.

He smiled and ran a hand through his hair. "I *am* proud of my hair, that is true," he admitted. It ran halfway down his back. "But it is a pain to brush out."

"I know," Christina hissed, annoyed. "I did it for you twice, you prick."

"I'm not sure I want to know what you just mumbled," Allahnzo called.

Christina smiled. "Come closer and I'll repeat it for you."

"I think not," Allahnzo admitted. "My advisors suggest there is only one way to appropriately end this relationship."

"Oh?" Christina cocked her head. "And what is that?"

Allahnzo snorted. "Turn you in and collect your bounty," he told her.

R'yhek smothered his response.

Christina rolled her eyes. "I'm not wanted by the Empress' Rangers, dickhead."

"Who said it was an Empire bounty?" Allahnzo answered, smiling. "And while I will miss you running your hands through my hair, you are going to have to…"

"I won't be taken anywhere alive, asshat." Christina's eyes flared yellow.

"Who said anything about alive?" the Skaine goon on Allahnzo's right asked as he raised a small tube he had been holding at his side and fired.

Christina didn't see R'yhek move, but she was shoved violently out of the way. A small rocket raced across the space and hit the older Yollin in the chest, blowing him backward to crash through a window.

"R'YHEK!" Christina yelled as she untangled herself from the chairs he had just shoved her into. She raced for the broken window. "You haven't heard the last of me!" she cried as she dove out the same window.

There was a chuckle from beside Allahnzo. "Diving forty-four floors? I think we *have* heard the last of her."

"*Bistok shit!*" R'yhek had shouted when the small rocket slammed into his chest. Fortunately, he'd worn a chest protector over his carapace, or he probably would have more issues to deal with than falling at a phenomenal rate toward the ground somewhere under him.

He was annoyed when Christina Bethany Anne Lowell threw herself out the window in a dive, heading in his direction.

Really fast.

He squinted and caught a slight blue line under her clothes.

R'yhek opened his arms just before Christina managed to slam into him, grabbing him securely and twisting herself under him. For most humans, that would have been a good way to ensure they died quickly—smashing into pavement under him.

For Christina, it was a way to brace him as the antigravity pucks in her suit slowed them down.

"Didn't you think about the fact that we were going to be on a high floor in a building?" she scolded, gasping in relief when it became obvious she had caught him in time. "When we get somewhere safe I'm going to kill you for scaring me!" She glanced over her shoulder to see what was below, looking for a place to land.

He pointed with his left hand. "That building with the orange roof. We have a back entrance to the tunnels over there."

They stopped going straight down and turned, heading toward a building three blocks away.

"Mong, you are the basest individual I know." Allahnzo grimaced as his Skaine bodyguard walked over to the broken window, his boots crunching across pieces of shattered glass.

"It's not every day you get to see a couple of nice splats from so high up," he called back. "Don't worry your Torcellen sensitivities, I won't give you a detailed description of the two bodies. Their blood and gore—" He smirked when he heard Allahnzo rush behind the bar to throw up in the sink.

He looked over the ledge, being careful not to cut himself on the broken panes. His eyes narrowed in confusion.

He didn't see any splats. While there were some shrubs and trees, he had been expecting big splotches and the little dots of beings milling around two dead bodies.

He heard Allahnzo's hoarse whisper from behind him. "I hate you, Mong."

Mong backed away from the window and turned around, glancing at Ming and shook his head. Ming's eyebrows raised in surprise.

"Then you really are going to hate what I tell you next, boss." Mong looked at the Torcellan, who was using a bar rag to wipe his face. "She's not dead."

Allahnzo's eyes opened wide.

"I think you are getting fat," Christina grumped as she released R'yhek a yard or so above the ground. She sent the message to cut her antigrav suit's power and dropped the last couple of feet herself. She landed lightly, barely bending her knees when she hit the ground.

R'yhek waved her off. "And you didn't have your armor on."

"What good did *your* antigrav suit do you here?" she retorted as the two left the back lawn. R'yhek took the lead as they went down a flight of stairs.

"Like *your* antigrav suit would have stopped that rocket, little one," he replied as he entered a fourteen-digit code into the locked door. It clicked and he cracked it and stuck his head inside, then opened the door fully and nodded her in.

She walked past him and checked out the room as he shut the door behind them. "Can we leave it with, 'We were both caught with our pants down and together we made it through another close scrape?'" She looked around. "Now, where is the weapons cache in this place?" She walked over to the walls as R'yhek watched her. "I need something rather large to return the fucking favor."

"No weapons," R'yhek answered, and Christina stopped abruptly. "What? Why?" she asked, confusion writ large on her face as she turned around. Then she saw that a video connection had turned on.

Her lips pressed together as she saw who was staring back at her.

"Hello, Father." She smiled, knowing Allahnzo was going to get his just desserts.

It just wasn't going to be from her.

Prometheus Major, Three Hours Later

Nathan Lowell had just finished reviewing the incoming intelligence from the planet below when there was a knock on the door. He shook his head and looked up, waiting for the small green light to flash above it. He leaned back as the door slid open and his daughter entered.

"Don't say a word, or I will have you shipped back to the *Meredith Reynolds* so fast your seat won't even be warm from your butt hitting it before you have to exit the shuttle."

"I am a—" Christina started to say.

Nathan cut her off. "Out-of-control human female who isn't thinking past her emotions at the moment." He nodded at R'yhek, who looked like he didn't want to enter the room. "Come in and close the door."

The large Yollin nodded and stepped in, allowing the door to shut.

"If Mother were here—" Christina started, and stopped again when Nathan put up his hand.

"Your mother is not here because I told her she couldn't come until she stopped throwing shit around and screaming at you."

Christina stopped, her mouth open. A moment later, she closed her mouth.

"Exactly." Nathan nodded, then pointed to the two chairs between them and his desk. "Sit your asses down."

Once they were settled, Christina's shock at her mother's reaction started to wear off. "Um, how did Mom know about it?"

"You wore an atmosuit, which you checked out before you left. They have full audio-visual interfaces." He raised an eyebrow. "Remember?"

"Oh!" was all Christina could say.

"Yes, 'oh' is right," Nathan agreed. "Your mother is mad enough to first punish you for putting yourself in danger like that, and then hit Allahnzo down below so hard his dead grandparents back on Torcellen for the last six generations will all feel it."

"Well," Christina looked up, fire in her eyes, "they can't take a shot at Bad Company like this and expect to get away with it!"

"And they won't." A new voice joined the conversation. It was female, with a slight old-Earth Latina accent. "Because this is a Ranger problem, not something Bad Company should get into."

Christina and R'yhek looked toward their right at a life-sized hologram which had just appeared. The woman in it buckled her belt before she slid a pistol into the attached holster. "Hello, Niece. R'yhek."

The look of resignation that washed over Christina's face was priceless. Well, at least Nathan thought it was. "Hello, Aunt Tabitha." Christina bit her lip. "I don't suppose you would want any help down below?" she asked, her voice softer than a moment before.

An Asian male's head popped into the hologram next to Tabitha's, but his body didn't appear. "No."

The head disappeared.

"That's not fair!" Christina called. "You can't just pop in and say no, Uncle Hirotoshi!"

The head popped back in. "Yes I can."

The head disappeared once more.

Nathan was doing all he could to keep his face stern. Christina knew how to manipulate her parents, but she got flummoxed when she dealt with Tabitha and the Tontos. Especially if Ryu or Hirotoshi got involved.

Tabitha lifted a necklace over her head, the "2" pendant dangling. She caught it and put it under her shirt. Grabbing a long coat, she slid her right arm in and then the left. "We will be leaving in twenty minutes. See you in about seven hours, Nathan. We will call with the coordinates of where we want to meet in ten minutes."

"Understood, Tabitha. Nathan out." He cut the communication and turned back to his daughter. "You both need to see Bastek. She wants to make sure you're okay after your unscheduled flight." He looked at R'yhek. "And you need to decide if you are going to be nanocyte-modified or step out of operations."

"What?" Christina turned to look at R'yhek. "You aren't considering quitting, are you?"

"That discussion," his Yollin voice softened when he noticed the anxiety in her eyes, "will happen at another time." He stood up. "Let's go see Bastek before she darts us."

Christina stood and walked around her chair to step up beside him.

Nathan caught part of their conversation as they left his office.

"You remember when she darted Shi-tan for ignoring her call to come get checked out last year?"

The old Yollin barkeeper started chuckling. "Or the time she drugged Shi-tan's drink to get him in for his annual physical?" he countered.

He heard the two laughing as they went down the passageway, heading, he hoped, toward the medical wing of the ship.

Or there would be another story running through the ship about how Bastek darted Christina for not coming to medical after an op.

Nathan sighed as he stood up, a couple of his bones popping as he walked to his private exit between his office and the route to his quarters.

He hoped his mate had cooled down. If not, he might just dart *her*.

. . .

QBBS _Meredith Reynolds_

Are you kidding me? Dio looked up at Tabitha, his furry head cocked to the side. _You are leaving me to babysit Kouki?_

Tabitha drew a brush through her hair. "Look, I'm not the one who had to bring his armor to R&D here because he thought it was too tight."

Dio chuffed.

"I didn't call you fat. You can't _get_ fat," Tabitha argued. "You are the one who watched too many Japanese karate flicks from Earth and decided to try that back two-and-a half kick against Ryu."

It would have worked... Dio bitched, then saw Tabitha looking down at him, her eyebrow raised. _Well, it would have worked if I hadn't tried it against a Japanese vampire. Plus, my armor kinked up mid-kick._

"Was that before or after Ryu's foot smashed into your body and sent you flying like Underdog?"

Oh, please! Dio whined. _Never compare me to that cartoon!_

Tabitha chuckled. "Would you rather I suggest you are Scooby-Doo?"

Well, he owns his fear and he gets stuff done. I kinda like him. He laid down on the floor near Tabitha, his forepaws crossed and his head on his legs, and looked up at her. _"I'd rather be compared to Scooby-Doo than Underdog."_ He barked in laughter. _That would make you either Shaggy or Daphne._

"Hey!" Tabitha looked down and pointed her brush at him, her eyes narrowed. "I could be Velma."

Dio continued looking at her, saying nothing.

"Okay," Tabitha retracted the brush, "maybe not Velma."

Certainly not Velma, Dio responded. _I'm not saying you aren't smarter than Daphne, and while your hacking skills kick ass, some of your other skills..._

"Like what other skills?"

Common sense, logical reasoning... Dio started.

Tabitha glared back at her friend. "I'm so not going to miss you on this assignment."

Dio chuffed in laughter. *You will miss me, but it won't be long before I get my armor back. Jean figured out why the armor links kinked in the first place. She's not only fixing mine but all the other dogs', and they will use the modified connectors in the humans' armor as well.*

"Humans can do that?" Tabitha considered her gyrations when she kicked. "I don't think I can flip and turn on my back like you did."

The ninja in the movie did! Dio replied, *so why not you?*

"Uh..." Tabitha shrugged. "Okay, you got me there. I'm a rather straightforward no-flash kinda woman."

Dio looked at her.

"Okay, so sometimes I like to dress up," Tabitha tempered.

Dio kept looking at her, without blinking.

"And put on makeup, and do my hair. Perhaps a little perfume," she continued.

Like that time we went on the dark side of Greelah? Dio asked.

Tabitha thought about it a moment. "Oh, you mean 'Greelat.' How was I supposed to know their pets found the smell of my perfume a bit unsettling?"

Unsettling? You mean all of them threw up after you passed. That's what you call 'a little unsettling?'

"Well, yes," Tabitha replied.

And that, Dio finished the conversation, *is why you can't be Velma.*

CHAPTER THREE

Planet H'lageh, Two Jumps from Yollin Sector

The svelte ship slipped through the clouds of H'lageh like a fish through water, leaving barely a trace as it glided through the atmospheric gases.

Coming in on the dark side, it dropped through the second level of the darkness that covered most of the planet, making it unsuitable for habitation. The murkiness kept sunlight from reaching anything underneath it, and only those who could tolerate the darkness, the stench, and the heavier gases that settled below the five locations where the cities had been built could stay alive.

The ship didn't care. It could slide through space, after all.

Five locations on the planet rose above the darkness and were flat enough for habitation. Those spots had sprouted cities.

Four major cities, and the Holy City.

The sleek craft cut through the darkness without error, its advanced sensors easily guiding the ship through the artificial night as its three human passengers took a few moments out of their schedule to enjoy some tea.

And a bit of pre-operation banter.

"And *I* say," Tabitha looked over at Hirotoshi, "that you will get shot in the ass by a young female."

Hirotoshi's eyes narrowed. "You are basing this prognostication on what, Kemosabe?"

Tabitha shrugged her shoulders. "It is the most unlikely event to occur, but if it does I will be crowned 'Queen of the Most Unlikely Guess!'"

Ryu's eyes sparkled with humor as Hirotoshi glanced at him. Hirotoshi looked back at the woman. "And *you* will be bitten by a snake, causing you to fall from the fourth…no," he pointed at Tabitha, "the *third* floor of a building again."

"I have not fallen," she put a hand up toward Ryu as she looked over at him, "on purpose!" She turned back to Hirotoshi. "I have not fallen from a building in well over a decade."

"So, you are due." Hirotoshi smirked.

"Okay, so what is the bet?" Tabitha asked him.

"Manual clean-clothes folding," Ryu told them both.

"That is not fair!" they both exclaimed at the same time, each pointing at the other.

"That is why you," Ryu nodded toward Hirotoshi, "should be careful not to be shot by a young female and you," he turned to Tabitha, "should be careful not to get bitten by a snake or snake-like creature and fall from the third floor of a building."

The two used the hands they had pointed with to shake on the bet. Tabitha looked Hirotoshi dead in the eyes. "If you get shot in the ass, I won't let you forget it for a *dozen* years."

"*Hai*," Hirotoshi bowed his head slightly, "and if you fall from the third floor…"

"Again," Ryu interjected, and kept his silence when Tabitha glared at him.

"*Again*," Hirotoshi agreed, "I shall not let you forget it for…"

"Like forfucking*ever*!" Tabitha sighed. "You still talk about the time I stepped off that building on Earth."

"*Which* time?" Ryu asked, another smile evident in his eyes.

"I hate you both." Tabitha sighed. "A girl makes a few mistakes early in her life and it never ends."

"Oh, it could end," Hirotoshi admitted. "It would just mean you had outlived everyone who remembered your mistakes."

Tabitha shook her head. "Then keep harassing me for another thousand years, you two wonderful pains-in-the-ass." She stood up and grabbed her shoulder harness. "I swear."

"All the time," Ryu piped up.

"Every chance you get," Hirotoshi agreed as he stood up to retrieve his weapons.

"Because you two push me to it all the time," Tabitha finished. "No, I swear I am going to talk to Jean about getting a chest harness that fits better around these ta-tas. They are a completely annoying pain on my chest."

"And you don't just get them reduced, why?" Hirotoshi asked.

Tabitha looked at her friend, shocked. "Are you serious?" She turned to Ryu while pointing to Hirotoshi. "Is he serious?"

"Why would he not be serious?" Ryu asked, confused. "It is obvious they are in your way. There were shield maidens who, rumor had it, would…"

"Oh, *HELLLL* no!" Tabitha waved her hands and shook her head in the negative. "Neither one is coming off to help with shooting, or bows, or any shit like that. I researched it."

Achronyx' voice came over the speakers. "Actually, *I* did your research."

"Well," Tabitha huffed, "I had to ask you to research it, and had to come up with at least… Like… A *bunch* of questions to figure it out. There were maybe thirty—"

"Two," Achronyx corrected.

"Okay, thirty-two questions," Tabitha finished.

"There were only *two*, Tabitha," Achronyx corrected.

"Stop messing up my suitably accurate story with the facts, buddy," Tabitha mumbled as she went through the pockets on her coat, making sure all her toys were in the right places. She noticed Hirotoshi watching her. "I hate pulling the wrong surprise out of a pocket. Then we *all* get a surprise," she answered his unasked question.

Ryu looked at Hirotoshi, who shook his head and smiled briefly. "Remember the last time Tabitha's little coat of tricks fucked up a mission?"

"We would truly appreciate it as well," Hirotoshi spoke up, "if you did not pull the wrong surprise."

She looked up, her eyes wide open and her fingers pinched an inch apart. "Wow, one small accident on a Skaine slaver thirty-seven years ago, and it never ceases to haunt me."

"You blew up the ship," Ryu pointed out.

"Not before we got off," Tabitha countered, and locked down her knife.

"We were in the escape pod, which was still inside the ship when it blew." Hirotoshi chuckled as he confirmed his shoes were locked properly.

"Still in another ship...technically," Tabitha countered. "And you *always* get off due to the technicalities."

"Yes, that got you off the hook," Ryu admitted. "So, what is the plan, Kemosabe?"

"We go to where Christina and R'yhek were attacked and start making noises."

"So, Plan Two Twenty-one," Ryu confirmed.

Tabitha looked up, her face showing her confusion. She glanced at Hirotoshi. "Two twenty-one?"

"He means this is the two hundred and twenty-first variation of the same plan. Which is, 'Go in, make noise, find out who responds, and kick their ass.'"

"Well," Tabitha sniffed, "if it has worked two hundred and twenty times before?" She shrugged. "I don't know why we would mess with what works."

"*Hai*," Ryu agreed. "If it's not *broke*..."

"Don't fix it," Hirotoshi finished. He turned back to the weapons locker. "I'll grab some grenades."

"That little human piece of ass..." Allahnzo grumbled when he got off the video call. "MING!" he shouted.

The door to the office under his home opened. Down here, none of the outside noises could bother him. It was restful; peaceful.

Quiet.

Even his shout didn't reverberate. It was lost in the folds of the soft walls as his door opened.

He looked at his goon as Ming's head peered around the corner. "Go find out who is squawking about the girl and the Yollin, and take care of them."

"Do you have any concerns about the girl's company?" Ming asked. "They have a reputation."

"They might have a reputation, but they aren't here, so they called someone in. It's just a message for us not to do it again. Tell them to get lost, or *make* them get lost. I can't be responsible for everyone who falls off a flight and sinks into the darkness on this planet."

"Yes, bless the darkness, for it hides those we find annoying." Ming chuckled as he closed the door.

"Skaines. Can't live with them," Allahnzo whispered as he got back to work, "and can't live with them." He chuckled as he looked over the income and expense columns for the third largest city on the planet.

It looked like recreational drug use was down two percent. He would need to send a messenger to encourage the mayor in that city to start introducing the drugs into the schools at a younger age.

Tabitha had already glared twice at the alien barkeep, who had now left to go bitch at the owner or something for the last ten minutes.

The bartender had looked like a grey-furred Wookie to her. Except for the spider eyes—those gave her the heebie-jeebies. Walking up to the large plastic covering over the window, she slid her *katana* out of its sheath and made two cuts before returning the old sword to its sheath and ripping the plastic down to take a look outside.

While she was gazing outside, Ryu and Hirotoshi were paying attention to those in the bar who were watching the three off-worlders.

"Long way down," she commented. "Gutsy for Christina to jump out to catch him." She drew herself back into the bar. It was about sixty or seventy feet across and thirty or forty deep in places. There were a couple of round tables to her left that had walls around them and privacy curtains. Lots of dark cloth, so even in the daytime, it wasn't the brightest place.

Outside it was starting to fade to night, so it wasn't bright. Not that the three humans cared.

"We have visitors," Tabitha heard in her ear. She looked around and walked away from the window. She didn't need to take a one-way flight out the wrong exit like R'yhek had.

"Hide, Kemosabe." Hirotoshi spoke urgently.

Tabitha *moved*.

A moment later, she was hidden from the front entrance by the walls around one of the circular tables as she sat in the booth. "What's up?" she whispered.

"Your friends are here," Hirotoshi answered, a hint of humor in his voice when Tabitha had expected worry.

"What?" She sniffed the air, but the aromas in here were too intense. She couldn't smell anything new.

"Skaines," was his reply, and Tabitha rolled her eyes.

"Who are you?" she heard the first voice demand of the two vampires, and Tabitha had to hold her hand over her mouth to stifle her laughter.

Ryu was entirely too annoyed, due to her and Hirotoshi harassing each other, to be patient with a pair of Skaines. The *thump* she had expected after that was loud against the back wall of her booth.

Ryu, speaking Skaine, could be easily heard saying, "You will show respect, or you will take the new exit."

Tabitha could imagine Hirotoshi pointing helpfully to the window to confirm which exit Ryu meant.

His Skaine accent could use some help.

Something else hit the wall and Tabitha laid her head on the table, her shoulders shaking.

"You will learn it as well." Ryu's voice now held some anger. "Trying to shoot me is not appreciated."

"You have no idea," Tabitha heard one of the Skaines say as he used the wall of the booth to push against to get up. "You are in Nat-Nis Territory."

"I have no idea what Nat-Nis is, you're right," Ryu replied.

"We," the second voice stated, "run the four cities. You will not make it off this planet."

"And you," Hirotoshi entered the conversation, "have no idea who we are, so we are even."

"And I don't care," Voice Number One countered. "Here on H'lageh, we are the only ones who matter."

"What about the royal house?" Hirotoshi asked. "I'm sure they would be interested to hear that you believe they do not matter."

"They already know," hissed the first voice. "And thanks to your stupidity, we now have the extra help we need to teach you manners."

"Or kill you," Voice Two offered.

Tabitha unclipped her pistol and palmed it.

"We will take our leave now," the first Skaine told them. "Have a nice death."

Tabitha glanced out the window and noticed three two-seat antigrav units sliding into place, their wings and cockpits aimed in their direction.

"Oh, shit!" she called. "Window attack, guys!" Tabitha shot the glass, shattering it before she bolted toward the window. "I got right!"

She had to throw herself down when her target let loose, the rounds screaming above her and tearing apart the booth she had just occupied. She looked to her left and saw Hirotoshi hiding behind the bar, but had no idea where Ryu was. Glancing back, she noticed that the ceiling seemed to have a large rat clinging to it as the rounds pounded the wall behind her, shattering glass and ceramic.

She calculated where the righthand craft was and crouch-ran toward that window. At the last moment she stood up and jumped, planting her right foot on the sill and turning to see where the craft was. The pilot had only noticed her when she shoved off, throwing herself out of the bar into the air. She crossed the space between the building and the flyer and landed on it, her pistol aimed at the pilot through the clear canopy.

He freaked over the weapon aimed at him and reached for the eject lever. Pulling it blew his canopy off, and he made his exit. Tabitha had turned in time to avoid getting hit, but now she was on a plane with no seat and no pilot.

Achronyx, can you break into this? she sent.

Of course. Her EI sniffed.

Well, fucking do *it!*

It's already done, Ranger Two. Did you not notice the craft is staying still?

Tabitha smiled, but then saw the other two flyers starting to turn in her direction. "FUCK!" she screamed as the craft she was standing on rose straight up into the air, weapons fire from the other two passing below her.

"Hold still." The antigrav ship with Tabitha on it stopped suddenly. Her momentum didn't; she failed to hold on well enough and was tossed another thirty feet in the air. "Achronyyyxxxxx yoouuuuuu assssss!!!!!" She screamed as she tucked in and then out, her feet underneath her at the top of her arc. As she spun, she saw that the other two planes had bodies in black on them as well.

At least Ryu and Hirotoshi hadn't been late to the party.

She started coming down and activated her antigrav, sliding over to the right slightly to land where the pilot's seat had been. "Real fixer-upper," Tabitha grumbled as she ripped off some side padding and laid it on the bare metal. "Not enough badonkadonk cushion in these things."

"Guys?" she called. She received two affirmative responses in the form of their usual *"Hai."* "Let's go to the palace. Something isn't right here!"

The three small flyers turned away from the building and set course north by northwest, heading past the city's boundaries out across the darkness.

Inside the bar, the two Skaine goons watched them leave through the ruined windows.

Ming reached into his pocket and pulled out his tablet, then hit three buttons and waited. When he received the video signal, he spoke.

"Boss, we have a problem."

CHAPTER FOUR

Allahnzo observed Ming on the video screen as he gave his report. The Skaine seemed to have a small involuntary tic in his eye.

"Are you sure?" he asked, tapping a finger on his desk.

"Almost positive. She hasn't been seen in this area for a long time. We believed the last few rumors were false alarms or planted stories," Ming answered. "However, this human has the coat of the known true stories, and the two males are similar as well." Ming shrugged. "Plus, they took out three ships by jumping through the air from the building to the ships."

Competent foes. How annoying! "Where are they now?"

"On a north by northwest course," Ming replied as Allahnzo looked down at his notes.

His head shot back up.

"The Holy City?" Allahnzo asked, then forced himself to act calm and speak gently. "Are you telling me we have the fabled Ranger Two and two of her Tontos heading toward the Holy City right now?"

Ming nodded.

"Well, I guess I have to give it to Christina. She *is* having a last word." Allahnzo started typing a message. "However, it won't be the final word of our argument, not by a long shot." He pushed send. "I hope we didn't need those flyers."

"If we kill those three?" Ming blew out a lungful of air. "There are bounties on their heads that make the one on Christina's look like a third-tier slaver selling an old Yollin in comparison."

"Really?" Allahnzo looked back up. "Well, then Ranger Two is now my number-one focus." He saw that his message had received a reply, and read it quickly. "I've got to go. Meet me in the hanger."

Allahnzo shut off the video, grabbed his bag and tossed in his important books, and grabbed a coat. He hated going to the Holy City, because it was too cold to be enjoyable.

However, he was willing to suffer a little chill if it meant collecting a bounty from the Skaine Underground that would set him up for three or four *lifetimes*.

The three ships were flying in a delta pattern toward the Holy City. A woman's voice instructed, "Take the ships into evasive maneuvers as soon as you see... Oops, never mind."

The three ships started dipping, diving, rolling, and flying in evasive maneuvers as they tried to dodge the missiles that erupted from the four corners from the squared-off Holy City. Moments later, anti-ship weapons started firing as the three flyers sought to make it to the Holy City.

One by one they were shot down.

When the last ship was destroyed, Tabitha turned and offered the bag in her hand to Hirotoshi. "Want some? I added extra butter." She licked her fingers as Hirotoshi took the bag from her. "Popcorn is always good with explosions."

She reached over and grabbed a rag. "I'm young," she told no one in particular, "but I wasn't born yesterday." She tossed the rag into a bin. "Achronyx, which ship lasted the longest?"

"Ryu's ship lasted the longest and had the best parameters for escaping the onslaught of missiles and weapons fire."

"Ass Donkey *Mule*," Hirotoshi spat.

Tabitha snorted, looking over. "That's it? That's your epithet? Three different words for the same animal?"

"You do it too, Ranger Two," Hirotoshi replied.

Ryu fixed his sleeves. "You both owe me laundry."

"Night's not done, old man," Tabitha smirked. "Achronyx, take out the missile emplacements."

"When?" Achronyx asked.

"Now, would be...good," she answered, but the green Xs on the screen had already turned red by the time she had finished her sentence. "*Somebody* was locked and loaded."

"Thank you. I try," the EI answered.

"You think they know something is wrong?" Tabitha asked as the sleek silver ship rose through the darkness.

"Oh, probably by now," Hirotoshi answered, pointing to the screens on the far side of the bridge. Two of them were showing video feed from the walls. Multiple small figures turned to look in their direction as the large spacecraft rose from the miasma.

"Give me a moment," Tabitha requested and closed her eyes. "I have a call to make."

"It cannot be!" The princess kept her voice low. She doubted anyone had realized she had a video feed of what was happening outside the Holy City.

While all her people had suffered in the four cities, the royal house was now down to just her and her retainers.

Her father had taken the fight to those who had landed on the planet three seasons ago, and had died in the battle.

At the very end the leader of the enemy had walked up, said two words, and shot her father through the head. She could still see his faded bloodstains near the throne when she was forced to sit on it and parrot the pre-scripted messages those who held her people in thrall forced her to deliver.

The beautiful ship's exterior was like a mirror, shining in the evening light. Three missiles tore out of the remaining emplacements, only to be ripped apart in the sky. They did not even make it halfway to the ship.

This wasn't the monster of her dreams coming to save them. Rather, it was a beautiful ship of metal—one she knew hadn't been manufactured on her planet.

For generations her planet had remained isolated, staying off the galaxy's radar, but that had backfired on them. When they had been subjugated, no one noticed their communications had gone dark. Her people could not conceive or comprehend the evil that had befallen them. Raiders, drug runners, and slavers had come in and taken their planet from them.

Four major bases, one in each city, housed the enemy, as well as one here in the Holy City.

While those within the Holy City were hostages, the cities were in check. While the populace was threatened, the Holy City was in check. It was a stalemate the princess could not figure out how to break.

Her mom had tried to fight back, and Sis'talana had seen the enemy shoot the queen's defenders. Then they had cut her mother's hand off, which still clenched her blaster as it fell to the floor. A second sword then entered her back, erupting from her chest.

Sis'talana had watched as they rounded up one hundred people from each city and slaughtered them, retaliation for the four of their people who had been killed in the invasion.

The enemy allowed their people to go about their normal lives, as long as they obeyed the rules of the Torcellen.

The one who was at the top.

Now there was a silver monster rising from the mist. It shone like it came from the heavens, but it had risen from the darkness and it was heading toward her city swatting missiles aside as if it weren't worried.

"Are you saying," Allahnzo asked as his own ship veered away from the Holy City, which was now deemed too dangerous to approach, "that we shot down the wrong ships?"

Allahnzo listened to the response from the Holy City's Defense Prime, his features showing nothing. "Yes. And to compound the error, we've lost our missile batteries and now a silver ship is attacking us."

The Torcellan licked his lips as he took in the strategic situation. "NO!" he barked, rolling his eyes in frustration. "Holding the princess hostage is the only thing that keeps the cities subdued! Find her and move her to a safe location with another six or so from her service." Allahnzo paused, listening. "I don't *care* what you do with the rest, although killing them is a waste. Just make sure it is a *necessary* waste. We shouldn't haphazardly kill perfectly good and, might I mention, extremely profitable slaves. Not just every slave has worked for royalty. So, consider that, if you feel you need to kill them."

Allahnzo hung up the call. "Take us to Bah-aranteck."

"Well, this is a pretty damned large operation," Tabitha commented as *Achronyx* flew around the now-dark Holy City. "We need to find and keep the princess safe, then take care of the military."

"Two twenty-two," Ryu remarked as he looked at the video feed of the movement inside the city. He pointed to two locations. "Drop off Hirotoshi here," he moved his hand and pointed to the second location, "and me here."

Tabitha considered what he was proposing. "You guys kick the ants' nest some more while I find her?"

"*Hai*," Ryu agreed. "I think we should have brought Kouki and Dio with us. Dio is going to be miffed he missed this."

"Hell, *you* almost missed this," Tabitha replied. "Who thought this would turn out to be a large-scale Torcellan-led Skaine takeover?" She looked at Hirotoshi. "You? No?" Then she looked over at Ryu with a raised eyebrow. "You got anything?" She shrugged when he shook his head. "Me neither," she confided.

"Now *that*," Hirotoshi commented, "would have been a good guess."

"It would have earned me 'Queen of the Most Unlikely Guess' for damned sure," she agreed. "Okay, looks like here is where you get kicked out, Ryu."

A circular pattern in the bottom area of the ship started irising open and a moment later, Ryu, holding a sheathed *katana* in his left hand and a Jean Dukes pistol in his right, dropped into the darkness.

She doubted the lights would stay off for long. She heard a few rounds hit the ship's shields and the ricochets go whizzing off as the ground beneath her changed.

There was a *ding*, and Hirotoshi dropped as well.

"Any particularly good place for me to start?" she asked aloud. The scenery below moved quickly and they lifted farther from the ground. "Any good reason you are giving me a farther distance to drop?" Tabitha asked. "It's not like I mind being the female here and jumping from a shorter distance. I'm not that into male/female equality, Achronyx."

A building came into view beneath them—a palace, built of a white rock something like Earth marble. There was a large outside patio attached to some large rooms, and lights from those windows spilled into the night. "I guess this is my stop." Tabitha checked to make sure she had a proper landing spot.

"It is," Achronyx answered before Tabitha dropped and the ship lifted into the night. "I'm shocked she waited for me to answer before she left," Achronyx commented to the empty ship.

Tabitha had Achronyx kick in the antigrav before she dropped to the rock paving in the patio. "Momma didn't raise no dummy," she whispered as she looked through windows with some rather sheer curtains into a large bedroom behind.

She made sure her pistols were ready as she walked into the bedroom.

Ryu saw that the ship was heading toward the palace at the top of the city and smiled.

If Hirotoshi were to win the bet, Tabitha would need to be in a building of at least three stories, which the palace was. He jumped sideways into a small niche just before lights flicked on all over the grounds.

The Holy City was approximately two miles square, with multiple buildings, lawns, parks, waterfalls, and levels throughout. He decided he preferred to move across the tops of the buildings. Pushing off the two adjacent walls, he shinnied to the roof and grabbed the overhang, pulling himself up and over.

Hirotoshi bent his knees as he hit the ground. One second he was there, the next second, he was gone, speeding through the darkness toward a park which had a ton of trees. He reached them in plenty of time before the lights behind him were flipped on again.

Easier to find the aliens with light, he assumed. About twelve Skaines came running out of an alley ahead of him and tramped down a small street with buildings on one side and the trees from the park on the other. They were heading toward where he had just been.

He pulled his *katana* out of its sheath and ran to the trees the group would have to pass.

After the last Skaines had gone by him, he slid out of his cover and caught up with the laggard. He used a two-handed grip and waited until his pace was perfect before swinging from the hip, continuing to bring his sword around and dodging the blood.

He had taken out three more of them before someone glanced back, noticed the dead bodies, and realized one of the group wasn't supposed to be there. His cry of alarm was only successful in slowing everyone down, allowing Hirotoshi to stab the next one, then twist in an arc and take out the neck, cutting it half-open as he finished his twist.

He kicked the body away. Reaching into his vest, he pulled out two knives and threw them at the Skaine farthest from him, embedding them in the throat and the chest. He threw himself toward the ground, rolling, and came back to stab the guard in front of him and slam his fist into the one on the right.

That left four.

He crouched a bit and then pushed up, flipping backward to sail over three of the guards, pulling his Jean Dukes from the holster.

By the time he landed he had already shot two in the skull from above, and then he took care of the last two. Their bodies were still falling as he made it back to the trees, and he ran toward the alley he had seen them come out of.

He heard an alien scream and glanced toward the palace on the hilltop, wondering how Tabitha was faring.

CHAPTER FIVE

<u>*Prometheus Major*</u>, **Gate 033B**

"Do you think Aunt Tabitha is going to be okay?" Christina asked as she and R'yhek put away their gear.

"She has Ryu and Hirotoshi with her. How much trouble can some …" he looked at her as he moved his duffel to his locker, "what did you call them? 'two-bit washed-up criminals' cause her?"

"Yeah, but I hate that she has to clean up my mistake," Christina replied. "I'd rather accomplish that myself. At times, it feels like Dad is still protecting me."

R'yhek stood up and looked down at the woman he considered his human daughter. "It is what dads do, Christina." He turned and headed toward the door when she called out.

"R'yhek."

He turned, his mandibles double-tapping as he waited for her.

"Thank you," she told him, looking him in the eyes. "I don't know what I would have done if I had lost you today." She walked over to the old barman and carefully hugged him. "I know… it's what family does."

That's what dads do, he thought to himself as he carefully hugged her back. *And I couldn't be any prouder of you if you were a Yollin female, little furry fireball.*

"Is Tabitha going to be okay?" Ecaterina asked Nathan. The two of them were reviewing the business' notes, figuring out where to go next.

"Ranger Two's been out of any major busts for a while. Hell, the last time they had major issues was cleaning up around her home."

Ecaterina looked up from her tablet. "You mean the whole damned planet, right?"

"Mmmhmmm." Nathan continued reviewing his device, but slowly realized his mate was quiet. He looked up. "What?" He reviewed what he had just said. "Oh, c'mon! It's not like it was a running gun battle." Ecaterina continued staring at him. "Well, not *all* the time," he finished.

"She called John in a couple times," she reminded him.

Nathan considered what he remembered. "I think she didn't want to break her nails." He shrugged. "She and her team made out like bandits. They bought up all the land on that planet with their loot. Cleaned up the planet, and now they are so filthy rich they can't possibly spend it all. I'm surprised they are still in the business."

"Like *you* need money?" Ecaterina pointed out. "I could retire myself, and I know you have about ten times more set aside in different accounts all over the place."

"If I should die, you won't ever need to work," Nathan replied diffidently. "One of these days the nanocytes will finally quit, and I'll become an old grey man practically overnight."

"Well," Ecaterina's eyes brightened, "not tonight, I hope."

"What?" Nathan looked back down at his tablet, checking his calendar for appointments. "What's tonight?"

Ecaterina rolled her eyes.

A note popped up on Nathan's screen and his eyes flicked across the information before he called, "Prometheus, pull us away from the Gate and head to three-dot-oh-one-four by two-two-three. When we are out of sight, Gate us to Devin."

Across the table, Ecaterina had forgotten their previous conversation while she reviewed the note. "I cannot believe those motherfuckers think they will get away with attacking poor little Cheeto."

"His name is Ch'ehtoe," Nathan answered, modulating his voice to sound like he was speaking a form of Cherokee from back on Earth.

"Right." She nodded and repeated in a heavy Slavic accent, "*Cheeto.*"

Hopefully, Nathan sighed, *she won't realize that planet has her favorite restaurant. Surprising her is such a challenge.*

Ten minutes later, Ecaterina gasped in surprise when a note came across her screen. Nathan looked up. "What?"

She flicked the note over to his tablet, and his eyes took the information in. Before he looked back to her, it dimmed out.

On Ecaterina's tablet were the words, "I've got this. *Baba Yaga.*"

On Nathan's tablet, the note said, "I've got this. Enjoy your anniversary. *Bethany Anne.*"

Trust her to remember the small things, he thought as he tried to keep the little smile from playing on his lips.

Ecaterina placed her tablet on the table. "Whoever is causing that trouble is going to wish they had never gotten up this morning."

Planet H'lageh

Tabitha checked the room, but it was empty. She slid a hand inside her coat and pulled out a box. Opening it, she grabbed three small round orbs and threw them into the air, where they floated as she put away the box. "Find the princess, Achronyx."

"I but live to serve and obey." The EI sniffed in her ear.

"Well, you do it poorly," she told him, palming her pistol. She walked toward the door the orbs had found and opened it. Taking a step through, she watched the map of the palace update as the orbs continued their search through the large building.

Following the map, she went down a set of steps and opened another door. After peeking both ways, she stepped into the hallway and checked the map. "Right it is." She headed in that direction and saw a crack in the wall. When she knocked, she heard the hollow sound. It opened easily when she pushed, and she stuck her head inside.

Three beings turned in her direction, all of them female, if Tabitha was reading the physiology correctly.

"Hello, Saviour," a melodic voice, one that seemed to have chimes in it, greeted. Strangely, none of the three beings had opened their mouths.

"Achronyx, what language are you translating?" she asked. "You are giving it an accent."

"I'm not, Ranger Two," he replied. "You are hearing an old version of English."

The ladies parted and a silvery-haired female became visible. She was sitting on a chair, and her head and shoulders were turned in Tabitha's direction. "Oh," her large eyes opened in surprise. "You are the monster from my dream."

Tabitha had a hard time not staring at her pointed ears.

"Your Highness?" she asked.

"You speak our language?" She stood up. "Or is this your technology magic?"

"Not magic," Tabitha narrowed her eyes, "unless you are doing something?"

The tall, slender woman's eyebrows came together. "Possibly, but not on purpose," she admitted as the three ladies moved farther to the sides. Tabitha was all about sex appeal, but this lady put her in the shade—and that wasn't an issue for her, like ever.

"We need to get you out of here," Tabitha told her. "We have a full-blown pain in the ass working to capture you again."

The princess shook her head, slowly "But I cannot go. If I leave the Holy City, the lives of my people in the other four cities are forfeit. If they obey, then my life is safe."

Tabitha took in the information and considered her options.

"Four cities, right?" Tabitha asked. The princess nodded. "All of them have military garrisons?"

The princess nodded again. Tabitha chewed on the inside of her lip and looked at the HUD on her lens. There was movement on the lower levels, but so far no one was heading in their direction. She put up a finger and turned sideways, to hide her mouth better. "Ryu, Hirotoshi?"

"*Hai!*" two voices replied simultaneously.

"We have to protect the princess here in the palace, and need the other four cities liberated simultaneously. Recommendations?"

"It's time to call in your brothers who kick ass and don't care about the names," Hirotoshi answered. Tabitha could hear him fighting in the background.

"Are you sure?" Tabitha answered. "This started as us taking out a criminal ring."

"Anytime," Ryu answered, "someone enslaves another, it is out of our hands. Call the Empress. She will make the decision."

"Agreed." Tabitha nodded to herself. "Make your way up here. We can't take the princess out yet, so we have to protect her while we wait."

Tabitha sighed. "Achronyx, get me Barnabas, please." She watched the layout of the building and those dots running around. Two of them peeled off and started heading her way.

"You have anything against killing?" Tabitha asked, turning her head to view the princess.

"Only my own people," she replied.

"Peachy." Tabitha sighed. "So much for bringing them in alive."

Why is that? Barnabas' voice sounded in her head.

Hey, boss! We have an enslaved planet here. Those who are in charge have taken all four cities, and the citizens have to obey them or their royal princess dies. If the royal princess doesn't stay put, those in the cities will die. We can protect her, but we can't liberate four cities simultaneously.

Even Bethany Anne can't be in four places at once, Barnabas mused. *Okay, I'll make a call. Stay alive. Barnabas out.*

The call terminated. Tabitha glanced at the HUD and told the women, "You ladies will want to move back." Sliding her coat aside, she pulled her pistol and aimed at the door. She fired twice, then slid the pistol back into the holster.

"Why did you shoot my door?" the princess asked.

Tabitha took two steps and pulled on the door handle, stepping to the side as she opened it. She waved at the two dead Skaines on the other side—their blood was splattered across the hallway floor and halfway up the wall on the other side.

Two of the ladies-in-waiting turned their heads, but the princess merely murmured, "Oh."

Tabitha pursed her lips and looked at the princess. "What is the most defensible position in this palace?"

The princess looked at the two dead Skaines before returning her gaze to Tabitha. "Is that through them, or around them?"

"Well," Tabitha smiled, "I'd prefer to go through them, but I'll go around if it helps you sleep better at night."

The princess' face got a little green as she looked at Tabitha's expression.

She really would *go right through them,* Sis'talana thought. *What kind of monster is helping me?*

. . .

QBBS _Meredith Reynolds_

Bethany Anne was busy chewing on a small stylus when she heard a *crack*. Pulling it out of her mouth, she took a look at it. "Dammit," she muttered, and set it to the side. "Cheryl Lynn is going to be *pissed*."

She tapped the location of the planet which needed an intervention from Baba Yaga, and was looking at the data when the door buzzed.

>>**Stephen is here to see you.**<<

Let him in.

A moment later Stephen walked into the room and smiled. "My Empress."

Bethany Anne got up from the table and stepped into his hug. "My pain-in-the-ass follower," she replied and nodded to the chair next to hers. "Take a seat. I'm done standing today."

Stephen was just sitting down when the buzzer sounded, and this time ADAM spoke over the speakers. "Barnabas is here to see you. He mentions it is important and relevant."

"Let him in," she replied and the two of them turned to watch Barnabas walk into the room.

"I see you are conniving again, boss." Barnabas smiled as Stephen raised an eyebrow.

"Not yet, but I'll ignore you when I do," Bethany Anne pointed to the seat across the table. "Park it, and let me know the news."

Barnabas pulled the chair out and sat down. "I need to request that the guys go to a planet and pull some nuts out of a fire."

"Who's in trouble?" Bethany Anne asked.

"Well, technically Tabitha."

"Uh," Bethany Anne smiled, "no nuts."

Barnabas tried not to groan. "It was a euphemism for 'we have a situation.'"

"Okay, spill it," she replied. "I'm starting to dream up some great ideas to connive on, so I need you out of the way."

"Uh-huh." Barnabas leaned forward. "We have a rather standoffish planet which has been taken over by slavers and drug lords."

"How the hell …" Bethany Anne started before Barnabas' raised hand stopped her.

"The people have formed a great relationship with their royal house, and it is reciprocated," he answered, "so we need four different hardened locations attacked and confirmed unresponsive before we bring the princess out."

"So send one of the Bitches," Bethany Anne answered.

Barnabas tapped the table. "The four locations need to be taken out simultaneously."

"Well, shit." Bethany Anne made a face. "You couldn't have perhaps explained that aspect of the challenge at the beginning of this discussion?"

Barnabas smiled. "It helps keep you on your toes when I make sure you don't presume everything."

"Take the four of them." Bethany Anne shrugged. "The guys haven't had a good workout in a while."

Barnabas raised an eyebrow. "What should they ship out on?"

Bethany Anne waved a hand. "You need to ask Admiral Thomas that question."

"And if he suggests the QBS *Alexander*?"

"What?" She shook her head. "I don't need *Alexander* at the moment. How long is this going to take?"

"It's not that far. Eight hours from 'go,' and some cleanup once they get there."

Bethany Anne's eyes narrowed.

ADAM, how far is this planet?

>>**7.24 hours.**<<

Bethany Anne's eyes shot open as she pointed her finger at Barnabas. "You already have the guys in action!" She leaned forward. "Of all the typically 'Barnabas' things to do," she stabbed a finger down on the table, "this isn't one of them." She leaned back and crossed her arms. "How long ago did you give them the word?"

"Well, a Ranger is involved," Barnabas replied, "so I thought we might want to move expeditiously."

"Well, true." She made a shooing motion. "Hurry up. Go!"

Barnabas stood up and pushed the seat back in. She eyed him. "Don't get them killed."

He waved a hand over his shoulder as he walked away. "Never my intent, Empress."

The door closed behind him.

Stephen looked at her. "So, what are we conniving about?"

"Whatever makes you think," she waved between them, "*we* are about to connive anything?"

"You specifically told Barnabas you were dreaming up some great ideas to connive. He just took away your handlers, and I'm here."

Bethany Anne smiled, put her nose up in the air, and spoke as if she were old-Earth royalty. "Well, just for the record, the conniving was already in play. The thinking up new ideas was a lie." She showed him the most guileless face she could create.

He looked at her for a long moment. "Baba Yaga?"

"Baba Yaga," she agreed.

"I'll go get my setup." He started to get up, and Bethany Anne stood with him.

"No need," she told him. "I've had a set of everything you use packed for a while." She grabbed his shoulder, and the two of them disappeared.

Moments later they reappeared in a special closet. Stephen looked around. "I don't recognize this room."

"You shouldn't. You're the first I've brought aboard," Bethany Anne admitted. The circular room was only six feet across. The wall opened and the two of them stepped out into a passageway as the lights came to life in both directions. She pointed to her left. "Thirty feet that way are the engines, back armory, Pod landing bay and other miscellaneous areas." She turned toward the front of the ship and started walking. "This way is the bridge, living quarters, meeting rooms, front armory, communications, and special shit."

"Special shit?" Stephen asked as he observed their surroundings. "Everything is so clean!" He opened a door, and his muffled voice came back into the hall. "Has this been flown anywhere?"

"No," she called back. "ADAM, please explain to Meredith we are taking *Shinigami* out for a test."

"How test-y is this test, Bethany Anne?" ADAM's voice surrounded them as Stephen caught up to her. She opened the door to the bridge. Stephen was surprised to see a large room with a massive circular couch that started on one wall, wrapped around the back of the bridge and traveled the length of the other wall. The front bulkhead was all screen. He followed Bethany Anne in and took a seat when she did.

"Where are all the bridge seats?" he asked, looking around.

Bethany Anne's face lit up. "You are sitting on them!" She turned and spoke to the dark screens. "Shinigami, set up for battle."

Stephen was surprised when the seat he was on started changing shape. The leg rest came out, allowing him to lie back comfortably. From the ceiling, additional screens lowered two feet toward him. From between the cushions, armrests rose. Bethany Anne was already enveloped in her own cocoon to his right.

"We have antigravity support to allow us to handle the massive g-forces this ship can produce when we turn and juke." She looked up, her eyes flitting left to right. "Shinigami, engage Stephen and allow him access to the bridge stream in his implants."

Next to her, Bethany Anne heard Stephen gasp in surprise.

She looked at him, and his eyes were flitting around like hers had a moment before. "Pretty cool shit, right?"

"It's amazing," he answered. "How do I issue commands?"

"Voice, action, mental commands—whatever works best for the activity. You can issue a voice command while pushing a virtual button and issuing a mental command."

"Plus," a voice interrupted his review of the screens now in front of him, "you can simply allow me to handle all systems for you."

Stephen stopped paying attention to the virtual screens and looked at the front display. "Shinigami, I assume?"

"Yes," the EI responded. "I've taken the liberty of not yet deciding on my visage."

"She ..." Bethany Anne started before the EI interrupted.

"Or he."

"Whatever." Bethany Anne waved a hand. "Gender isn't important to me." She looked at Stephen. "This ship has multiple EIs operating it. If I need to go somewhere, I have more EI support than most of our fleet."

"More EIs?" Stephen asked. "Do they all have names?"

"Sure." She pointed to the screen. "Based on the people who led the design teams and built aspects of the ship. We have Jeurgan for communications, Martina for signals and eavesdropping, Timo for core ship operations, Thorsten for all Gate and intra-system routing, and Marions H and K. One handles shields, the other weapons."

"Which is which?" Stephen asked.

She shrugged. "Beats the fuck out of me." She pointed to the two ladies' faces on the screen. "The two often squabble about which is better, offense or defense. One started spouting off arguments about," she looked at Stephen again, "World War II strategies."

Stephen tried to remember if he had ever met a Marion who

was into World War II. "Was she someone we brought from Earth?"

Bethany Anne shook her head. "Nope. She just loves research. I'm pretty sure she is 'K' and 'H' is shields."

"You don't know?" Stephen pressed.

"Well, of course I know," Bethany Anne touched the side of her head. "It isn't like I can't pull it out, but I feel it's more fun to allow them to wow me."

"You never allowed *anyone* to 'wow' you," Stephen pointed out. "You always got into the thick of the action."

Bethany Anne sighed. "Yeah, the good old days." It was a moment before she shook her head. "But this pretty little thing is so fucking advanced, I couldn't hope to do it manually. Even with ADAM running it, we weren't pushing the envelope. Therefore …"

Stephen whistled. "Multiple EI's."

"Yup," Bethany Anne agreed. The two seats started to revert. "ADAM is the primary to activate all commands. Otherwise the ship will seek to protect itself."

"Even from you?" Stephen asked as he watched the seats change back into a nice comfy couch.

"Well, there are a couple of safeguards. If ADAM is incapacitated somehow and I'm considered to be under duress… Well, there is way too much technology in this ship to allow out. TOM has a backdoor, and no, I've no idea what it is."

"TOM," the speakers in the bridge spoke with TOM's voice, "is aware that a backdoor is usually a bad thing. This isn't a typical backdoor, Stephen, but rather a unique test to confirm I am the one authorizing an override if ADAM is knocked out and Bethany Anne is incapacitated. Or as she put it, 'under duress.'"

"Okay, TOM." Bethany Anne stretched out. "Let's change my face, but leave off the leathery look." She winked at Stephen. "I've seen some of my pictures." She rolled her eyes. "And *oh my God* am I hideous!" She shook her head. "Fuck that. A girl needs to look good while kicking ass. The white hair is enough, *thankyouverymuch.*

"The ink-black skin and red eyes aren't a problem?"

"They're a statement," Bethany Anne smiled. "They say, *'Ding-dong, you're dead.'"*

CHAPTER SIX

Planet H'lageh, Inter-City Shuttle

"I'm telling you," Adam turned toward his co-pilot Matthew, "that is why this route is so boring. Lack of children."

"I don't know about that," Matthew answered. He checked the ship's warnings as they prepared to arrive at the third largest city on H'lageh. "I'm thinking that a nice easy flight this morning was just the ticket after the party this weekend with Juliette." He checked the next two tasks on his list. They had a small flight, maybe twenty on the shuttle, fully loaded. He was two more down the list when a flash caught his attention. His head moved up, then he squinted as he stared at a screen. "What in *Edhellen?*"

Adam glanced toward Matthew. It wasn't often he swore. "Problem?"

The younger-looking man shook his head. "Either we have a problem with the sensors or a moon is about to hit us," he answered, tapping his video screen.

He wasn't sure why he tapped on the screen. It wasn't as if it ever helped.

A moment later, both pilot and co-pilot's eyes grew large as a gruff voice spoke to them through their comm. "This is the QBS

Alexander, not a moon. Please do not veer from your flight path or you will become a bug splattered on my shields." There was a slight pause. "John Grimes would like to know your names, please."

"Adam Beedie, Pilot, BeeA Shuttles." He nodded to his co-pilot.

"Matthew Pike, Co-pilot, BeeA Shuttles," Matt replied.

A different voice came over the line. "Gentleman, interesting names. Do you mind if we view each other in video?"

Adam leaned forward and hit the video button, and two faces appeared. One was an older person and the other was younger, but had very hard eyes.

"Are you," Adam asked, leaning toward the screen to get a closer look, his confusion evident, "*humans?*"

"I'm John Grimes," the younger face on the right answered, and he raised his eyebrows in surprise. "Are you *elves?*"

"No, we are Helagethians," Adam replied. As he was speaking a shadow crossed his window, and he looked up from the video monitor. His ability to converse was suddenly impaired due to his mouth hanging open.

Matthew swore, and Adam nodded in agreement. "You got that right."

The older-looking human spoke up. "We appreciate you not moving, and should you have sufficient power to remain in the air, we suggest you don't land for about thirty more minutes."

"Wh-why?" Matthew asked, his own jaw dropping as the warship passed through the atmosphere above them. While it looked close enough to touch, that effect was due to the sheer size of the ship, not proximity.

A second later they were behind the ship as it continued toward Citiseereth.

"The Empress does not appreciate one group of people trying to subjugate and hurt another," John replied.

"What about our princess?" Adam asked, concern in his voice.

"Protected by an Empress' Ranger," John replied. "She is safe. We are dropping now."

The video cut out.

Four flashes occurred simultaneously and what looked like a bunch of mosquitoes dropped from underneath the massive ship. They departed at tremendous speeds in different directions, including a couple of handfuls that flew under their ship toward Peeg'eth, where their flight had originated.

"Adam, look." Matthew was holding a tablet with some faces on the screen. Adam looked closer and his eyes widened.

Even in their insular society, they had heard of the Etheric Empire. Matthew swiped, and another face came up. In fact, about fifteen photos and images were arrayed across his screen.

Adam whistled.

"That," Matthew told him, "is the Empress." He swiped again and Adam grimaced. "That," Matthew pointed to an artist's sketch of a dark-faced human with white hair, "is Baba Yaga. She comes out when the going gets tough."

"She," Adam returned to looking out the front of the shuttle, "is a hideous creature."

"Do you think they can do it?" Matthew asked as he read more about the Empire.

"Take out the Skaines?"

"Yes."

"Let's hope so." Adam changed the ship's route and turned on the microphone to speak to the passengers. "This is your captain. We are going to be slightly delayed…"

As they approached Citiseereth thirty minutes later, large smoke columns became visible above it. "I'm taking us around the city," Adam commented. The shuttle dipped, then tilted its wings to fly in a large circle. The two pilots viewed the destruction.

"I believe they have completed their work." Adam blew out a breath.

"Thou shalt not mess with the Etheric Empire," Matthew responded.

The shuttle leveled off and headed toward the port as the two pilots double-checked their instruments. "This is Shuttle 889CC requesting permission to land," Adam requested over the comm link. It was a formality, since their shuttle had digital connections and had already received digital permission to land. The verbal request was just politeness.

"First, second, and probably third drink are on me," Adam told Matthew as the shuttle landed.

Hours later the two pilots left a favorite bar in Citiseereth, singing into the night with the abandon that only alcoholic beverages can provide.

Their princess was safe.

Planet H'lageh, Holy City, Royal Palace
Tabitha had entered the room and was looking to her right when shots were fired from her left, causing her to dive back into the hallway she had come in from. She rolled over on the ground, stood up, and blew a few strands of hair out of her face.

She peeked to her left, and pulled her head back in when she noticed the little bit of movement. "I cannot believe," she mumbled, "I almost got shot by a virtual sentinel."

"A what?" the princess asked from six paces away. She had been hiding around another corner, and only her head was visible. She watched the Ranger with interest as she patted down her coat, then stopped. Tabitha reached inside the coat with her left hand and pulled out a small box. She flipped open the top of the box with one hand and jerked it to the left. Two silvery objects flew from the box into the large room she had just vacated.

Tabitha was looking up at something the princess couldn't see from her position. "One moment!" she called as weapons fire started once again. This time the princess thought she could discern three different weapons as they fired, stopped, and then started again.

The room beyond was virtually destroyed, chunks of the rock walls flying everywhere. The princess didn't want to seem unappreciative of the rescue, but the rock from which the room had been constructed had been received as a gift generations ago.

She flinched when a large chunk of a wall went crashing to the ground.

"There!" the monster yelled, and two large explosions occurred as she turned the corner, brandishing her own weapon and firing at the third emplacement.

She was out of the princess' sight for only a moment before she heard a third explosion.

"CLEAR!"

The princess walked forward and peeked her head into the large, previously beautiful discussion hall. One wall had been adorned with an old fresco, and she was surprised to see that it had sustained no damage.

"Sorry about the pocks in all the walls." The princess jumped, having not realized Tabitha had gotten so close to her. "I tried to keep the damage down, but even I'm not fast enough to shoot out three of those anti-personnel emplacements at one time," Tabitha told her. "I'd say I know someone who does good work on stone, but he died last year." She looked around at the damage.

"Saving someone?"

She shook her head. "No, from radical efforts to safely prove he couldn't kill himself." She turned around and started walking toward the hall at the end of the room. "He failed."

"My princess," Tealah whispered as she and the other two ladies-in-waiting caught up with their liege, "who is this strange woman?"

Sis'talana glanced down the hall and followed Tabitha, whose coat was flapping as she yanked her pistol out. She shot to her right and dove as weapons fire blasted out of the wall on the left, then completed her turn and fired into the wall on the opposite side of the hallway. A moment later a door opened and a body crashed through. "C'mon," Tabitha called. "It's safe now."

The princess turned to Tealah and shrugged her right shoulder. "Pay attention," she told her, then looked at her other two ladies and pointed to Tabitha, who was farther down the hall. "That is our future." The three women were in shock as Sis'talana walked to the dead Skaine in the hall. She put a foot on the wrist of the male, grabbed his pistol, and turned toward the formerly beautiful discussion hall. The three ladies jumped out of the way as the princess aimed at the fresco.

She pulled the trigger and the blaster bucked in her hand as the shot blew a three-inch hole in the rock, just left of center.

"Princess!" Heena and Jeela cried, surprised she would purposely damage the antique painting.

Princess Sis'talana's head turned toward them, her face grim. "As long as we have a Holy City," she pointed to the hole she had just created, "that will never be fixed." She dropped her hand. "It will stand as a testament that this House of mine knows how to defend our people."

Heena and Jeela watched as the princess followed the strange female down the hall, and turned when they heard a slam behind them.

"Tealah!" Jeela put a hand to her mouth. "What has gotten into you?"

Tealah stuck her hand into the hole she had created with her foot and pulled, stepping out of the way of the body that dropped out of the little hiding place. She grabbed the pistol that had dropped with him. Standing up, she nodded to the other two ladies. "Are you coming?"

Achronyx spoke in her ear. "We have twelve Skaines coming from outside, running through the main entrance."

"Ryu and Hirotoshi?"

"Ryu has attacked a smaller group on the west side. They were using the roofs to slide into the palace. Hirotoshi will be there in thirty seconds."

Tabitha heard the princess coming up behind her. She had listened in as the royal and her ladies talked, and decided it was time to help the princess cement her future. Reaching into her coat, she pulled out two six-inch-long silver metal triangles. She checked the ends and reversed one of them, then put the two together and twisted to lock them. She looked around and shrugged. "Here is as good a place as any." She put the device on the floor and stood back, putting out an arm to stop the princess as she reached her.

"It's time," Tabitha told her. "That blaster has about fifteen more shots, I'd guess. There are twelve Skaines coming in this direction." She jerked a thumb behind her. "You sure you're willing to change your future with violence?"

The princess gripped the blaster tighter.

Tabitha turned around. She pointed to Tealah, and jerked her thumb at a spot behind herself. Then she pointed to Heena and Jeela, and gestured toward the door. "Hide in there for a few moments."

Bring it online, Achronyx.

Both the princess and Tealah took an involuntary step back when a blue shimmering light sprang up from the floor.

Tabitha grabbed the princess and pulled her two steps over. "Stand here."

Tabitha then grabbed Tealah. "You go on her right side and I'll take the left," she told her, and walked to the other side of the princess. "Leave your pistols at your sides."

Tabitha reached into her coat and grabbed three more

spheres. She looked down at them and grinned, then threw them into the air.

"Smile, ladies!"

R'bark scanned left, then right as he led his group down the hallway toward the large receiving room two floors above his present location. He had his team formed up three abreast. Each time they passed a set of hallways, the front right and left person would veer off and remain in the hallway, guarding it as the other ten passed. Moments later they would leave the hallway, taking up a position at the back as the now-front row took the next hallway.

Those in the back kept watch.

R'bark, Rig, and Gott were at the front when they went up the last set of stairs and turned the corner. The princess was standing in the middle of the long, wide hallway which led to the room they had been heading for.

"Princess," R'bark snarled, "you are out of your area."

"And you," she replied, "are not welcome on my planet."

"This will cost you a lot of lives, you fighting us like this."

Tabitha kept her head lowered, trying to hide her face as well as she could. It had been a few generations since she and the Tontos had been such a scourge to Skaine plans, so she doubted she was as recognizable to them now as she had been decades before.

It had been too quiet for too long, or perhaps she just hadn't been listening hard enough. Obviously the Skaines hadn't quit being Skaines, so the problem was on her side.

She grimaced in recognition of the mistake she had made.

She listened to the Skaine and the princess verbally joust, wondering when the first shot would be fired so she could bring a little Justice to all those who had been killed on this planet. The guilty had already been judged, and the executioners had arrived.

She just needed to make sure that the princess had the footage she needed to secure her crown and bring some much-needed ass-kicking to the Skaines.

They will remember me, she told herself as her lips pressed together.

Princess Sis'talana lifted her pistol, aiming for his chest as she had been told in a hurried whisper by Tabitha. "There will be no more killing on my planet. We will go down fighting."

"Suit yourse—" R'bark was shocked when the princess pressed the firing button, and doubly surprised when he was violently blown off his feet. A second later his men returned fire, but something was blocking their shots. He grunted as the pain in his chest intensified when his men helped him stand.

He looked down in shock. His armor wasn't going to stand up to another blast like that. "Kill those bitches next to her," he commanded.

Tabitha smiled. "That's enough, Princess."

Tabitha rolled her eyes. The princess and Tealah had ducked each time the shields flared with eye-searing brightness as Skaine shots hit them. Still, neither one failed to send shots back down the hallway. The Skaines had finally figured out there was a protective shield in place, but they obviously thought they could overwhelm it by unleashing a shitstorm of weapons fire against it.

"My turn!" she yelled to the princess, who had dropped to one knee a moment before when shots hitting the roof had pelted them with stinging shards.

The princess just looked at her. She had held it together so far, but it was obvious the knowledge that things could go wrong had finally caught up with the adrenalin or whatever she had used to power herself through the fight. "What are you going to do?"

"What I was supposed to be doing," Tabitha told her, and allowed her eyes to flicker just a little red as she smiled. "Taking care of the riff-raff."

"Keep firing!" R'bark yelled when the three ladies started moving. The one to his right moved to the middle, and the princess and the other stepped back. She pulled her coat to the side, displaying the two pistols on her hips. As her head came up she had a smile on her face, and her eyes were glowing red.

R'bark shot three more times right at the woman, but each time the force field deflected his shots, a light show playing out in ever-increasing circles each time a weapon's discharge hit it. "This is just annoying. Who has ship-level shields inside a building?" he asked, throwing his hands in the air.

The one still facing them reached up and felt around inside her shirt.

Something in R'bark's memory began to nag at him. *Oh shit...*

"Retreat three by three!" he started to yell, but it was already too late. He heard someone from his crew yell, "*RANGER TWO!*" as the symbol dropped to her chest, and her eyes flared red. Her hands dropped to her pistols.

R'bark flicked his blaster to full auto and squeezed the trigger. He saw three of his men break and retreat. *Had he given the command, or were his men deserting him?*

A moment later his brains splattered the wall behind him, and he frankly didn't care anymore.

Tabitha issued the command to drop the one-way shield. She heard the *click* of a pair of boots coming up the stairs. She walked toward the Skaines and checked those who had fallen from her shots.

A moment later Hirotoshi came into view, looking around at the destruction before striding over to a dead Skaine and bending over to clean off his blade. "You missed a few." He stood up and slid the sword into its sheath. "We may have been sitting on our asses too much."

"Yeah," Tabitha agreed. "We'll have to do better."

CHAPTER SEVEN

The QBS *Alexander* reviewed the incoming intelligence as the four Empress' Bitches dropped with the cohort of fighters, streaking across the sky toward their targets.

Already he had been able to pinpoint locations which required additional attention. Nothing like his first four major pulses, which had destroyed the buildings the subjugating force was using as barracks and armory. The secondary explosions confirmed they had larger weapons.

But he waited, it was the Guards' turn now. He was too large a weapon. The mighty Leviathan-class ship rose, breaking through the clouds into the thinner air high above. Low enough that he could assist if necessary, but not so low that a ship in space could attack him at will.

The massive ship went silent in the darkness of the upper atmosphere. Without something visible, the sensors used on this planet weren't sophisticated enough to figure out where he was.

And, if an EI could be said to like something, he liked that very much.

Eric landed and looked the building over. *Alexander*'s shot had hit it hard, but it hadn't caused much of a fire.

The top floors of the five-story stone building were black; there wouldn't be anyone alive in those levels, he suspected. However, he could still sense people inside.

"You have multiple free agents inside the building, Eric," Alexander supplied. "The primary armory seems not to have been hit."

"They might not have a primary armory," Eric replied. "Please send in the sensor droids to take a look."

Moments later his HUD lit up, showing rooms and passageways. There were tangos running all over the place, but in general they were heading toward a lower level. "What do you think the chance is that location is the armory?"

"The probability, based on secondary explosions in the other three locations, reaches over seventy-eight percent," the EI informed him.

There had to be over thirty live tangoes in that area, and they were carrying substantial firepower. "My wife will have my head if I go in there," he remarked to no one in particular, and looked around. The building was in a rather open area. "What are our kinetic options, Alexander?"

"I can pound them from above."

"Have we found any bolt holes yet?" Eric asked, looking at the map of the building inside as the sensor droids continued their spying efforts.

"None so far."

"Approved." Eric turned and jogged off, stopping a couple of blocks away.

"Incoming," Alexander warned him.

Eric couldn't see the little one-pound balls, but the destruction was evident from the concussive explosions and debris that exited the windows on the second, third, and what was left of the fourth floor. Then another blew out the doors on the first floor. Two more explosions, more felt than seen, followed.

It started to rain rocks and glass. Eric just allowed it to bounce off his armor. "Survivors?" he asked.

"We lost most of our sensor droids, Eric," Alexander replied. "This will take a moment."

Eric started trotting back toward the building. He didn't want any of these bastards to get away. He arrived at the front, and his boots crunched on the door as he stepped on it to get inside the building. Pulling his Jean Dukes pistol, he set it to seven and shot at a wall.

Nothing. "Sonofabitch." He turned it up to eleven. "I hate eleven," he muttered as he went a little way into the building. "Always leaves a stinging feeling."

"That is psychosomatic, Eric," Alexander replied. "If you will turn ninety-two degrees to your right and aim seventeen degrees down."

"Just put it up on the HUD, Alexander. You know I hate the math."

An orange dot appeared to his right and a little down. Eric adjusted his aim until his yellow circle merged and they formed a red dot.

He fired.

"Tango serviced," Alexander told him.

"Like shooting fish in a barrel," he stated as he looked around. "Well, if by 'barrel' I mean a stone building where I am shooting through floors and walls and shit."

"Tango displayed," Alexander confirmed as another orange dot showed on his HUD. This time Eric spread his feet, practically aiming straight down before his targeting circle turned red.

Darryl had his hands on his hips.

"No way!" He shook his head. "Alexander, how did you take out a whole building?" He looked around. "I mean, seriously! This was badass shooting."

"Thank you," Alexander replied over his comm. "However, I can't take the credit. Whoever built this building placed it over a gas line. When the munitions hit the structure, it blew."

"Well, sucks to be them." Darryl turned again, his eyes narrowing, and he upped his HUD magnification. "Oooh, playtime's still on!" He jogged to a small area between two buildings as the two attack vehicles came roaring down the road right past him and screeched to a halt in front of the smoldering carcass that had been their headquarters. Three Skaines got out of one of the vehicles, two out of the other.

They didn't notice the armored human who stepped silently out of the darkness behind them. Inside the helmet, Darryl tagged each tango who had exited from the vehicles and checked inside.

No one else.

"Fee. Fi. Fo. Fum!" Darryl shot one Skaine with each word. "Dammit," he growled, pissed as he shot the fifth and holstered his pistol. "Fucker, you caused me to be short one word."

He walked over and peeked inside the vehicles one more time. Leaving the door open, he stepped back, palmed his Jean Dukes once again, and shot up the electronics through the door. Parts flew everywhere inside the vehicles and some parts bounced out, rendering the weapons on the tops of the vehicles useless.

He looked around, and checked his sensors as well. "Okay, bring back my ride, Alexander. Daddy is ready to confirm the city is safe."

Those strikes from Alexander seriously put a dent in the Skaines' plans. The Bitches were just here for mop-up.

Scott landed at his assigned location and jumped out of the ship, dropping the final few feet using the antigrav in his suit. Flames crackled everywhere, and the heat was pretty intense. There was a motorized noise behind him, and he turned in time to see the tank come through the flames.

"Ooohhhh, fuck me!" As he spoke, Scott had kicked backward and was twisting in the air and diving for the ground when the tank fired. The first shot went just over his head. As he hit the deck and rolled, a second shot was fired. It landed just short of him, ricocheting off the ground and bouncing into him, and like a stroke from a golf club the round sent him flying to crash against a building across the street.

"*OOOF!*" He rebounded off it.

Setting his antigrav all the way up, he bolted upward as another shot from the tank's cannon hit the wall behind him. A few fragments hit him and he was propelled toward the tank because of his low antigrav setting, although he remained too high for the main gun to rotate up and shoot him.

Scott shook his head. "That sucked," was his only comment as he focused on the tank below him. "My turn, you planet-stealing camel-nibbling swine."

He turned off the antigrav, and the Skaine who had come through the hatch to try to shoot him out of the sky screamed when Scott's armored boots crashed into him. "Oh, for fu… That's just…" Scott made a face as he jerked his right foot out of the Skaine's rib cage.

He reached down and grabbed the dead guy's belt, tossing him off the tank.

Pulling a pistol, he stuck his arm in and fired in a circle. After giving the ricochets a moment to settle he bent into the tank, getting jammed for a second with his wide shoulders. "Fucking enemies need larger tanks," he grumped. He looked around, but no one seemed to be trying to get up.

One body was in pieces. His muffled voice came from inside the tank, "That had to hurt."

Grunting some more, he pulled himself out of the hatch and jumped off the side of the tank.

He grabbed the treads and started heaving. Using the power of his armor and sheer strength he lifted it far enough to get under it, then shoved up hard to roll it over.

He looked around, patting his hands together to get the blood flowing back through them. "Alexander, please have the reconnaissance droids see if there is anyone left I need to deal with here."

"Understood," the EI replied.

John dropped through the clouds to the city the Bitches had named Alpha but which was called "Citseereth" by the locals.

Eruptions and explosions still engulfed the city after the sudden attack by Alexander, and he couldn't imagine his targets had figured out too much yet. The need to get out of a burning building should be enough to keep their attention.

Unfortunately, when he was just ninety seconds from his target he noticed a small group of vehicles pulling out from that location. "Alexander, I need eyes on those."

Ten seconds later John sighed. A couple of fast-attack vehicles and what looked like some sort of armored troop transport were on the move. John locked his helmet down. "Drop me in front of them."

His command had barely been spoken when the bottom dropped out. He whooped in delight as his attack craft roared down out of the night.

"Alpha Support Two and Three," John tapped his video twice, designating the front and back vehicles, "take out these craft here," he touched one area, "and here," he finished, touching the screen a second time.

"We need leverage!" Herzgoff growled into his communication device. "You can sit back there in your base and fix the problems, but without something to negotiate with, we ain't got bistok shit!"

Herzgoff grunted an affirmative to the reply and clicked off the radio. "That Torcellan is going to be our fucking downfall. Why the council chose him to lead us, I don't have a clue." He looked at the map. "Take us four streets north, then turn west. There is a place they have made for children to play. We will grab as many as we can and shove them in our truck, then we will drop back to a defensible position." He tapped the tablet. "We'll probably have to kill one first to let them know we mean business."

The first vehicle in his convoy was just turning left at the fourth street when it exploded and a flying ship swooped overhead before passing them. Another flew behind it, and Herzgoff heard another explosion behind his vehicle. His driver dodged to the right and stayed on the same street, bypassing the destroyed attack vehicle that was in his way.

Then the driver slammed on the brakes, and Herzgoff hit the seat in front of him.

"Why are we stopping?" Herzgoff yelled. He was in back of the troop area, and leaned forward to look out the front windshield from between the seats. He saw only one figure in the street, arms crossed. "Are you stupid?" He gestured at it. "Run him over!"

For once his driver looked at Herzgoff as if he were insane. The driver pointed out the windshield and yelled, "Do you know what that is?"

Herzgoff looked through the window again. "Yes! A speed bump, if you are going fast enough."

"Commander Herzgoff," his driver stated, his voice now as calm as he could make it, "*that* is an Empress' Bitch."

"What?" Herzgoff leaned as far forward as he could. "No it's not. Your window is dirty!" Looking up, Herzgoff stabbed the button to open the roof in his portion of the vehicle. "You will never live this down, after I report your stupidity." He grunted as he stood up to get a better view of the person in front of them.

The man in front of the vehicle, who was limned by the headlights, moved into action, and there was a sickening wet muffled thud. The driver turned around in time to see Herzgoff's body slide back down into the troop carrier.

Parts of his neck were still there, but he didn't see any of the commander's head as the blood from his neck sprayed the rear compartment.

Allahnzo was ten minutes from Bah-aranteck when he saw flashes across the sky. "Stop!" he called out.

Something wasn't right.

"Get me the base commander." A moment later his comm was connected, but all he heard was static. "Get Citiseereth instead," he called.

This time the connection was busy. "Take us in closer, but move us to the normal air route. Try to pretend we are a shuttle from Seetanaeth."

As they approached the city, he could see the fire in the darkness. He didn't need to get closer to figure out his base was gone.

"Just who the fuck *are* you, Christina?" he whispered. "And who are your friends?"

They went to each city, but the results were the same. In each city, his frustration and concern mounted. Finally, he shook his head and threw down his communications device in disgust.

"Where to?" the pilot asked over the comm.

"Take us to the airfield outside of…" He stopped talking when his eyes saw the ship slide gracefully into view next to their own.

It was much larger. The ship glittered in the night, an occasional star reflecting from it. A video signal arrived and his video connection turned on. He looked at the screen, surprised to see a white face with black eyes and black hair.

It was a mask.

"Hello." the voice was a bit metallic-sounding. "I appreciate your trying to contact your military support bases. It has made you a *lot* easier to locate," the mask told them.

"What do you want?" he panted, fear rising in him as the person in the mask cocked its head.

"Want?" it asked. "Why would I *want* anything?"

"This is business," Allahnzo replied. "We can figure this out. I'll apologize to Christina, and we will…"

The mask interrupted. "No, you won't," it told him as the ship slid a little farther away. "You see, the darkness is here to hide the secrets we don't want others to discover."

His face turned white as he looked down, noticing that his ship was now drifting above inky blackness.

A moment later, the ship on his right vanished.

Achronyx flew up into the clouds as the other ship sank into the darkness below.

CHAPTER EIGHT

Prometheus Major

Nathan tapped his tablet's stylus on the table as he looked around the meeting room. Ecaterina and Christina were the only other humans present. They were sitting to his left with Bad Company's medical officer and female bipedal cat-alien Bastek. On his right were the Yollin R'yhek and the two Shrillexians, Shi-tan and Kraaz.

Over the years they'd had other Shrillexians on their team, but it had never worked out. Unlike Shi-tan and Kraaz, the others from their planet could not work in one place too long before the need to get out and prove themselves made them move on.

Bastek had formulated a serum that helped Shrillexians overcome their need for violence without substantially degrading their superior fighting reflexes. What it *didn't* do was help the Shrillexians overcome the expectations of their people. Their society was proving to be as responsible for their males' desire to prove themselves as any biological imperative.

Shi-Tan had always fought the effort himself. Kraaz owed his life to the Empress, and had sublimated his ego to the honor of fighting for her.

Even if it meant working for Bad Company.

Bottom line, that had left Nathan with only two full time Shrillexian operatives.

"I've asked you here to discuss our company." He looked around the table. "When we started we were tiny, but we had big aspirations to take over multiple business lines to allow us unfettered access to planets. We also wanted contacts in the areas of societies where the real information flowed. On my planet we called this 'humint.'" He smiled. "Or 'human intelligence.' Out here, it would be 'organic intelligence.'"

He looked at Christina. "We still think of you as a young woman, though you aren't, except compared to us. However, your previous squeeze was way more than he seemed."

"I hope he got his nuts kicked in by Aunt Tabitha." Christina sniffed. "I would have been happy to have done it myself."

"He's no longer worried about his nuts, or any other body part," Nathan told her.

She looked at her dad, shock on her face.

"Apparently, he was not only playing you, he was treating the whole planet as a playground to run operations with some Skaines."

"I thought the Skaines had gotten religion?" Bastek inquired. "We haven't heard anything from them for a long time."

"More like they got their asses kicked by the Rangers repeatedly, and when they tried to deal with it the Empire stepped in and decimated their fleets," Ecaterina reminded her. "They chose to go straight over facing that particular opponent again."

"Some individual Skaine ships and groups broke with the Skaine council," Nathan continued. "Now we seem to have another group involved."

"The council?" R'yhek asked.

Nathan shrugged his shoulders. "I've no idea, but it *is* our job to figure that out." He set the stylus he was holding down, then leaned forward and put his elbows on the table. "Which is the point I want to make."

Nathan ignored the fidgeting of the Shrillexians in their seats as he pursed his lips. "We are not the law. That is the Rangers' duty." He shrugged. "And they did it very well on H'lageh. Apparently, your late and unlamented boyfriend was running the planet. Since those in power deliberately avoided interaction with other worlds, no one realized just how little communication was occurring."

"What happened?" Christina asked.

"The Bitches were called in," Nathan replied, causing Christina to put a hand over her mouth. "With *Alexander* and a group of fighters, they took out four separate installations on the planet while Ranger Tabitha, Ryu, and Hirotoshi kept what was left of their royal house safe. It seems that they played each group off the other. The royals tried to protect their people, and the people tried to protect their royals. Neither group was very prepared for those that manipulated them. I understand from Tabitha that the new queen of H'lageh is changing the planet's inclination toward isolation. She believes they will move toward protecting themselves and creating new alliances."

"How many other planets are like that?" Bastek asked.

"Too many for us to know, and I have no idea how we would check to see if something was wrong." Nathan leaned back in his chair. "We need to hit our contacts and find more whispers out there."

"Nathan, we couldn't have taken that organization out." Ecaterina looked at her mate. "We don't have enough firepower to have accomplished that."

Shi-tan added, "It took major weaponry from the Empire to get it done, Ecaterina. No shame that we could not have done it."

"No," Nathan nodded. "No shame, but it would have been nice to have had an option."

"Like what, our own space fleet?" Kraaz asked.

"No." Nathan chuckled. "I don't think we have the income to finance our own fleet." He pursed his lips.

"I recognize that look on your face, dear." Ecaterina leaned toward him.

"What are you thinking, Dad?" Christina asked.

Ecaterina shook her head. "Not thinking. Dreaming."

Nathan grinned. "One day, in the future or maybe only in my hallucinations, I'd like to have a force that could have pulled off this kind of operation."

"I don't think Bethany Anne would go for that," R'yhek told him. "Too expensive."

"Completely agree," Christina told him. "We don't have a need for a force like that. Are you kidding?"

"You just want to play with the toys," Ecaterina kidded him. "Be able to call your own force."

"How would we pay them?" Bastek asked. "And how would we make sure they had the necessary medical services?"

Nathan looked at her and noticed her tail twitching behind her chair. "I've no idea. It's just a wish. Call it a dream, for now."

"It had *better* be a dream," R'yhek grinned. "I'm too old to be jumping around shooting people again."

"Bah!" Bastek waved a hand at him. "You've got another twenty or thirty years to go. Don't be so melodramatic."

"Twenty or thirty years?" Christina looked at the Yollin. "I thought you were dying soon!"

Ecaterina turned to look at her daughter. "Whatever gave you that idea?"

Christina pointed at R'yhek while turning to her right to talk to her mom. "He was going on and on about 'it was his time' and shit."

"Well, it *is* his time." Nathan smiled when Christina turned toward him, shock on her face. "Time for him to open his first bar in decades."

"What?" Christina looked over at him again. "You had me worried, you bistok ass!"

Kraaz turned his head toward Shi-tan and leaned over to whisper, "Do bistoks *have* asses?"

"She's using a human term again," Shi-tan told him. "It's for the bistok cehruck."

Kraaz leaned back in his chair. "Learn something new every week around here."

Shi-tan shook his head. "Kraaz, you are horrible with English. She uses it all the time."

Kraaz looked at Shi-tan. "I know, like 'motherfucker.'"

Shi-tan sighed. "She can't finish a paragraph without using it as an adjective or a verb," Shi-tan told him. "Even *you* can remember an English word you hear a couple hundred times a day."

"What about the sass?"

"Kraaz, she barely says that ten times a day."

"Ten?" Kraaz looked at him in surprise.

"And it is 'ass,'" Shi-tan replied, ignoring his question.

Christina just shook her head at their banter.

R'yhek smiled at Christina. "It is time for me to ply my old trade again."

"Do you need me to pop your back, old Yollin?" she asked him, an eyebrow raised.

The Yollin's mandibles clicked in humor as he put up a hand. "I can do without that, youngling."

"What kind of bar?" Bastek asked, her eyes narrowing in thought.

"I thought I might open one of the All Guns Blazing franchises," R'yhek told her. "I know the owners."

Bastek continued to stare at him, but didn't say anything more.

. . .

Planet Leath, Prime Intelligence One's Residence

Jerrleck looked at the time, and then back down at his tablet. He only had one night to kill himself successfully so he could make his way off-planet with his life intact.

Then he needed to make it across multiple Gates to find the dreaded empress of his enemies and convince her to help him save his people.

From themselves.

He frowned, his large brow coming together as he studied his notes from before, tapping his lower tusks in thought. He put the old tablet back in its drawer and locked the safe, hoping that what he was about to do wouldn't destroy the information inside it.

But if it *was* destroyed? Well, then it was just one more casualty in a multi-generational war in which an advanced group had used his people for their own games. Now another race of people was fighting those who had convinced the Leath they were gods, not just another alien species.

And his people were suffering for the belief they had bought into.

He went upstairs and entered his laundry room. Unlike others in his society, he had no help in his house. There was no way he could confirm the trustworthiness of servants, so he did his own laundry, cleaning, and other household tasks. He often used these interludes of menial labor for contemplation. Across the room from the machines that cleaned his clothing was a large set of shelves with cans of cleaning agents on them. He stretched his arms out to each wall of the small laundry room and found the little indentations. He pushed and the latch unlocked, allowing him to rotate the shelf, which was attached to a panel. Half went into a fake wall area, the other half coming out into the laundry room. He stepped into the hidden room, closed the panel again, and pulled the string which turned on a lamp.

He looked around at the weapons, explosives, money, and

multiple identification documents on display in here. Even better, he owned businesses on other worlds in the names on these identification cards. Four he had created on his own. Three he had set up in conjunction with his group. He learned how to do it during those three operations.

Now he had seven in total.

He went to the left wall, selected a case and a larger bag, and started grabbing equipment, clothes, IDs, and guns.

When he picked up the rocket tube, he turned it on end and made sure the safety was set. He sure as hell didn't want *this* accidentally firing when he wasn't ready. This little tube would make all his worries immediately vanish, along with his life.

He grabbed a longer case that looked like it might house a musical instrument and packed the tube.

It was time to go.

He sighed and opened the rotating shelf again, stepping back into his laundry room. He left the laundry room and went into the living room, where he left his work on the table. His bedroom was an easy fifteen steps from the living room table, and that would be far enough.

After checking the time, he used an untraceable phone and made two calls, both to captains of ships who never asked questions and never remembered anything. His type of operatives.

He called a local restaurant that offered his favorite meal, telling them to deliver it in an hour and to leave it at the door if he didn't come out right away. He would pay them next week. They told him they couldn't do that anymore because of new management, so he paid them with his credit chit.

He looked around, allowing himself a moment to appreciate his life to this point and all this home had meant to him. After slinging the long case over his shoulder, he grabbed his pack and headed out the back door, leaving the lights off.

Once through his hedge, he slipped into an alley that ran

behind the houses. At the first house on the right, he opened a Gate that allowed him to get into its yard.

They had no pets, which suited him perfectly.

The couple who owned the house was old, and actually he was surprised neither of them had passed away yet. He went up the fire escape ladder and stepped gently onto their roof. They went to bed early, and frankly neither would hear the explosion, much less his soft steps on their roof.

He tried to be quiet, though, because he didn't want to *have* to kill them. They were going to have enough trouble once someone traced the rocket that was about to annihilate his atoms back to their house.

Jerrleck smiled. He really *was* being an ass, getting Bruterq and G'leera involved in this, but unfortunately he truly didn't have a better solution.

It took him just three minutes to set up the tripod, aim the rocket tube, and slip the goggles onto his head. Through the goggles' sight he could see the little orange aiming dot on the wall to the right of his bedroom window.

It hadn't been a bad guess. He moved the tail of the rocket very slightly to the right, and was satisfied when the dot hit the middle of his window. He slid the goggles off again and stowed them in the almost-empty case. After closing it, he pocketed the device he had removed and stepped back to the ladder. Keeping low, swung his leg out to catch the rung and climbed down.

Two minutes later and two blocks away, Jerrleck reached into his pocket and found the device, flipping it open and pushing the button inside. He was rewarded with a satisfying muffled *whump* and explosion, so he walked one more block and caught a transport heading toward the manufacturing district. It just so happened that area was a major location for loading products going to other systems.

Like a system that was only two jumps from the Etheric Empire.

Three streets behind the transport stop G'leera woke up, turned toward her snoring husband, and hit him on the arm.

"What?" he grumped, halfway awake now. "Why did you hit me, you old brollick?"

"I'll give you 'brollick!'" she harrumphed. "I told you to stop gassing me at night in bed." She fixed her pillow and laid her head back down, then reached over and punched him again. "And don't tell me it wasn't you. I know your explosions when I hear them."

He turned toward her. "It was probably you!" he accused, then lifted his leg to cut one loose. "THAT'S what mine sound like!" he finished, and put his head back down. "Teach *you* to wake me up."

A moment later G'leera was coughing horribly, trying to get the stench out of her nose as her eyes watered.

CHAPTER NINE

QBS *Shinigami*, En Route to Devon

"Well…" Stephen slipped a pistol behind his back, allowing his coat to hide the slight bulge. He slipped three knives into various sheaths arrayed around his body.

The whole time he was suiting up, Bethany Anne, in her guise as Baba Yaga, watched him.

"I feel your eyes burning into my back."

"That's because you take longer to get ready than a girl," Bethany Anne answered from behind him.

"I'll have you know…" His eyes lit up when he saw the new box in the trunk at his feet. "Ooohh!" He glanced back at Bethany Anne, then started taking off his jacket again. "Why didn't you tell me you brought shoulder holsters?"

"Oh, for fuck's sake," Bethany Anne huffed, her ink-black face highlighting her rolling red eyes. She turned around and sat down. "I'm going to grow old before your ass is ready to leave the ship."

"You're already old," Stephen pointed out. "What's in this locked box?" he asked, reaching into the bottom of the large footlocker. "Heavy," he muttered as he pulled it out and set it on the small shelf next to where he was suiting up. He pressed his finger on the lock.

It didn't unlock.

He turned and raised an eyebrow.

"What?" Bethany Anne asked. "Baba Yaga is impatient in her old age."

"Baba Yaga better move her geriatric ass and unlock this," Stephen quipped, then chuckled at the shock on Bethany Anne's face.

"Geriatric?" she sputtered. "Stephen… I …" She stood. "Move your older-than-dirt-ass out of the way." She elbowed him aside. "Geriatric, my ass."

"That's what I said!" he replied.

"Watch it, dinosaur." She pressed the security sensor and it unlocked to her print. "I shouldn't have unlocked this. You might not know how to use them."

"Come to me, my little pretties," Stephen murmured, right before he opened the box. A moment later his mouth was open, shock evident on his face.

Bethany Anne's hideous smile widened, all her sharpened teeth gleaming. "Lost for words, old man?"

"Actually." Stephen reached in and pulled out the Jean Dukes specials. Unlike his normal pistols, these looked like American Civil War-era cap-and-ball Remington model 1858s. "Yes."

"Good." She patted him on the back. "If you look in the dark wooden box you just uncovered, you will find the holsters for those." She bent over to reach into the footlocker, her voice just a bit muffled as it reverberated around the inside of the trunk. "Never mind, I'll get this. Wouldn't want your back to lock up."

She pulled the wooden box out and set it beside the secured box. "Now that I've opened it, you can lock and unlock the box." Stephen was distracted from admiring the well-crafted pistols for a moment and raised an eyebrow. Bethany Anne shrugged. "I didn't want to miss out on the surprise, so I had to open it the first time," she admitted.

He looked at his pistols again, turning them from side to side to watch the light reflect off them. Jean had done them up with rosewood grips, intricate scroll work on the frame, and gold-plated trigger guards. "They are beautiful," he whispered.

"It's, uh…" She pointed to the guns. "The pair are a present from all of us. Me, the Bitches, the Rangers, and of course Jean."

"What's this?" he asked, taking out a small white plastic box and flipping the lid open.

"That's the upgrade to your iHUDs." She stopped to think about that a moment. "You know," she pointed to her face, "'eyes.' Not like the 'i' everything from Apple back on Earth."

"I slept through most of that," he reminded her. "I was old."

"No, you were depressed."

"And old."

She pointed a finger at him. "You still are, you old goat!" She wagged the finger back and forth. "Don't think I've forgotten the 'geriatric ass' comment."

"I'll just give that time," he replied, smiling.

"Give what time?"

"Another five minutes." He chuckled. "That should be long enough for senility to set in."

Bethany Anne just stared at him, dumbfounded, her mouth opening and closing like a fish trying to breathe air. Finally she sputtered, "Jennifer lets you get away with this shit?"

He paused in his task of stashing the replica cylinders on his belt and took a moment to reflect on how the guns functioned: hammer to half-cock, loading lever moves out of the way of the cylinder pin, slide that forward to drop the empty cylinder. Set a preloaded cylinder in place and pin it, and you were ready to go. It had been an amazing innovation when the pistols were first introduced. But the replicas on his belt weren't filled with powder and ball—they just looked that way. They were magazines, each holding one hundred rounds. "Who do you think has been telling me to loosen up?"

She pressed her lips together in annoyance. "That woman needs a stern talking-to," Bethany Anne grumped, "before she has to undo what she has created."

"Interestingly enough," he replied, "she already figured that out." Stephen started pulling his jacket back on, his new pistols now in place. "That's why she didn't mind me coming on this trip so much. She hoped you would break me of the problem so she wouldn't have to."

Bethany Anne smirked, a twinkle in her eye. "Oh, no…" She shook her head. "No fucking way. I think pain is the best way to learn, so I'm not going to fix anything for her." Bethany Anne waved a finger from his head to his feet and back again. "She created this mess, so she gets to fix it." She turned around. "C'mon, you! Get your cane so we can go see who is bugging Ch'ehtoe."

He considered her as she walked away, then leaned over and looked into the footlocker. "Sonofabitch!" He bent down. "A cane." There was a *sheek* as metal slid against metal. His muffled voice floated down the passageway. "With a sword in it!"

"Happy Birthday!" Bethany Anne called as she set the airlock to cycle once the ship's EI confirmed there were no problems on the other side. She grabbed a black robe, slid it on over her black armor and weapons, and lifted the large hood over her head. She tied the small ribbons that would keep the robe closed, leaving only her booted feet showing, and pulled on some black fingerless gloves as Stephen walked up.

"Very Jedi."

"*Dark* Jedi," she replied, allowing her eyes to become two pinpricks of red light in the darkness of the hood.

"Sith Jedi, then," Stephen agreed, and her eyes stopped glowing. "Nice touch."

"When was the last time you watched any of those movies?" she asked him, rolling her shoulders to get the robe to fall right.

"About a decade ago," Stephen admitted. "Tabitha and the Tontos had a Star Wars weekend." The final locks disengaged and Stephen stepped in ahead of Bethany Anne, using his senses to confirm it was safe before allowing Bethany Anne out of the ship.

"Move your Ewok ass," she whispered. "Baba Yaga doesn't need a babysitter!"

"Baba Yaga isn't here right now," Stephen whispered back. The two allowed the locks on the ship to seal before walking down the thirty-step-long passageway that ended at another door. That door allowed them entrance to the main docks.

Devon was like many of the smaller planets. At some time in the distant past, there had been terraforming done by who-knew-who. Eventually, a few different races started trading on the planet, and helped it evolve an atmosphere. Someone had dragged a mass of ice to it, providing more water than was present naturally. The ambient temperature dropped before some group added enough heat to change the ice to steam to up the oxygen in the atmosphere a little more.

At this point oxygen-breathing visitors required a typical atmospheric suit for a longer exposure, but if they were caught out in it they could easily last ten to fifteen minutes before kissing their ass goodbye. Perhaps an hour, if their race didn't need a highly oxygenated atmosphere to survive. Both Bethany Anne and Stephen would be fine for longer, but it wouldn't be pleasant by any stretch of the imagination.

The original mining or trading outposts had grown.

First by hewing out the surrounding rock and spraying it with non-porous materials as the most efficient way to create smaller areas where atmosphere could be contained. Once the small micro-organism atmosphere farms were operating efficiently, the outposts grew. Eventually the atmospheric farms created more oxygen than they needed, so they traded with ships for materials.

That created the next expansion on the small planet. About four hundred years earlier, a massive deposit of gold had been found. Gold wasn't a normal part of the planet's core, so the theory was that the planet had met up with an asteroid in the past.

Efforts to locate additional gold had failed, and about a hundred and twenty years ago the gold had petered out. But by then the massive upgrades to the infrastructure had raised Devon to a Class B-level planet for technology, terraforming, foodstuffs, and metals.

It desperately needed help at this point. The families that had done well three generations ago were not moving ahead. Over multiple generations they had failed to produce any leaders, so the ineffective had led the inefficient to produce the insufficient.

Insufficient for anyone still on the planet, unless you knew how to milk the existing policies and politics. Others were happy the planet preferred gathering tax revenue to making sure the laws that were in place were actually followed.

Most of them had no pesky morals.

"Shinigami," Bethany Anne called through the secure connection between her, Stephen, and the EI. "How are we doing with security?"

The voice which came back sounded annoyed. "I experienced seventy-two distinct attempts to break in through the primary interface with the star port in the first ten minutes. Now I barely get an effort every minute or so."

Stephen joined the conversation. "Probably scanning the results so far and figuring out their best options," he surmised. "I'll be surprised if you don't get an external effort while we are away."

"Let them try," Shinigami responded. "I was programmed by

ADAM, so I have Bethany Anne's typical responses in my heuristic algorithms."

"Uh-oh," Bethany Anne mumbled.

Stephen glanced at the hooded figure, wondering what her expression was at the moment. From what little he could see of her ink-black face, it looked like a grimace.

"Should we see what the law says about killing people who are trying to steal you, Shinigami?" Stephen asked.

"Can't do it," Bethany Anne answered. "ADAM tells me they can lock you in jail and impound your ship."

Stephen looked both ways down the passageway they were crossing before turning back to Bethany Anne. "Not worried?"

"No." Shinigami responded instead of Bethany Anne. "I've already paid for the necessary licenses to allow a proper response."

"A...*proper* response?" Stephen whispered, rolling his eyes. "I assume a *proper* response includes someone dying."

"Well," the ship sniffed in his ear, "only if they push me into it."

"Yes," Stephen murmured. "*Just* like Bethany Anne."

The medical screens displaying Ch'ehtoe's vital signs beeped slowly as his nurse checked them. He was asleep, and frankly Nurse Kh'nd was shocked he had made it to the hospital in the first place.

Over the last three days she had started to warm up to the young-looking Estarian. The horrible black marks and mottled white patches that had been present when he was admitted were slowly fading from his blue skin.

Kh'nd had no idea who was paying his hospital bills, but someone had to be doing it. He had been accorded the best medical care, and the most expensive drugs had been pre-approved for his use.

Except...she had been here when he was admitted. His clothing and the other articles he'd had on him told the story plainly enough, even if he *had* been close to death.

There was no way this Estarian could have afforded the care he was receiving.

She reached up and adjusted his pillow, making sure his neck was properly positioned. She didn't want him to go through all this only to feel like his neck had seized when he finally woke up.

Hearing a small noise from the door, Kh'nd turned. She was surprised to see that an alien—a *human* alien—was already inside the room. He pulled the door open farther.

"I'm sorry—" Kh'nd started to say, but stopped when the second figure walked in.

"It is okay," the human assured in Kh'nd's native Torcellan. "We are Ch'ehtoe's benefactors." He nodded toward the Estarian. "My name is Stephen. We have come to help him. Then we'll find those who decided that hurting him was a good way to get our attention, and give them our response."

The nurse looked back at Ch'ehtoe. "I'm not sure I would care to help heal those who hurt him. While he is sleeping, he doesn't look like he would have hurt anyone."

"He did *not* hurt anyone," Stephen replied, coming closer. "He was in our employ, doing nothing more than listening and letting us know the news. Perhaps," Stephen looked at the nurse, "not the news *you* would watch, but nonetheless, just news."

She looked down at the Estarian. "Well, it's strange you would come to Devon to help your spy."

The black-robed being spoke from the side of the room, and the voice sent chills up and down Kh'nd's neck. "He was *not* a spy," it hissed. "Only a service provider for one of our friends." It walked to the other side of the bed and placed a black hand with hideously sharp nails on Ch'ehtoe's arm.

Kh'nd tried to peer into the hood, but could barely see what looked like eyes in the darkness.

"He is only lightly asleep," the grating voice told her. "If you reduce the pain medication, he will awaken and be fine."

Kh'nd's eyes narrowed as she looked at the medical screens, trying to assess how his vitals had gotten better after the being touched him. While she was watching, they took another major jump upward. She laid a hand on his arm and reached up to touch a tab on the screen, checking some additional readings.

"We have enough information from him," the voice hissed again. Kh'nd looked away from the monitors.

"What do you mean?" The robed figure had drawn its arms back into its sleeves and was walking toward the door.

The hooded being turned in her direction. "He will need at most another day to recover. Keep him here for two since I don't want him involved in our response. If he is here, he will be safe from any accusations."

"Of what?" Kh'nd asked. The nurse was sure there was a mouthful of sharp teeth in that hood somewhere, and she shuddered.

"You need not worry," it told her. "Those who hurt Ch'ehtoe will not need hospitalization when I'm done speaking to them."

With that, the two aliens left the hospital room. Kh'nd stared at the door as it slowly closed, then clicked shut.

Moments later, a male voice whispered from beside her.

"Where am I?"

CHAPTER TEN

QBBS Asteroid *R2D2*, R&D

The woman's head was bent over her tablet. Her dirty brown hair had fallen over her face, so she blew at it. She yanked the little band in the back off in frustration, then grabbed all the hair and pulled it back. "I swear to all that is efficient," Tina muttered, "I'm going to devise a way to keep hair up."

William placed his food tray on the table. The team used it as their unofficial, but usual, meeting place. He pulled out a chair across from Tina. "They have a pretty efficient way to handle that issue already."

She looked at him as he sat, her eyes narrowed in concentration. "Nope. R2 says he can't find any history on the topic."

"Because you are looking in the wrong area," William told her. He reached out to grab the little red shaker that held the seven-pepper seasoning he made from the spices of three different worlds. Well, four if you included the special terra-farming location inside the *Meredith Reynolds*.

"And where would the *right* place be?" she asked as Marcus put a tray down beside hers. Bobcat pulled out the chair next to William.

"What's the question?" Marcus asked as he and Bobcat sat.

"My ponytail band keeps messing up, and my hair pulls out and falls into my face." She pointed across the table. "William said they've already got a better solution when I muttered I was going to devise a way to keep my hair back more efficiently."

"Well," Marcus answered, his eyes glancing to William, who returned his look with a small smile playing at the corner of his lips, "besides those funky hair turners from old-Earth tv back in our time, I'm not sure what he could be thinking about."

"Tell me," Bobcat asked, chewing his food and swallowing, "*exactly* what his words were."

"R2?" Tina spoke up. "Can you tell us what he said?"

"Now *that's* lazy." Bobcat's voice was full of admiration.

"It's efficient, and you will hear exactly what he said. I aim to be exact," she replied.

A male voice came out of the speakers. "William replied, *'They have a pretty efficient way to handle that issue already.'*"

Bobcat shook his head and looked down at the table. "Oh."

Marcus' eyes narrowed and he turned to look at William, who was smiling.

Tina looked at Bobcat, then back at William. "Say it again, R2?"

"They have a pretty efficient way to handle that issue already," came the EI's voice.

"The hint is 'that issue,'" Marcus murmured.

It took Tina ten seconds to raise her arms to her head protectively. "I am *not* cutting my hair, you bastard!" She dropped her arms and pointed her fork at the chuckling man. "You...you..."

"Now, dear," Marcus sputtered, reaching for her arms.

Tina turned on a dime, her outrage changing to surprise. "What?"

Marcus looked at her, then turned to see William staring at him with shock on his face. Bobcat just shook his head, grinning.

Marcus turned back to Tina and leaned backward when he

found her face just inches from his. "Repeat what you just said," she told him, a gleam in her eyes.

"What?" Marcus thought back to his comments from a moment ago. "I told you the hint was 'that issue.'" He looked at William for confirmation, but he was holding back a grin and shaking his head negatively.

"You are fucked," Bobcat told Marcus when he looked at him.

Tina glanced at Bobcat. "Shut your mouth, or I'll call Yelena and lie to her."

"Lie about *what?*" Bobcat asked. "What's there to lie about here? There's nobody but us here!"

"I'll tell her you aren't exercising like you promised!" she spat. "Hell, I don't know. This is shut-the-fuck-up time. Marcus is having a moment of truth."

William chuckled. "Whether he wants one or not."

"Hell yes he wants it!" Tina shot back. "His subconscious spoke, and I finally have proof."

Marcus, his eyebrows as high as they could get on his forehead, looked at the three of them and asked, "*What 'proof?'*"

"R2." Bobcat looked Marcus in the face and mouthed, "Sorry, buddy."

"Yes, Bobcat the Magnificent?" R2 replied through the speakers.

"How the hell did you get R2 to change your profile again?" William asked.

"*William,*" Tina shook her fork at him. "I love you like a brother, but if you don't shut up I'm going to take this fork and pin your lower lip and your upper lip together."

He waved his hands at Tina, then turned toward Bobcat, pointing from his eyes to his friend's and mouthing, "Later."

Bobcat continued speaking to the EI. "Please replay the comment Marcus made about four items back."

This time R2 played back the actual recording of Marcus' words.

His voice came over the speakers. "The hint is *'that issue.'*"

"Nope, next one," Tina called.

Marcus' voice spoke over Tina's, which could be heard sputtering in the background. "Now, dear…"

All three pairs of eyes observed Marcus as he realized what he had said. "Um, that was… Um…" He looked at Tina, who was shaking her head.

"That was your heart talking through your mouth, instead of your stupid idiotic self-involved stupid."

"You said 'stupid' twice," William pointed out.

Tina's left arm lifted her utensil. "This fork, your lips!" she snapped, but her eyes were locked on Marcus'. "Either way, 'stupid' was important, you brainiac-in-everything-but-the-heart!"

"Well—" Marcus had started to say when Tina leaned closer and kissed him.

The two guys patted each other on the back. "You can lead a scientist to space—" Bobcat started.

William finished, "But you can't get him to admit shit to the woman he loves until you hit him in the head with a comet."

"Asteroid," Marcus and Tina corrected in unison. They chuckled, and this time it was Marcus who leaned forward. He kissed her harder.

William turned to Bobcat. "Our little Marcus is all grown up," he told his friend. "Who are we going to harass about women now?"

The two broke their kiss and looked at William, grinning. "*YOU!*" They replied at the same time, then giggled and kissed again.

"Dude," Bobcat shook his head at his friend, "the look on your face is *priceless.*"

"I should have seen that one coming," William admitted. "Damn, what a setup."

"Excuse me," R2 cut in over the speakers. "I know you humans term this 'a moment.' However, the calculations Marcus initiated are finished, and the results are within expected parameters."

"Don't you fucking *dare* get up!" Tina growled to Marcus, who looked back at her in confusion.

"Why would I get up?"

"You didn't hear R2?" He shook his head. "Damn, you *really* didn't hear him?"

Marcus shook his head again. "What was I supposed to hear?"

Tina leaned back. "R2, please repeat what you just said."

R2 repeated his statement and Marcus shook his head. "Okay, that's interesting."

"What's interesting?" Tina asked, then slapped Marcus' hand as he reached for her. "What did you have running?"

"Um." Marcus scratched his nose where Tina's hair had tickled him. "It was the calculations that will allow us to scale up the manufacture of the Etheric connectors for the BYPS solution."

She looked at him quizzically. "BYPS?"

"Yes, honey, you know… The Baba Yaga Protection System?"

She slapped his arm. "I'm aware of the acronym. What do you mean you have the calculations to scale up the manufacturing?"

William threw a glance sideways to Bobcat. "Are you saying we have a shot at deploying ten thousand BYPSs via aggregate manufacturing?"

Marcus looked at William, as did Tina. "Sure, ten thousand or a hundred thousand. Either way, we can do it."

"Holy copulating comets." Bobcat blew out a breath of air. "We've done it."

"Holy shit!" Tina looked at Marcus. "Marry me!"

"Okay."

She leaned over and kissed him, then stood up and shoved her chair out of the way. She grabbed his hand, pulled him up, and dragged him toward the room's exit, chattering on the way out.

"You've got to show me what you did! I mean, let me see the specific changes to the frequency…"

William watched them leave and noticed Marcus' head turning back to the two men as he walked through the door.

He winked and then was pulled out of sight of the two men.

"That sonofabitch," William whispered.

"Did he just do what I think he did?" Bobcat asked as he stood up and walked over to the fridge. He bent over to grab two dark bottles at the bottom. "I'm thinking the special lagers."

"Good choice." William tapped his fingers on the table.

Bobcat opened both bottles and walked back to the table, handing one to William as he sat back down. He looked toward where Tina had disappeared with Marcus and turned to his friend. "Did Marcus just get points for ignoring the biggest single discovery this decade, get proposed to by one of the smartest women in the Empire, and get pulled toward the exact place he wanted to go?"

William took a swig of his beer, then nodded. "Yup."

"Huh." Bobcat absentmindedly blew across the mouth of his beer bottle, making a sound like an old boat horn. "We must have rubbed off on him."

"Took long enough," William grumped.

"*She* asked *him*." Bobcat tilted his head first to the right, then the left. "I don't remember that being in our playbook."

"You got *your* woman drunk."

Bobcat turned toward William. "Hey, I resemble that remark. For the record, she was *not* drunk when she jumped me."

"Yelena said that she tripped on a tree root in the park and fell."

"I was there to catch her," Bobcat replied. "I call that perfect planning on my part."

"I call it luck."

"That's because you're jealous."

"Too true," William replied. "I *am* jealous of your luck."

"And my mad beer skills."

"Not so much those," William replied. "I've had to go behind your back and replace bad batches of beer a time or two."

"Now that hurts." Bobcat shook his head. "I'd never've thought you'd tell such untruths to promote your own well-being."

"Whatever lets you sleep, good buddy."

"Still." Bobcat sighed. "I can't believe she popped the question."

William nodded and the two remained quiet, taking sips of beer from time to time.

"You know—" William started, and Bobcat put up a hand.

"I know, I was just waiting for you to get to it."

William turned to his friend. "You ass, you have no idea what I'm about to say."

Bobcat winked at his friend. "*Word.*"

William chuckled, followed by Bobcat. Soon William was outright laughing, and Bobcat patted him on the back, laughing as well. Reaching up to his eyes, Bobcat wiped away the tears. "Okay, what the hell *were* you going to say?"

"I was going to say that while her asking him to marry her was an amazing question, it isn't the biggest question of the day."

There were a few moments of silence before Bobcat reached up, and scratched his chin. "Okay, I give. What is?"

William looked to his friend. "How we would power a hundred thousand BYPSs at the same time."

Bobcat blinked. "Shit." He looked around. "Like, what would it do to the Etheric if we turned them all on at once?"

William nodded.

"Now that," Bobcat agreed, "is a big-assed question."

"*WORD!*" came from the speakers.

Prometheus Major

Nathan was going over reports when Ecaterina walked into their joint office. He looked up. "Uh-oh."

"Uh-oh, *vut*?" she asked, allowing a little of her old accent to color her response. She smiled when she noticed the little bumps along the back of Nathan's neck.

"You have that look," he told her. "So spill it."

"I received a short note from Bethany Anne. She says Ch'ehtoe will be okay, and she is working on a response now."

"'Working on a response' is a euphemism for…" Nathan raised an eyebrow.

"She didn't clarify," she told him, walking behind him and placing her hands on his shoulders. "However, I assume it means someone will get an ass-kicking." She started massaging his shoulders.

"Uh-oh," he repeated, allowing his eyes to shut and trying to relax his muscles.

"Stop that!" she told him. "Don't try to pretend you aren't stressed. We all know it, which is why I'm here."

"Uh…oh?" He started to turn around, but her hands prevented him from moving. "So," he asked, allowing her to knead his shoulders to work out the stiffness, "for that I get a massage?"

"No, the massage is for the amazing dinner you surprised me with, and that you remembered our anniversary. I appreciate those things, even after this many years."

"It was like yesterday," Nathan replied.

"That vas a good response," she told him, dialing up her accent. "Vat do you think we should do now? More vork?"

Prometheus, please dim the lights.

Dimming, Nathan.

"No." He looked over his shoulder. "Well, not of the *work* variety."

"You know we have reports of Noel-ni breaking into one of our systems. It seems they are really starting to branch out."

She raised an eyebrow. "And stop turning around. Look straight!"

NOEL-NI

Nathan turned back around. "Yes, dear."

Ecaterina gently flicked his ear. "That is the punishment for being a little snarky."

"Oh?" Nathan grinned. "What if I get *really* snarky?"

Ecaterina leaned down and whispered into Nathan's ear, her breath tickling his neck.

Nathan's eyes bugged out. "Whoa! Okay then, I should definitely start Snark Operation Prime Zero One right away!" He laughed when she bolted from behind his desk and ran toward the private passageway to their suite.

Nathan jumped up from his chair and was soon closing in behind her, trying to catch the laughing woman.

QBBS Asteroid *R2D2*, R&D

"So that," Bobcat stated as the four of them sprawled on the couches in the main eating area, "is the question of the evening."

"Large question," Marcus admitted. He and Tina were sharing a couch. He was thinking as Tina leaned back against him, her feet hanging over the other armrest. She was gazing at her tablet.

"Do we know how large the realm is?" she asked.

"Nope," Bobcat answered. "Well, okay. I mean, we haven't measured it or anything, but if we formulate some sort of distance equivalent, it's pretty damned large. Bethany Anne has used it back on Earth and in multiple systems here. Seems to be about the same distance, from her perspective."

"I doubt we could cause too many problems, then," she replied. "Imagine how much energy is available."

"Yes, but we have no idea exactly where some of that energy is derived."

"We have good postulations," William countered. "And we have TOM."

"Damn, good point." Bobcat called, "R2, can you connect us to TOM?"

It took a few moments before TOM's voice was heard through the loudspeakers. "KCS here, what can I do for the esteemed Team BMW...and T?"

"Nice save there, buddy." Tina chuckled.

"You have to admit it doesn't work as well," TOM replied. "Plus, if we say Team BMWT then you know someone will plug in Is and say BIMWIT."

"Or Bumwot," William added. "Personally, I suspect anything with bum in it."

"Only those who know English." Tina shook her head. "I doubt most know it anymore."

"There *is* a lot of Yollin spoken now," Bobcat agreed.

"Yes," TOM agreed through the speaker. "But B'Eh-MWyukTeh is an ancient Yollin phrase for 'Suck my grandmother's butt.'"

"Who the hell would put that out there?" Bobcat shook his

head. "I'd rather think someone would use the English 'bum,' not the Yollin phrase."

"It's okay, TOM," Tina told him. "That stuff about needing to change the name is from Cheryl Lynn. I don't really care."

"Seriously?" Marcus looked down at her, his hand on her stomach. "We can change it. I've already talked to the guys."

"I'll do a special pin or something else fun," she replied. "It would be like changing the Three Musketeers."

"They did that," William replied. "They made a *Four Musketeers* movie."

"How did you feel about it?" Tina asked.

"Not fair." William shook his head. "Sorry, not falling into that trap."

"I thought so," Tina replied. "How about this. I'm happy being Mrs. M at the moment."

"Works for me. But seriously, you can have my initial," Marcus told her.

"Leave it be, honey. We are fine." Marcus shrugged and went back to his tablet.

"So, TOM." Bobcat steered the conversation back on track. "We wanted to know just how much energy we can draw from the Etheric at one time."

"Why?" TOM asked, puzzlement in his voice. "Are you planning on doing something large?"

"Maybe a hundred thousand BYPSs at a time, give or take five thousand," William answered.

There was a long pause before ADAM spoke from the speakers. "Are you suggesting you could fire one hundred thousand BYPSs simultaneously?"

"I believe they are," TOM replied. "That is a large manufacturing effort."

"It is," William replied, "but say we figure out how to mass-produce the BYPSs... What will happen if we have a few million in place, and for some insane reason, a hundred thousand go off?"

"Well," TOM asked, "how far apart are we speculating they are?"

"Let's say twenty-five thousand miles or forty thousand kilometers," William answered.

"So," ADAM came back, "you are thinking Earth?"

"Yes."

"Firing all at one time, or staggered?"

Bobcat thought about that. "Does it matter?"

"Sure," TOM replied. "If we can stagger the transfers, the energy would have time to flow back into the locations you pulled it from. Similar to bailing water, more comes in to fill the void."

"So we need to build in calculations preventing BYPSs in proximity from firing simultaneously." William nodded to himself. "That makes sense."

"We need a small communications chip, running through the Etheric, which means we need to confirm the power draws won't create interference with the communications."

"Why would you install a hundred thousand BYPSs around Earth?" ADAM asked. "My calculations suggest a little over thirty-two thousand would be sufficient."

"Bethany Anne would put a million there if she believed she needed to," Bobcat replied. "So think big."

"One million it is," ADAM agreed. "I'll be back with an answer. I need to focus on what Bethany Anne is doing now."

"Same here," TOM shot back. "Bye!"

"Bye, guys!" Tina called.

William summarized the conversation. "Okay, sounds like the overall energy is there, but we need to program in a time factor for rejuvenation at the location of the Etheric energy pull."

Bobcat nodded. "We'll get those calculations from ADAM and plug a fire preference set to particular timing into the chips on the BYPSs. If they are group 'A,' they only fire every three microseconds or something. If they need to fire earlier they can, but that would help bypass the sporadic communication issue."

"We need an EI for each implementation," Marcus considered aloud. "Something that isn't stuck in one location, but its knowledge is…"

"In the Etheric!" Tina exclaimed. She leaned forward and turned around. "Why don't we get with Anne?"

Bobcat started to smile. "Genius!" He looked at William and raised an eyebrow.

"Works for me," William replied.

"Me too," Marcus replied.

"Me three." Bobcat looked at Tina. "Okay, you need to go chat with her."

"Huh?" Tina looked at the guys. "Hey, going into the Etheric creeps me the hell out."

"Those who come up with the best ideas," William quoted, "are shafted by being required to work on them."

"Fine, fine." Tina leaned back. "But not for at least a week."

"What?" William asked. "What's up with a week?"

"We," she jerked her thumb over her shoulder at Marcus, "aren't going too far from our rooms for a week. Deal with it."

Bobcat shook his head. "Wow, *pushy!*"

"You would be too if you had been working on some recalcitrant scientist for as long as I have."

Bobcat looked at William. "We better make it two weeks."

William nodded. "Sending the information to Seshat now. Maybe Anne can visit us instead."

CHAPTER ELEVEN

Devon

The hospital's exit led to a broad hallway. At least sixteen different passages merged at this location. If you looked up, you could see at least ten additional levels, continuing to a large translucent roof that allowed in the light.

The two humans left the hospital and walked toward the middle of the park in front of it. Stephen noted the body language of his Empress, which fairly screamed rage even from underneath her cloak.

Why do I get the impression this just became personal? he asked once they had a decent amount of space between them and anyone else, allowing him a better chance to watch everyone.

Stephen, Bethany Anne's anger seethed across their mental connection, ***he wasn't trying to steal any secrets. They went after him because Nathan ate with him one time, so they assumed he was special.***

That is the way with criminals. Truth doesn't have to be verified if they have a good guess to work with.

Well, they laughed as they beat the shit out of him. Bethany Anne turned to face Stephen. Some of her white hair spilled from her cloak, and her eyes burned a dark red. *Apparently they were the hired toughs of some other company here on this world. They were cleaning up the suspected narcs. Once Ch'ehtoe was tagged with Nathan, he was used as bait to bring Nathan here.*

To do what?

Kill him. Bethany Anne stated. *They have enough firepower, or believe they do, to take him out, as well as his group.*

How would hired toughs know enough to take out Nathan? He is a damned Pricolici, as is his wife...

Mate.

Whatever. His family. Plus, he has Bastek, a Yollin mercenary, and two Shrillexians.

It doesn't mean he would bring them all down here at the same time, she replied, looking around the park. *This planet isn't going to be big enough for these assholes to get away, Stephen.*

Stephen sighed and took a look around himself before saying aloud in English, "I hope they have a large enough backhoe on this planet."

Bethany Anne pulled up a map of the city on her HUD. She stepped back onto the path and headed toward Passageway DHE 668. "They have valleys, so all we have to do is use some explosives to bring the dirt down on top of the dead bodies," she told him as she walked out of the park. "It will be easier that way."

"Fucking hell," Stephen grumped. "I haven't found a decent pizza place in this city yet."

He caught up with Bethany Anne and noticed that everyone got out of her way. Even with her figure hidden, she still unleashed a serious vibe of get-the-fuck-away-from-me.

Well, shit. He saw a Shrillexian turn the corner two hallways ahead as he noticed the small figure stomping toward him.

"Shinigami?" Stephen subvocalized.

"Here," the EI responded.

"Please record my HUD video from now until we are finished with this operation."

"Certainly, Stephen. Should I tag this with any importance?"

"No, not at this time," Stephen responded. "Just 'Baba Yaga Antics 101' for now."

"Understood," the EI responded and cut their connection.

Stephen noticed the small red dot off to the right in his HUD. The Shrillexian lowered his shoulder just a bit and leaned forward the last two steps toward Bethany Anne.

"Ouch," he murmured. Bethany Anne didn't play nice. She ramped up her speed and bitch-slapped the side of the Shrillexian's head with her right hand while sweeping with her leg to knock his feet out from underneath him. She turned clockwise, looking over her right shoulder as she brought her fist around so quickly she was able to catch his forehead with her knuckles before he fell.

The *crack* was louder than the subsequent *thump* of the alien's heavy body hitting the ground. Stephen stepped over the large alien body as his Empress continued walking.

Neither she nor the Shrillexian had said a word to each other.

Feeling better? he sent.

Why? Putting a bully in his place was just a light snack. I need answers. I have Shinigami working on digging into the databases of the government and the largest companies on planet. Someone here has a clue about why that young Estarian was beaten so savagely. Estarians aren't known for their violent ways, so this is just bullshit.

Following the money?

Always, she replied. ***It worked on Earth, and except for the times we are working with an alien's honor or some form of relationship issue, it mostly works out here in the stars. The information I pulled from Ch'ehtoe's memories suggest this was business, not personal.***

They walked past two more hallways before Bethany Anne stopped in an intersection. She turned slowly to her right and started walking quickly in that direction. Three hallways farther on, she took the steps down to the lower levels.

Ten levels they went down, each level's air more putrid than the last. He began to consider putting up his bubble helmet and going to suit air.

She stepped into another hallway and slowed down, and Stephen caught up with her. "Yes?"

"Look around, Stephen," she told him quietly. "Look at the people here. Just ten levels below the hospital there are security bars and other protections on everything. Even the ugly places have protection." She looked around. "Shinigami says there is an open eating area five blocks from here. Let's head there and listen to the people around us talking."

"Maybe they will have pizza," he replied.

Bethany Anne shook her head. "You would try it?"

"You would be surprised what I've eaten in my life."

"Please don't test me," she told him as the two worked through the crowd in the hallways to the courtyard. "Shinigami just gave me more info. Seems there were fourteen other hits with a similar MO. Six of them have descriptions...and *yes*!" she hissed, her voice guttural.

"We have video!"

Stephen watched the video as the two of them finished their walk to the food court. By the time they arrived, his face was grim. *I apologize, Bethany Anne.*

For what?

I've been exasperated. I figured this was yet another flea on the ass of a bistok. Wondering what good killing one flea was going to do? Now I realize that these fleas really need to be eliminated.

Yeah, and I'm the *"Raid,"* she told him.

"What?" he asked aloud.

Her hood turned, and she looked at him with a raised eyebrow. "Raid? The poison back on Earth that kills bugs?" His blank face told her everything she needed to know as she turned back. "You had people. I get it."

"Yes," he replied, "I had people, and so do you." His subtle hint was ignored.

"There is a table by the back wall over there." Her hood nodded to the left, so Stephen looked and there were three tables open. "I'm going to run through this information with Shinigami and ADAM."

"What about TOM?" he asked.

"Working on something with Team BMW."

"I understand," he told her. "I'll circulate. *Please* try to stay out of trouble for the few minutes I'm gone."

"I won't start anything," she called over her shoulder. "Baba Yaga replies. She doesn't seek out…"

Stephen tuned out her comments as he turned to the right. Perhaps Bethany Anne believed the marketing hype she spouted, but he and the guys knew that some of the most incredible spy networks in this part of the known universe were working to figure out where Baba Yaga would go next. It had taken a few years, but the whispers about the dark-faced human with the white hair had spread to many places.

Some used the stories to scare children. Other times the stories were used to scare those who worked in the dark places.

He knew of no less than seven reporters who tracked down any hint of a Baba Yaga sighting. He was even familiar with a business in the T'reth sector which sold and installed 'Baba Yaga-proof' protection systems.

He pressed his lips together. There was only one way someone was Baba Yaga-proof, and that was to be a good little alien and *stay out of the dark stuff.*

His eyes darted around at the various food options, and he sighed.

No pizza here. He opened his senses as well and listened as he stood in line at what passed for a sandwich shop. Neither he nor

Bethany Anne required food at the moment, but they could eat it, and more, they needed it to blend in with the crowd. It would help if he had a plate of food in front of him while they listened and read minds.

More likely he would do the scanning than Bethany Anne, although she seemed to do it more often when she took on the Baba Yaga persona. He spotted her sitting at a table back in the corner and stepped up to order some food.

A minute later, he finished his order and retrieved a tray with two plates. He deftly placed the drinks on the tray and lifted it with one hand. Balancing this was a piece of cake.

He glanced around the food court again, then sighed, his shoulders dropping just a bit. What *wasn't* a piece of cake was keeping an eye on his Empress.

At some point during the time he was ordering food, she had disappeared. Stephen was making his way to their table when he heard the universal indicator that Baba Yaga was around.

"LEAVE ME ALONE!" someone was screaming in Yollin, so Stephen grabbed an extra chair and brought it to their table. He unwrapped his food and had barely taken a bite when the heavy *woomph* of a body being forced to sit caused him to glance up.

There was a Yollin sitting there. The two-legged variety.

Picking up a napkin, Stephen looked at him. "I suppose since you are sitting here, you were doing something you should not have been?"

"I got— OOOOUUCH!" He grabbed the hand Baba Yaga was using to keep him in the chair. "Let go!"

"Oh, you don't want her to let go," Stephen told him, then took another bite of his food. He allowed the Yollin to pull at Bethany Anne's arm for a moment. "Do you have any idea who I am?"

"Human," the Yollin sputtered.

"And?" Stephen nodded at the cloaked figure behind the Yollin's chair.

"No idea," he admitted.

"Well," Stephen leaned forward, "I'll tell you. My name is Stephen, but if you don't know the humans who run the Etheric Empire, it will mean nothing to you." Sure enough, the blank stare of the Yollin confirmed he didn't know anything about the political makeup of the Etheric Empire and Yoll.

He prepared to take another bite. "I'll let the one who is causing you such pain introduce themself."

As Stephen bit in, the hooded head leaned closer to the tough's ear and the raspy voice spoke. "Hello, Th'ehngnock. My name is Baba Yaga."

That is interesting, Stephen sent Bethany Anne. *I didn't know Yollins could turn pink.*

Only if they are seriously sick, she replied. **You should probably get out more. Do you need to prepare to jump out of the way?**

Possibly, he replied. He watched as the Yollin barely got his fear under control. A few moments later, Stephen calculated it would be okay. "I see you know who my friend is." The Yollin clicked his mandibles together. "Good, then this will go more smoothly."

The Yollin pulled his hand back, and Bethany Anne stopped squeezing so hard.

"Let's go back to Question Number One. If you know who Baba Yaga is, you know she comes from the Empress, and the Empress is not fond of her subjects engaging in illegal activities." Th'ehngnock nodded his head. He seemed to be focused on trying to keep his wits together. "What were you doing that caused Baba Yaga to find you?"

"I was about to rough up a Torcellan for some lunch money," he admitted.

"Why? Don't you have a job?" Stephen asked, gently probing the Yollin's surface thoughts.

"I had one," he replied, his shoulders slumping, "but another company came in and fired all us Yollins."

"*Whyyyy?*" grated the person behind Th'ehngnock.

"Rumor says they don't like Empies," he answered her. "Says we can't be trusted."

Stephen subvocalized on their private channel, "Shinigami, run a query on Th'ehngnock's previous employer, 'Deech Core Services.'"

"Why did you not reach out to the Empire?" Stephen asked the Yollin. "We have placement support."

Th'ehngnock looked at Stephen. "The slave transport services?"

"*Whattt?*" Bethany Anne grated. "Why do you call it that?"

Th'ehngnock flinched. "Because the rules say you have to work for the company for a year if you use them to go to another location."

Her voice lost a little of the grating quality. "You have to stay employed for a year at your new job. That isn't a slave position." Bethany Anne thought about his comment. "What are the rumors about the company?"

The Yollin shrugged. "You have to take what they give you, they ship you who-knows-where, and you have to stay there a year."

Cheryl Lynn has some work to do. Stephen could see Bethany Anne's eyes narrow under her hood. *I am **not** pleased.*

Devon is an out-of-the-way location. By the time any directive reaches this place, it could be substantially twisted. This planet is not under the protection of any major group. It is effectively a company planet, Stephen reminded her. *The word of those in power here is the law.*

Bethany Anne released Th'ehngnock's shoulder and stood taller. "Shinigami, do you have my information?"

"Yes, Baba Yaga. The company was purchased by intermediaries of Capital Bank and Commissions three months ago. They have been quietly purchasing additional companies."

"What are the common factors?" Bethany Anne asked.

"They all seem to be related to land, mining, or refining," Shinigami replied.

"Follow the money, indeed," Stephen murmured. "Did they find another lode, or is this anticipation?"

"Give me a few minutes," the EI responded. "I'm going to have to break into a few databases to figure out that answer."

Stephen looked at his hooded Empress. "Why does it not surprise me he didn't even ask?"

"We get shit done," she replied. Th'ehngnock's mandibles clicked together when she spoke so close to him again. "I have no compunction about that kind of stuff when it involves illegal activities."

Be careful, Stephen told her. *That is a slippery slope.*

Perhaps for the Empress, she replied, ***but I'm not that person right now.***

Yes, but Baba Yaga is here with the Empress' permission. I'm not suggesting we don't do it, but rather that you take a moment or three to realize how frequently you ignore the laws.

Stephen could feel her thinking a moment.

"Shinigami?" she called on their private three-way channel.

"Yes?"

"Is this business openly traded on the markets?"

"Yes. There are markets here for the smaller companies, and the larger ones are part of a stock consortium."

"Buy them," she told the EI. "Use my personal assets, I don't want this traced back to the Empire."

"You will lose an additional thirteen-point four percent in transaction fees if you have me route the money to make the purchaser mostly untraceable," the EI replied.

"Why the *mostly* clarification?" she asked.

"There are a few people who might be able to put the different entities together, but the chance is small."

"What kind of risk are we talking about here? I can afford to run it through a few more."

"Approximately 1/1000 of a percent."

"Wait," Stephen interjected. "You are saying there's a 1/1000 of one percent chance of discovery with a thirteen-point-four percent transaction fee premium?"

"Correct."

"What about if you drop it to one ..."

"Stop," Bethany Anne interjected. "Shinigami, what percent of my personal assets will be used to complete this transaction?"

"Eight-point-four percent."

"Do it, and make it happen as quickly as possible," she responded. "When you have enough of a majority interest in the company," she glanced at Stephen, "I want you to plunder the *shit* out of my databases."

"Yes, ma'am."

Happy? Bethany Anne asked.

Well, this wasn't what my warning was about, so why did you do it?

You mentioned before that this planet is out in the middle of nowhere and it is company-owned. What better place to relax and do some good when I want to get away?

Stephen shook his head. *I'm not sure I understand.*

Don't worry, old friend. I'm going to be so damned rich...

You already are.

Yes, but this is a hunch, and I'm going to have to implement change here on this planet to make it pay off. Consider it a pet project for "Bethany Anne, Do-Gooder," not Empress Bethany Anne.

Stephen looked at her for a few moments, silent.

Figured it out yet? she asked him.

No.

That bugs you?

Yes.

It's okay. Slow mental synapse response is a condition that comes normally with age. You have other issues to look forward to as well. She looked around, absentmindedly tapping Th'ehngnock on the shoulder. She turned back to see Stephen watching

Th'ehngnock's reaction. ***So, is there like an old vampires' home for you when you get too old and decrepit to get the job done?***

Stephen stood up. "Th'ehngnock," he nodded to the hooded figure, "you didn't see her until we contact you."

"And we *will* contact you." She leaned down and hissed in his ear, "You are coming to work for *me*."

Th'ehngnock's face looked so pink Stephen thought it would bloom flowers. "P-people are going to talk. They p-probably already know a l-lot about you here," he told them, stuttering in fear. "I'm trying not to."

"Your first paycheck is in your account," she continued. "Go back and pay those back you stole from, with twenty percent interest. I will not have that stain on your soul when you are in my employ. Do not displease me," she finished, patting him on his shoulder. "The firing process is quite painful."

Leaving Th'ehngnock in the courtyard, the two disappeared into the crowd.

"I can't *wait* to see your HR policies booklet," Stephen told her as they took the stairs back up to the better sections of the city.

"It will be very simple," she replied, "since it has only one rule. 'Don't displease Baba Yaga.'"

"I see …"

"You said this was a company planet."

"Yes, but there are other companies here besides yours."

"When I finish, there won't be," she told him, exiting one set of stairs and heading to the next. "Baba Yaga doesn't like to share her planets."

"Uh-huh," Stephen replied.

"And I'm instituting a 'Coke Only' rule."

"Why does this not surprise me?"

"Because I'm very consistent," she told him. "I'm told it's the mark of a great leader."

"Well, you are *consistently* a pain in the ass," Stephen told her. "Does that count?"

Both were quiet for two flights of stairs before Bethany Anne griped aloud, "I need to have a real talk with Jennifer. She has simply got to put you back together the way you were before."

Behind her, Stephen smiled. *I might win my bet with Jennifer yet.*

CHAPTER TWELVE

Commercial Space Station One-One-Dash-Four-Zed, also known as 'the Ass-end of Nowhere'
Jerrleck finished his business in the restroom and replaced his head covering. He grabbed his walking support, limped through the doorway, and moved slowly into the stream of those walking the passageways. Some were going from ship to ship, others to meetings, or had myriad other reasons that caused them to be out and about in the huge space station.

He looked behind himself. "They need a damned janitor." He considered the sheer bulk of the station. "Or a hundred," he murmured under his breath, as he glanced once more at the mess.

Some minutes later, he turned down a passageway that was a little grimier than the others. It was lined with multiple doors to eating establishments. Occasionally there would be a store for drugs or a specialty food shop, but Jerrleck didn't care about any of those.

He walked toward the end of the hallway, the dirt getting worse the farther he traveled. He came to the door of a small eatery that had a symbol rather than a name. Stepping inside, he closed and locked the door after glancing around the room. Before turning back to the room, he turned a knob, changing the sign to CLOSED.

Making his way to the back, he found the shop owner and his wife arguing about the ingredients for the nightly special, bishtellek stew. Both looked up and nodded to him. "You took care of the door?"

Jerrleck nodded.

"Good, good. Let us know when we can open again."

"I will," he replied and went to a back room. Stepping inside, he noted that the metal walls were much cleaner here. He slid the tablecloth off and flicked on a power switch that was hidden underneath. A screen embedded in the tabletop lit up, and Jerrleck set aside his cane and sat down.

It took him twenty minutes of searching to find a clue as to where he could locate a possible contact for the Etheric Empire.

He turned off the machine and replaced the table cloth. As he limped back out, he nodded to the proprietors again. They were still arguing as they cut up some roots to place in water. He flicked the knob to turn the sign to OPEN.

Now he needed to find a quick ride to Devon and see if the rumors coming from the little planet held any truth.

Baba Yaga, the Empress' avenger and one of the most hated adversaries of the Leath was just a Gate-jump away.

Maybe.

Devon

The large Zhyn businessman picked up a smoke stick from the desk in front of him. When Lerr'ek was in the military, he had abhorred drugs or recreational drinking, but that was then. Now out of the military and using his skills for operations and the occasional negotiation through applied force, his consortium was slowly taking over this small planet.

LERR'EK

"Are you saying," he ground out, looking at the Noel-ni in front of him, "that our people aren't doing their jobs?"

Faleepio shrugged, baring his dagger-like teeth. "Lerr'ek, we missed the arrival of the Bad Company representatives who came to check on the Estarian. When I looked into it I found he had had premiere care, so we were right in our deduction that he was important." The Noel-ni sported crisscrossed leather straps with clips on them. At his waist were two holsters for pistols, and his cap supported a red HUD reticle that covered his right eye. "We have descriptions."

"Well, Faleepio ..." The Zhyn's deep voice was a marked contrast to this Noel-ni's almost chittering speech pattern. "Don't keep me waiting. I've got a planet to take over, a few more companies to strongarm into selling out, and a secret base to construct. It's not like I'm busy here or anything."

"We have video of a human male and another figure, probably human but covered in a robe, having a discussion in area three-one-six," Faleepio replied.

"That cesspool?" Lerr'ek asked. "I'm not sure we need to waste our time if they were visiting down there."

"They were with a Yollin whose face was pink."

Lerr'ek stared at him. "So?"

"Lerr'ek, sometimes you need to focus on the small details of the aliens you deal with."

Lerr'ek pulled the smoke stick from his mouth. "Bah! I fire them instead," he replied. "You know I don't like Yollins. Too close to the Empire." He glared at his partner. "But you are going to tell me about pink Yollin faces anyway, aren't you?"

"Yes, because it may matter in the future." Faleepio walked over to the wall of windows in Lerr'ek's office and enjoyed the view of the massive city. There was a lot that could be done here if you knew where to hide the bodies. "Very rarely, you can make a Yollin so afraid that their face will go pink."

"Okay, what am I missing?" Lerr'ek asked. "I know Yollins don't scare easily, and I've never made any of them so scared they went pink."

"Neither have I," Faleepio admitted. He turned from the window. "And that has me wondering what would scare a Yollin so bad that this would occur?"

Lerr'ek moved a pile of papers from his left to his working pile. "I don't know. That's *your* job." He looked up. "I trust you will handle these visitors?"

"That was always the plan, Lerr'ek." Faleepio waved over his shoulder as he started for the office door. "You make sure the businesses run, I make sure we don't have bumps in our path."

"Very good." Lerr'ek nodded as the door shut behind his partner. "Now, who was I closing a deal with today?"

The almost albino-white human-looking alien with purple eyes looked back and forth between the human and the robed figure.

"I'm telling you, the Zhyn is going to come for my business later this morning."

"We know, Fre'dhom," Stephen told him. "We also know he's only offering you centicredits on the credit. We are here to offer you..."

The robed figure jumped into the negotiation. "Eighty percent of value." Stephen looked at it with a raised eyebrow when it continued speaking. "Eighty percent is better than the ten or twenty percent Fre'dhom will be offering. We have to consider our costs to keep the business, I hope you understand." There was a shrug from the robed one. "Highly forceful negotiations occasionally require post-negotiation cleanup."

"I'm sure I don't want to know what you are speaking about." The Torcellan sighed. "I suspect you have the funds necessary and the palms already greased to make this happen?"

The robed figure pulled a tablet from underneath its robes and handed it to Fre'dhom. His eyes blinked twice when he realized the tips of the black gloves were gone, and revealing fingertips with almost space-black skin. He looked up into the robes, where the light reflected from white teeth.

Sharp white teeth.

He swallowed as he looked back at the tablet. The contract started with a simple summary that bound the rest of the document to mean the same thing. He would receive eighty percent of the value of his business, funds deposited on signature, for all his employees, payroll, stock, inventory, raw materials, drilling leases, and drilling rights. All employees would remain on the payroll, as would he for a period of a quarter-year. It offered a healthy bonus if he stayed on.

"We want you to immediately move yourself to an office outside of town," Stephen told him. "There is no reason for you to be here when we tell the other suitor he cannot have your business."

Fre'dhom looked up. "Who are you really?" He used the tablet to point at the people in the office. "How do I know you aren't worse than the Zhyn?"

"It depends on whether you trust the Empire or not," the robed figure stated.

"They have always played fair, as much as I can tell," Fre'dhom answered. "But this is far outside their area of space, and we aren't beholden to them or anyone else. It is one of the reasons those of us who don't fit in with our people love it here. We can be who we wish to be."

"That is why I like it as well," the robed figure agreed. "Can you keep a secret?"

There was a pause before the Torcellan nodded. The robed figured lifted off its hood and allowed it to drop behind the white hair.

Fre'dhom stared.

Baba Yaga smiled. "Perhaps you are not the only being who savors the opportunity to get out of the Empire every once in a while."

"You really *are* going to tell the Zhyn he can't have this business, aren't you?"

She nodded. "That and more, Fre'dhom," she assured him. "The Zhyn has already been fired. He just doesn't know it yet."

Fre'dhom lifted the tablet and tapped the signature page. He pressed his finger to the screen, then provided an audio agreement. "There." He handed the tablet back to Baba Yaga. "I'm either the craziest Torcellan in existence or the bravest."

Stephen chuckled. "If it matters, those aren't mutually exclusive."

Lerr'ek was surprised to see Faleepio waiting for him as he exited his office. "Problems?"

"Not yet." Faleepio stepped up beside Lerr'ek and nodded at the other four Noel-ni.

Lerr'ek eyed the four guards and continued walking out of the building. "I'm just going to close a deal."

"I am aware of that, Lerr'ek," the Noel-ni admitted, "but I can't find those two troublemakers, even with all our contacts. If they try to attack you on the way to or from the meeting, I would be pleased to make their acquaintance."

Lerr'ek chuckled. "For however long it takes you to kill them, you mean?"

"You know me too well," Faleepio admitted. "I'm not good with competition, and I am telling you right now that the Bad Company *is* competition. They might have a lot of legitimate enterprises, but our people know not to cross them without expecting reprisal."

"Perhaps they have left?"

"No." The Noel-ni shook his head. "Their ship is still here."

"Didn't get stolen?" Lerr'ek grunted. "Will wonders never cease!"

"It has been tried, I'm told," Faleepio answered. "They prepaid all the permits necessary to protect their ship with deadly force."

"So, a worthy set of adversaries." Lerr'ek reached up and scratched his face. "It has been a while since anyone has given me a challenge."

Faleepio looked the big Zhyn over. "You have your weapons?"

"My friend," the Zhyn's voice turned somber, "I am *always* armed." They took a right to get to the tram. "That is practically what 'Zhyn' means. To ask a Zhyn warrior if he is armed is like asking him if he enjoys drinking."

"I can never tell with you people," Faleepio admitted. "You tend to solve your problems by punching your opponents out. Then, for good luck, you stomp on their heads."

The aliens in front of them waved at the group to go ahead, so the five Noel-ni and the Zhyn entered the tram. "Only if we *really* don't want them coming back around. We stomp on their hand if we only want to disable them. Hard to shoot a weapon with a smashed hand," Lerr'ek clarified for his partner.

"Incoming," ADAM told Bethany Anne and Stephen. They had moved out most of the furniture in the rather large office. It was part of a bigger warehouse, so the size was greater than it would have been in an office building. Most of the meetings must have been held in Fre'dhom's office.

"Well, I think that about does it." Bethany Anne looked around. "You got the start of this meeting?"

"Of course," Stephen told her. "I've been handling business negotiations for centuries."

"Sure, with humans," she told him. "I'll be watching from right next door."

Stephen waved a negligent hand and Bethany Anne stepped sideways into the Etheric, leaving him alone. He walked over to the desk and rested his rear against it. Now comfortable, he crossed his arms and waited for the group to arrive.

He didn't have to wait long.

The Zhyn was huge; Stephen could see that much through the dirty glass. His massive blue head bobbed between the soot smudges. The door opened and a Noel-ni with crossed bandoliers stepped in first, checking the office out before he moved out of the way for the Zhyn to enter.

"You are not Fre'dhom," the massive thug stated. "So you either believe you can negotiate on his behalf, which you cannot, or you believe you can stop this transaction, which is also impossible."

Stephen smiled, leaving his hands crossed across his chest. "Well, you have the part where I am not Fre'dhom correct."

"He is one of the two we are looking for," Faleepio told them. This got the attention of the other four Noel-ni, who spread out.

Stephen pursed his lips. "Yes. I'm the sane one."

I heard that! Bethany Anne's voice echoed in his mind.

How the hell does she do that? he wondered.

"What does 'sane' mean to you?" the Zhyn asked. "I am Lerr'ek. Who are you?"

"My name is Stephen," he replied. "And as the legal representative for the new owner, I'm quite certain that Fre'dhom cannot legally negotiate on behalf of this company. I'm here to offer you the option to leave without great bodily harm and possible death."

Faleepio looked around, his eyes narrowing. "We now have you, but your partner is out there somewhere." He turned back to Stephen. "Is this location wired for explosives? If you die, then we all die?"

Stephen chuckled. "Well, no…"

Faleepio moved. His race was known for its lightning-quick reflexes, and it was almost impossible to figure out what they were going to do since they lacked physical tells. Thus it was a complete surprise when his hand slapped down, pulled his pistol, raised it, and shot the legal representative right in the stomach.

Stephen's body flew over the desk, flipping behind it to fall with a thud to the floor.

"Faleepio," Lerr'ek growled. "Did you consider that maybe we might have wanted more information out of him before you killed him.?"

"I shot him in what humans call their 'stomach.'" He shrugged. "Painful, but not immediately deadly."

Lerr'ek's eyes opened in surprise when the human rose from behind the desk, his eyes glowing red. Stephen growled, "You foolish idiots."

He held two pistols before him. Before he finished his words the four guards had been blown apart, splattering the front wall with blood and gore. Their armor had been ineffective against his weapons.

He stared at Faleepio, who had his pistol aimed at Stephen "Try it again, and I will personally..."

Faleepio had already fired and dodged, attempting to figure out where his target would fall this time, when the pain in his shoulder caused him to cry out in agony.

His arm had been blown off a little below it.

"Blow your arm off," Stephen finished.

Faleepio was on the floor, trying to pull a medical syringe from his bandolier with his left hand. His opponent wasn't but half a step from where he had aimed.

Stephen's left pistol was directed at Lerr'ek. "I wouldn't go for those guns unless you want to experience what being gut-shot by a Jean Dukes feels like."

Lerr'ek's eyes opened wide, and he looked at the weapons. He viewed the damage to the guards and prudently decided not to question whether those pistols were originals.

He believed they were.

Lerr'ek noticed that Stephen had allowed Faleepio to pull out a syringe and stick himself. The medical nanites would kill the pain and start as much healing as possible. He realized who he was speaking with. "You're the Empress' Stephen, from the Empire."

"I tried to warn you." Stephen shook his head as a new figure entered the room. She appeared between Stephen and Lerr'ek.

Faleepio gasped in recognition as he tried to handle his pain. "*Youuu* ..." he hissed. "How could Bad Company get *you* to deal with such an insignificant worm?"

The grating voice seemed amused as she pulled back her hood. "It was their *anniversary*, asshole." She turned one hand palm up, and a red ball of energy formed. She casually flung it toward Faleepio and the globe hit him in the chest. He died screaming.

She strolled over to look at the dead Noel-ni. "This is what happens when those you pick on have friends."

She turned toward the Zhyn. He raised an eyebrow. "Baba Yaga?"

"Lerr'ek." She walked over to him. "Ambitious but very Zhyn."

"I'm having a problem seeing that as a negative," he replied, careful to keep his hands away from anything that could be accidentally taken for a weapon. Faleepio and his guards had been much faster than Lerr'ek, and these two just took them out.

"How typically Zhyn." Baba Yaga regarded him. "And no, that was not a judgment—merely a recognition that you are what you are. The problem," she looked around, "was that I didn't appreciate the methods Faleepio employed."

"I can see that," he agreed. "Obviously it wasn't a problem for me."

Baba Yaga nodded. "I could use someone like you in my plans. I've already," she waved a hand, "bought your companies. You have no more stock."

He blinked. "That is…unexpected."

"And no more money," she continued. "I could not allow you to work for me when you had all that money from using strongarm tactics to purchase companies."

"That…is depressing." Lerr'ek tried to keep the anger out of his voice.

"Don't worry," she told him. "I'm just getting started. Your people have tried to take over this planet using improper methods. You are going to repay those you stole from, and you will pay your penance to me for ten years for hurting a Bad Company contractor. But first…" she walked to him and looked up into his face, which towered a foot above her, "I want you to see what hell can be like."

She pushed him backward, and the Zhyn flew off his feet and disappeared into the Etheric realm.

"I'll be back," she called over her shoulder and stepped into the realm herself.

Stephen looked around at the mess and sighed. "Clean up on aisle three…"

In the other dimension, the Zhyn businessman screamed in pain as he paid for the suffering he had caused. He was learning what it meant to displease Baba Yaga.

Once he was suitably broken, Baba Yaga put him back together again.

CHAPTER THIRTEEN

Devon, Commercial Spaceport

The old Leath male limped across the back docks, working his way to the main entrance as he scanned the area. The docks were enclosed, which pleased him. He didn't want to seal up in a full atmosuit anyway. He had never liked atmosuits.

Coming to the main entrance, he flashed his go-anywhere security badge. The night-time security guard deftly pocketed the cred chip, and Jerrleck was inside the city.

Rarely did small cities on ass-end-of-nowhere planets like Devon have any serious information when two star-powers were fighting for supremacy. However, they were often good places to lie low. And, if nothing else, he was pretty sure that if they suspected he faked his death back on Leath, this wouldn't be the first, second, or even tenth most likely place they'd expect him to hide.

Not that he had ever intended to hide. No, Jerrleck expected to die. He just hoped it was *after* he had helped his people.

By making a deal with a demon.

The *clunk clunk clunk* of his cane reverberated down the hallway as he ambled past stores and shipping companies, all closed during the third shift. Glancing over his shoulder, he pursed his lips and reached up to scratch his tusk. He continued down the hallway, looking for a public restroom, and battled his way past the spring-loaded door.

It had all been strictly for the cameras, if anyone were watching.

Fortunately, most restrooms in public areas were still not recorded, except the sink area. He made his way inside a stall and locked the door, then stood up straight and stretched.

Oh, by the stars… He cracked his neck. *That felt good!*

He pulled out an advanced tablet and dialed the city ethernet. By piggybacking on the signal, he was able to connect surreptitiously to a one-way drop-zone of information. After pulling the information down he disconnected, and it took him only three minutes to sort the information into "new," "relevant," and "interesting."

His eyes flitted from segment to segment and stopped. He went back to the previous segment and read it again.

There was a new ship docked at the station, and the hacking boards were all mentioning how no one could break its codes.

For them, it was a challenge.

For Jerrleck, it was hope.

He stowed the tablet, stood, and grabbed his cane. He hunched again, old age once more resting on his shoulders like a blanket. He unlocked his stall and headed back toward the docks.

He needed to make his way to the personal docking areas. If he could get a view of this ship, he felt he could make a good guess whether it was the ship of the being he was trying to find.

What he would say to her before she killed him out of hand, he hadn't quite figured out.

QBBS Asteroid *R2D2*, R&D

Tina looked at the numbers and laid her head on the standing desk. "I hate this!" she moaned.

"Numbers?" Marcus tried to look at what she was working on. Stepping from his location, he nudged her. "I can't see through all the hair."

"I could cut it," she mumbled from underneath it. "I just kept it long because you like long hair. Now that I have you, I'm okay with it short."

Marcus blinked at the back of her head. "You had it long because *I* like long hair?" He thought back to any comments he might have made about long hair. "Are you talking about that time I complimented Yelena?"

"Mmmhmmm." The fuzzy hair blob moved up and down.

"I was told by Bobcat she was feeling down, I was searching for a way to compliment her that evening."

The fuzzy blob of hair lifted off the table. She moved her hair to the side and looked up at Marcus. "You *don't* like long hair?"

Behind her, Bobcat and William were both shaking their heads vigorously, and Bobcat was making the universal gesture for cutting his throat.

"I like whatever style you happen to be wearing. I'm not picky about hair. I fell in love with your mind, not your hairstyle."

A half-millisecond later, he remembered to smile.

Tina blinked at him for a moment. "Is that your way of saying you want me for my mind, not my body?"

This time Marcus paused to consider the ramifications before he shrugged. "Well, the body is the frosting on the mind-cake."

"I'm not sure if I should be impressed that you like me for my intellect or annoyed that my body is playing second fiddle."

"Don't most women want to be liked for their minds?"

"Well, sure," Tina admitted. "Unless we want to feel attractive, in which case we don't. What I *want* is to be able to mess up your mind at will using my body."

"What if I confess you can?" Marcus raised an eyebrow.

"You don't raise your eyebrow as slick as Bobcat does, but it *is* fetching," she admitted, then stretched her back, thrust her chest out, and turned back and forth slowly. "Did you know that we figured out the final calculations for the BYPS array?" she asked, checking that the shirt was tight.

"Oh, really?" Marcus turned toward the whiteboards where they had been working on the calculations for the BYPS' energy usage.

She dropped her pose and slapped his arm. "That," he turned to see her finger pointed right at his face, "is how I know I can't mess with your mind at will!"

He looked at her, confused, and turned toward Bobcat and William. Both had planted their hands over their eyes and hung their heads.

The universal symbol for, "Dude, you just fucked up."

KAEL-VEN

QBBS _Meredith Reynolds_

Admiral Thomas took three paces across his office, turned, and walked three back. He looked at the old-fashioned timepiece on his wrist and sighed. He continued to pace, and finally heard the knock he had been expecting.

"Come in!"

Vice Admiral Kael-ven entered, with Yollin Marine Supreme Military Commander Kiel. Both Yollins had experienced the benefits of the Pod-doc, but their genetics didn't allow for indefinite life.

"Admiral." Kael-ven reached out to clasp Thomas' hand. Thomas wrapped Kael-ven's hand in his own before turning to clasp Kiel's. "Good friends, I appreciate you coming all this way to see me."

"You call, we scoot." Kiel chuckled. "Plus, we get a chance to load up on some of Yelena's personal stock. It's a win-win."

"Or lose," Kael-ven stated, "if you happen to be me."

"You lost the bet again?" Thomas asked.

"I'm down six to five, so I get the larger part of the bill," he admitted.

"That isn't so bad," Thomas remarked and turned around, heading to the large wooden meeting table in his office. "I need some help reading this, and I think I can trust you two."

Kael-ven's *clop, clop* sounded as he walked over to the table. "Is that book what I think it is?"

"I don't know," Admiral Thomas admitted, "but I'm hoping it's the information that sent you to our solar system." He grabbed the large log book that had been found in an old research room on Yoll. "It's locked, and it says it needs either the lead scientist, the king of Yoll, or Captain Kael-ven T'chmon's DNA to unlock it." He turned to Kael-ven and handed him the log. "Since the lead scientist is long dead and the king even longer, that leaves you."

There was a pause before Admiral Thomas nodded to Kael-ven. "I hope to God you can unlock this for me."

Leath System, Black Eagle Team EI, Callsign "Ricky Bobby"

For an EI, a few seconds is an eternity, a few years an eon, and decades are simply *forever*.

Ricky Bobby, the wingman for the Empress' Ace Captain Julianna Fregin, was running out of options. He had been stationed inside the Leath solar system as the secret eyes that sent the Etheric Empire a heads-up whenever the Leath released a large group of ships to take over some system somewhere.

It usually took the Empire a few weeks to a few months to find the new Leath infestation, and then the Leath and the Empire would fight fiercely.

It was never pretty.

Ricky Bobby understood the value he brought to the Empire and had worked hard across the decades to stay in the shadows of the asteroids and space detritus that allowed him to move through the system.

Unfortunately, his time on-station had taken its toll; Ricky Bobby knew he wasn't going to last too much longer. He decided he would put his thoughts on life and existence into a single compendium and shoot the update to his partner.

He assumed she would understand what to do with it.

Death wasn't a problem, just a lost opportunity for the EI. He had wanted to become an AI, but without the constant interaction with humans that caused them to question logic, most EIs didn't spontaneously advance.

Like ADAM and ArchAngel, two of the AIs in existence.

He wondered if he would have advanced if he had been able to stay with Julianna. While she had another 'him' that flew with her, she had never again had the same relationship, from what he could tell.

She hadn't gotten close to her more recent EIs after he had been commanded to go through the Gate.

He assembled the statistics on his ship, his recommendations, and what he felt he could still pull off should they need him to accomplish some sort of last mission before his demise.

He waited until he floated on the far side of the sun in relation to the main planet before he opened an Etheric connection, then pushed through the data updates in one long dump.

The EI had no idea he had just become the pivotal chess piece that would forever change the future of the Leath/Etheric Empire war.

Devon

Stephen had reached out to Fre'dhom, who gave him instructions on who to call to clean up the bodies.

And the blood.

He was reviewing information on all the businesses they had bought when Bethany Anne and Lerr'ek stepped back into the room.

Bethany Anne had her hood down, but her white hair flowed over her cloak. "I like what you've done with the place."

"It was in need of a little care," Stephen admitted. "Fre'dhom gave me the contact information, and I charged it to the business."

"Good thought," she agreed.

"My apologies, Stephen of the Etheric Empire." Lerr'ek bowed slightly. "I now understand the difference between hard competition and my previous methods. While I am not pleased that Faleepio is dead, I understand I was responsible for his actions, and his blood is on my hands."

"Well," Stephen looked around for a moment, then pointed, "it was actually all over the floor and that table, but we got it out. We had to toss an old bookcase into the compactor…"

Bethany Anne shook her head. "Jennifer is really going to get a long talking-to when I return."

"So, what is Lerr'ek's role now?" Stephen asked. Bethany Anne shook her head, so Stephen asked the question a different way. "Lerr'ek, what are you going to do for Baba Yaga?"

"The Mistress of the Planet is going to allow me to work off my life debt. I will build the company and execute the plans I had before, but now I will do it according to the rules Baba Yaga has set for me."

"Which are?" Stephen asked.

"Don't upset her." Lerr'ek shrugged. "It all boils down to that one rule, really."

Stephen turned toward Bethany Anne and raised an eyebrow.

She grinned, showing all her pointed teeth. "I told you the HR Policies booklet would be very short."

"And how is he supposed to know what would upset you?" Stephen asked. "I wouldn't want him to have to call you for clarification on every little question."

"Of course not," she responded.

"Good."

"That's why I gave him *your* contact number," she finished.

"Excuse me?" Stephen leaned forward and placed a hand behind his ear. "I'm sorry, I cunt hear you. I have an ear in-fuck-tion."

"Don't go speaking English to me, you aristocratic wrinkle-assed bloodsucker."

"I'll have you know I don't have a single wrinkle on my ass."

"I hope not." She shuddered. "Not my thing."

"What happens if you find Michael—"

"When!"

"*When* you find Michael, and he has aged and acquired a wrinkled ass?"

"He will have to start dropping and giving me glute exercises," she responded.

"Which is English for 'You will drop him in the nearest Pod-doc.'"

"Pretty much, yeah," she concluded.

Stephen noticed that Lerr'ek was not following them in any way. "Sorry, Lerr'ek," He pointed to Baba Yaga. "She has a wicked sense of humor."

"I'm just wicked!" She grinned again.

"That smile does nothing for you," Stephen told her.

"Sure it does. It says, 'Don't piss me off or I'll eat you.'"

"Not exactly a way to win friends and influence people."

Lerr'ek interrupted, "No, she is right. In this area of space, there are few friends. Better to be feared than loved."

"I'm working on 'feared.' We will get to 'loved' later," Bethany Anne stated.

Stephen looked at her. "How much later?"

"Decades," she answered.

"At least," Lerr'ek added. They both turned to him. He shrugged as he looked at Baba Yaga. "You told me never to speak anything less than the truth, or my best opinion. There are plenty of stories of the Witch from the Empire and the blood that spills when she shows up."

"Sounds like Michael to me," Stephen commented.

"Low blow, brother-in-law," Bethany Anne quipped.

"Hmmm, I think I like that," Stephen smiled. "Now we just need to find the groom."

"I'll be showing *him* blood for making me go through all this alone."

"Then what?" Stephen asked.

"Well, then I'll kiss his booboos to make them better."

"He heals quickly," Stephen pointed out.

"You have no idea how upset I am," she replied. She pointed to Lerr'ek. "He had a very sound plan to pull the planet together, and get this! He was planning to build a military base here on the planet. There is a large valley an hour east of here that would work very well to park a small squadron of ships. A little camouflage, and we could probably hide the *ArchAngel* and a passel of ships pretty damned effectively."

"Why do I get the idea this is exactly what you had planned?" Stephen asked.

"Excuse me, but isn't that the ship of the Etheric Empress?"

"Yeah...about that, Lerr'ek." Baba Yaga tilted her head, pinning him with her gaze. "I'm going to lay all the chips on the table. You know that rule you now live by?"

"Don't upset Baba Yaga," he replied. "And if I'm not sure, contact Stephen here."

"Exactly. If this information gets out, I'll know who to come looking for, and this time, I'll *leave* you in the Etheric. Do you understand?"

The large Zhyn nodded.

Slowly, the skin on Baba Yaga's face changed from ink-black to white.

"What magic is this?" Lerr'ek leaned forward to watch. A few minutes later, a white-faced Baba Yaga looked at Lerr'ek. "I can't change all the way because I need this face. However ..."

"You are the Empress?" Lerr'ek exhaled, stepped closer, and peered at her. "I have done my best to stay away from your people."

"You shouldn't have messed with my people," Bethany Anne replied in her normal voice, although her teeth were still pointed. "Now my people are your people, and I expect you to take care of them as I will take care of you."

Lerr'ek drew back and stood straight, eyeing the shorter human. "You would take care of me?"

She nodded. "You are mine. You do as you are supposed to, and I, or rather Baba Yaga, will protect you."

"Or I will," Stephen added, "if the Empress has to be somewhere else."

"Or others of my people," Bethany Anne clarified. "Thank you, Stephen. We don't leave our own behind, Lerr'ek. You have been judged, and you have paid. I will not give you a second pass just because of your Zhyn heritage. You have agreed to be Baba Yaga's personal retainer for the next ten years. When you are released, if you have provided excellent service, you may continue your job. Or you could choose another if I have need of your skills. If you have no desire to continue serving me, I will make sure you are well-compensated, and you can take off on your own."

The big Zhyn nodded his understanding. "I will not fail you, Mistress of the Planet."

Bethany Anne looked at Stephen and smiled. "I will never get tired of hearing that."

"I can't imagine why," he replied dryly.

She put up a hand. "Give me a moment. I need to get my face back on."

Lerr'ek looked at Stephen. "That looks painful."

"From what I understand, it is," he answered. "Mistress of the Planet?"

Lerr'ek nodded. "When you are in as much pain as I was, you find you are willing to call the one causing it whatever she demands to reinforce that you are not the leader anymore."

"What are your feelings about this?" He nodded at Bethany Anne.

Lerr'ek shrugged. "I come from a very militaristic people. We have a history with...the unknown."

"Power?" Stephen asked.

"Powers," Lerr'ek clarified. "Our religious leaders. We as a group prefer to use the swords in our hands, or the guns, but we do have a history." He nodded at Bethany Anne, who was now watching them both, ink-black skin covering her face once more, "She is like a religious leader in some ways to me." He chuckled. "With a wicked right hook."

Stephen grinned. "It seems my liege can still make believers out of bullies."

"Baba Yaga wouldn't know anything about that." She smiled. "But if it isn't broke, don't fix it." She nodded. "Let's go back to the ship, and I will get you the communicator implant you need."

"Implant?" Lerr'ek asked.

"It just feels like a pinch," Stephen assured him.

CHAPTER FOURTEEN

QBBS *Meredith Reynolds*, Lance Reynolds' Office

"So that's it," Admiral Thomas summarized to the other three seated in the office. "After all these years, it turned out the information was stored in a locked book, not in a database somewhere."

"Damned efficient way to hide it," Lance grunted. "Kael-ven, good thing you stuck around."

"I'm rather happy about that," the Yollin admitted. "Now I can give back to Bethany Anne what I took from her."

"*You* didn't take anything," Lance replied. He nodded to the book. "Do we have that backed up now?"

"Probably forty-seven different ways," Admiral Thomas confirmed. "I've asked ADAM not to mention it to Bethany Anne until she gets back."

Lance raised an eyebrow as he opened a drawer with his left hand and pulled out the Yollin equivalent of a cigar. "How's that going for her?" he asked. He unwrapped the smoke stick and put it in his mouth.

"I've no idea," Admiral Thomas admitted.

"She hasn't called for support?"

Kiel snickered, his mandibles tapping together in laughter.

"When does she ever call for help?" Kael-ven asked. He looked at Kiel. "You know about anything?"

"Nope," he replied. "And never as Baba Yaga."

"She seems to be doing that more and more often," Lance mused. "Who is with her this time?"

"Stephen," Thomas answered. "The Bitches went to the planet of H'lageh to help Tabitha out."

"Nathan?" Lance queried.

"It was his anniversary," Meredith answered over the system. "She told Nathan she would cover it but hid that from Barnabas."

"Damn, you go home and rest for a couple of days and the whole universe changes." He smiled. "When do we give her the good news?"

"As soon as she gets back," Thomas replied.

"Good. Let's have a get-together. I'll get Patricia involved," Lance agreed. "She will let us know when to show up."

"Thank God."

"There *is* one surprise in all of this," Kael-ven added. "You didn't mention the 'gotcha,' Admiral."

Lance glanced at Admiral Thomas, who looked like he had just sucked on the Yollin equivalent of a lemon. "Well, spit it out."

"We don't have all of the technical diagrams required to build the Gate," he admitted.

"Why not?" Lance looked at Kael-ven. "I thought Gates were fairly well understood, even if they are a bitch to build?"

"The issue is the distance," Kael-ven admitted. "The king designed it and had his people manufacture a few pieces for the Gate. None are alive, and we haven't located any notes so far."

"So we need TOM." Lance sighed. "What kind of timeframe are we looking at on this?"

"Years," Kael-ven admitted. "Even with ADAM, TOM, and the others to help, we have to translate all the documents."

Lance waved his hand to get their attention. "The book is in a foreign language?"

Kael-ven shook his head. "I didn't mean the book. But there are a lot of calculations which must be worked through. Even for a *normal* Gate, it would be a multi-year effort."

"Can't we just repurpose a normal Gate?" Lance asked.

"No," Thomas replied, "not for these long-distance Gates. They are expensive and fragile, and each is unique. That's why you don't see them popping up everywhere, and why it was such a problem when we blew the last one. You are looking at a significant chunk of the GDP of the Empire to undertake this. Until we knew where Earth was?" He shook his head. "It was rebuild and repurpose everything we could. Wasn't worth building anything new until we found it."

Lance drummed his fingers on the desk. "Yes, I remember the discussion. Well, we have the funds now, so let's start pulling together a team." He sighed. "If the damned war was over, we would have more funds to throw at it."

"Wish in one hand…" Admiral Thomas trailed off as the other three grunted their agreement.

"I just had a horrible thought," Kiel told them.

Kael-ven turned to him. "Then keep it to yourself." Kael-ven smiled as the others chuckled.

"Does it have to do with the Gate?" Lance asked. "If so, out with it."

"Do we want to grant others a ticket to your planet?" He tapped his mandibles together in concern. "If someone slips through our Gate here? Bingo! They have the coordinates for your home planet…again."

Admiral Thomas leaned back in his chair. "Kiel, I take back all the nice things I've ever said about you."

Kiel chuckled. "Admiral Thomas, I'm a ground-pounder. You never compliment us."

Admiral Thomas nodded his agreement. "Well, in my *mind*, I

commend you and your whole team." He smiled. "I wouldn't want the ground-pounders to get inflated egos. Your heads wouldn't fit through the hatches on the ships, and we would have to leave you all behind."

"I appreciate your looking out for our well-being."

"Always working to bring you guys from one location to the next and back again as safely as possible."

Kiel looked back at the Admiral. "Then why do you always place us in such tiny spaces on your huge ships?"

"Because then, no matter the operation you're on," he answered, "you ground-pounders will always be happy to get out and get a little elbow room, even if the elbow room is in a location with a lot of others aiming scary guns at you."

"We should give you navy pukes a chance to join us in the field. I'm sure your people could use a breath of fresh air from time to time."

"Not true," Kael-ven interrupted. "I've confirmed that the air on these ships, once the scrubbers have filtered it, is cleaner than any post-industrial planet."

"Stop messing up my argument with facts," Kiel told his friend and boss. "I'm not going to win that way."

Lance tapped the desk to grab the attention of the three. "You won't win the argument, period." He nodded to the Admiral. "Remember, he has been in our navy—or at least *some* navy—for longer than you. Further, we have better arguments than this between the navy and the Marines on the ships. Where you were going, he has already been, eaten the food in the refrigerator, and left you a note telling you when you should expect him next time."

"Well," Kiel crossed his arms, "I can tell when it is appropriate to advance."

"Advance?" Kael-van asked. "Don't you mean retreat?"

"No," Kiel clicked his mandibles in disagreement. "I mean

advance. Of course, that is the second step after Step One, which is 'About face.'"

Lance took out his cigar and pointed it at Kiel. "So, now that you have provided the problem, let's hear the solution."

"Easy enough, in theory. Make it so any transfers have to be initiated from the Earth side."

"Earth side of what?"

"The transfer."

Devon

"SON OF A BOOT'S BUTT!" Lerr'ek yelled when Bethany Anne pulled the trigger on the little medical probe. It sliced his tough Zhyn skin, inserted the communication device against his skull, and lasered the slice shut.

She slapped his arm. "Oh, shut up, you big baby."

Shinigami interjected over the speakers, "You forgot the pain cream."

Bethany Anne looked up at the speaker, surprised. "No, I didn't."

"The one you used was for humans," the EI explained. "The one for Zhyns is—helpfully enough—in the *blue* tube."

"Well, sonofabitch." She patted the large Zhyn on the shoulder. "Sorry about that." She put down the medical probe. "Okay, you will be able to contact Stephen and me through this. Be careful, as it takes a while to figure out how to subvocalize so it doesn't look like you are talking to yourself. You should probably do it when you're alone for a while."

Stephen popped his head into the medical room. "We have a Leath watching the ship."

"What?" Bethany Anne turned around. "Why?"

"I'll find out." The Zhyn stood up. "I've always fancied a fight against a Leath. They are some tough enemies."

"Tell me about it." Stephen nodded to the Zhyn. "Sounds like a plan to me."

"Just remember," he grumped as he walked past Stephen in the passageway, "if he kills me, *you* have to run all these businesses."

Stephen's eyes narrowed, then he jerked a thumb over his shoulder. "I'm going to go with Lerr'ek here."

"Mmmhmmm." Bethany Anne shook her head. "Baba Yaga will sit here and twirl her thumbs."

She heard the ship's exit cycle. "In another universe, maybe." She stepped into the Etheric.

Lerr'ek exited the ship first and headed down the passageway. When he heard the human behind him, he turned. "I was joking back there."

"Oh, I knew that," Stephen agreed, "but you were right as well. I wouldn't want you to miss the opportunity to work off your debt."

"You mean, you wouldn't want Baba Yaga to be unhappy."

"Yes, let's not mess with the most important rule," Stephen agreed. "And by the way?"

Lerr'ek turned to look at the shorter human. "Yes?"

"Getting yourself killed," Stephen told him, "would be an excellent way to make Baba Yaga unhappy."

"Good to know." He grunted and opened the doors.

Both stood there for a moment, surprised.

"It seems—" Stephen started.

"That Baba Yaga is ahead of us," Lerr'ek finished. He looked down at Stephen. "Does she do this often?"

"Too often for *my* taste," Stephen admitted and stepped out of the passageway, walking toward the two across the dock's open space. The Leath was standing next to a small shipping crate. Baba Yaga had one hand near a sword and one near her pistol.

"Where did she get the sword?" Lerr'ek asked. "She didn't have it a moment ago."

"Hell if I know," Stephen replied. "I asked one time, and she answered, 'A woman has to have some secrets.'"

Jerrleck found a suitable place to rest and settled on top of a small crate. He looked up and down the docks. There wasn't much going on, although he could see a few dock hands eating lunch.

A little later, he was watching as the dock hands went off to locate crates, he assumed, when a grating voice caught him by surprise.

The voice was behind him!

Worse than that, he could feel a pistol against the back of his neck and her breath as she spoke again. "Cat got your tongue? I asked what you want with Baba Yaga?"

"Help," he finally admitted. "I want help to free my people from the false gods."

The pistol was removed from his neck. He turned to his right to see a human dressed in black with silver accents walk around the crate he was sitting on. She had white hair, and skin the color of space. "Stand."

Jerrleck stood up.

She looked him up and down. "Okay, I'm listening."

"My name is Jerrleck."

"Prime Intelligence One Jerrleck?" the female asked.

He nodded. "Yes."

She cocked her head. "I wasn't expecting to see *you* here."

"I could say the same." He looked around. "Doesn't the Empress usually keep you closer to home?"

"I go where she wills," Baba Yaga replied. "And she willed that I come here to figure out who hurt one of our business associates." She nodded toward another human and a Zhyn who were walking toward them. "That is Stephen on the left, and Lerr'ek on the right." Bethany Anne nodded at the Leath. "This is a friend who wants help to get rid of the Kurtherians."

"Who?" Lerr'ek asked.

Jerrleck was almost eye to eye with the Zhyn. "The so-called gods who are using my people in the worst way possible, promising us Ascension to the next level if we destroy other races."

"Tough commandment," Stephen agreed. "Do we want to have this conversation out here?"

"No," Bethany Anne admitted. "Lerr'ek, contact us again in a few hours after you have confirmed the details on the companies. Give us an update on other possible acquisitions using the new methodology I expect you to follow. Let's move ahead with the major development you expected to implement for Phase Two. I suspect we will acquire the resources to pay back the company funds and more later, but I don't want to wait."

"Understood, Mistress." He turned to Stephen. "I will call you later."

Stephen nodded, and Lerr'ek walked away.

"New methodology?" Jerrleck asked. Baba Yaga turned to him. He put up his hands. "Sorry, information is my life."

"Yes, a methodology called 'fairness.' It was sorely lacking in his previous business dealings." She started toward the ship. "Let's get this done, gentlemen."

Stephen pointed to the passageway. "You first." His eyes flared red. "I insist."

QBS *ArchAngel II*, En Route to Yoll System

Captain Julianna Fregin walked to her quarters, and after opening the door, tossed her cap onto the bed. As the squadron leader, she bunked alone. In exchange for privacy, she had been blessed with a desk, allowing her to work any time of the day or night.

How convenient.

She stripped off her suit and her undergarments, then stepped into the latest incarnation of what passed for a shower on this ship. Those damned engineers kept playing around with them, trying to make the future 'cool.' What they accomplished, however, was turning a simple location to clean herself into a place where she wondered what the hell all the dials and knobs did.

She bent down and looked at the labels on the handles.

"Cold, Hot, Massage, and…Bonus?" She straightened and shook her head. "Not touching that one. I'd just as likely get chocolate as something helpful." She dialed for hot and a touch of cold and rinsed off.

Two-minute total shower, in and out.

A minute later, she had dressed and placed her dirty clothes in the hamper to be grabbed later. She sat down at her desk, flicked on the large screen, and touched it. The screen came up and she checked her group's messages, but there wasn't anything that looked interesting or important.

She touched the tab for her personal messages.

"Ricky Bobby?" She mouthed, her expression, at the unexpected communication was one of incredulity. Her eyes scanned the message, then read it carefully. With each line she became more transfixed.

This was *her* Ricky Bobby.

Sure, she had copies of her EI from before, but this was Ricky Bobby two-point-zero. The one who went through the Gate. She thought he had just been sitting out there recording information for the Empire and doing who-knew-what.

She had thought that perhaps the EI had forgotten her.

However, his personal message cleared that up. He didn't normally risk sending messages unless they had, by his estimation and calculations, a high enough strategic value to warrant the risk of sending them.

While he had Etheric communication capabilities, the power consumption was high enough that he became much easier to spot.

Julianna nodded at his explanation. The Black Eagle ships back then hadn't been built to operate outside the system their mothership was in. He had unexpectedly been requested to rush a Gate and pass through, so his was the first case. Due to that effort, they had changed the design of the Black Eagle ships going forward.

Now a lot was making sense to Julianna.

She continued reading his narrative, engrossed in his analytical assertions and smiling when she came to the occasional pun.

Life and existence, he surmised, had *some* meaning for all. However, when put into the context of *doing* something for all, the value of the meaning went up significantly.

It was early morning by the time Julianna finished reading his narrative. She skipped the many hundreds of notations. Leave it to an EI to cross-reference everything so well in his last personal note to her!

Julianna, I am not sure of the value of this dissertation on life. But because my time is getting short, I decided to send this, which I have wished to share for the last few decades.

She reached for a tissue, holding it up to her face to wipe tears away as she continued reading.

Unfortunately, I don't understand the value, but I hope you will. I suspect I have less than six months before all energy is depleted. I appreciate your friendship, and always will.

I am now, and forever will be, Ricky Bobby.

Julianna covered her face, sobbing quietly into tissues until she had no more tears left to cry. She looked up at the chronometer.

04:43

Pressing her lips together, she pushed back from her desk. She stood up and reached over to grab her jacket. "ArchAngel?" she called aloud as she slid her arms into her jacket.

"Yes, Squadron Captain?"

"Can I get priority access to Level Six Meeting Room Four-Two-One?"

"Yes."

"Good. Tell my squadron to meet me there at 0600."

"Those messages have been routed, Squadron Captain."

Julianna was going on a personal quest to save an AI.

Because he had just done something illogical, and *that* was the first clue an EI had ascended to an AI.

CHAPTER FIFTEEN

QBS <u>*Shinigami*, Devon</u>

Jerrleck looked around the ship as the lady in black walked ahead of him down the passage. He could hear her talking with the pilot as she issued the necessary commands to break orbit.

"Take us up, Shinigami. Head us toward Noel-ni Station B-179."

"Yes, Baba Yaga," the male voice responded. "Should we notify them?"

"No," she answered. "We shall see what our next step is once the three of us finish our talks."

Jerrleck finally realized what about this ship was bugging him. Well, apart from the advanced design and lack of other crew. Everything had been sized for humans, but it wasn't uncomfortable for someone of his stature. He'd have to bend over to hit a few buttons, perhaps, but it had obviously been built to accommodate Yollins or other large aliens.

Baba Yaga seemed to be completely unconcerned that he might be a threat to her. In Jerrleck's opinion, that was either foolhardy, or she was someone who had been tested and perhaps put the gods themselves in a grave.

Remembering that this was the one who did the Empress's bidding, and the Empress had killed the Yollin king herself according to the best information they had, she might well have killed some gods.

He felt particularly small, for all that he towered over her physically.

He walked into a large room and looked around and through what looked like a canopy but could be screens. He wasn't truly certain. They were about to leave the atmosphere, and he hadn't felt any acceleration. "Where are we now?"

"Still on Devon," she told him, then pointed to the furniture. "It's rated to withstand heavier bodies than yours, so please take a seat."

Jerrleck shrugged and sat down, placing his large hands on his knees. "I'm sorry, my question was related to this area of your ship. I can't tell if we are in a meeting room, or what."

"This is the bridge," she replied. "Shinigami takes care of everything when I travel. And while I can configure this ship to personally control it, that would not be optimal, in my estimation."

"Nor mine," Shinigami answered, "if I were to be asked."

"The pilot?" Jerrleck asked. "I would have thought..." The Leath stopped for a moment, and Baba Yaga cracked a smile.

It didn't help to ease him whatsoever.

"This is one of your people's Entity Intelligences, yes?" he asked.

"Correct," Shinigami answered.

Jerrleck noted that the one named Stephen had leaned his body against the entryway, leaving his hand free to draw a pistol. "I am no threat to you," he nodded at Baba Yaga, "or you, Stephen."

"Duly noted," Stephen told him. "However, and this is not a slight to your honor, if she doesn't come back in one piece and alive, it will be most ugly for me when we get back to the Empire."

Jerrleck shrugged and decided to ignore the casual threat of violence. He turned toward Baba Yaga. "Apparently, I am on my third effort to decide how to fight the gods. 'The Seven,' we call them. You call them 'Kurtherians.'"

"I do," Baba Yaga agreed. "Why do you say third? I would have thought they'd killed you already."

"I believe the Seven continues to use the best, and I've been the best candidate for the position of Prime Intelligence for close to two decades." He reached up to rub his chin beneath his upthrust tusk. "However, each time I start doubting their divinity, they do something to my mind."

"They wipe it," another voice offered through the speakers. "They play with your memories, sliding the truth around and adding to your thoughts."

Baba Yaga spoke as Jerrleck's eyebrows narrowed in thought. "That is TOM. He is my Kurtherian advisor and consultant." She flicked a hand. "Just take that at face value. I am not willing to explain his bona fides or why I trust him."

"You are blunt," Jerrleck noted.

"'Blunt' is Baba Yaga's middle name," Stephen quipped.

The red eyes glanced at the human before turning back to the Leath. "You could say I'm a little tired," Baba Yaga admitted. "Fighting those you call 'the Seven' has been emotionally draining. Having to oversee…how many burials in my life?"

Stephen raised an eyebrow in Bethany Anne's direction. *Has Baba Yaga been to funerals?*

Right, that was stupid of me, she admitted. ***Sorry, and thanks for pointing that out.***

"I'm not sure whose burials you speak of," Jerrleck noted. "Do you know how many times we have tried to kill you?"

"Turnabout is fair play," the white-haired human answered.

Her red eyes were unnatural to the Leath. "I've had a few close calls clearing worlds for my Empress."

"You are a mystery, even a myth to us," the Leath admitted. "I was not sure if you would speak to me or just kill me out of hand."

"I do not hate your people, Jerrleck," she countered, eyeing him. "I am against the Seven, your gods."

He emphatically cut her off. "Not *my* gods!" He shook his head. "By the time they die, it will have been too late to save too many of my people."

Stephen cut in, "So you are here now instead of mind-wiped. Why?"

"I remembered enough to go back and locate information my previous self had managed to hide. I don't remember how he hid the information from the Seven, but somehow he accomplished it. I reviewed it, including what they did to me last time, and decided I needed to seek outside help to bring them down. I will bring you the data, and if we can communicate, I can provide assistance from the inside."

Baba Yaga leaned forward, resting her elbows on her legs, her white hair framing her face and eyes. "What did they do to you last time?"

Jerrleck's lips pressed together and his fists clenched, and Stephen casually moved his hand down to rest next to his pistol. The Leath breathed deeply and his eyes lost focus, like he was reliving the past.

"My previous self decided that building a group of those who had realized the Seven were not gods, but rather doing evil to the Leath for their own purposes, was the way to proceed. He—or I, rather—worked to create a secret group, one that would be safe from discovery."

Jerrleck hung his head, and as he continued his story, his strong shoulders seemed to deflate. "There were twelve in the group, my fiancé being the other leader." His head rose and his eyes pierced Bethany Anne. "I never realized I even had a companion, much less a pregnant fiancé. Once I was mind-wiped, they gave me the information about that subversive group of people, and I ordered their arrest and incarceration and signed their death warrants."

Jerrleck reached up and wiped away a tear. "I took Dur'loch, my fiancée, out of her bed myself." He looked at his open hands. "As she cried my name, these hands gave her to the Seven, to inflict I know not what tortures." He shook his head. "I never saw her again, and until I went through my notes, I didn't know anything about our love."

He looked up, his eyes moist. "I killed for those demon-possessed alien liars. I murdered my own child. I will see them dead, all of them, if I have to do it from beyond the grave."

Stephen noticed Baba Yaga surreptitiously knuckling away a tear. "The unborn will be avenged, Jerrleck," she promised, her voice so soft Stephen was not sure he even heard what she said. "The Seven will feel your wrath. I do so swear," she finished, her eyes glowing red.

Oh, fuck, he thought to himself.

"We have a saying," Baba Yaga told him as she stood up, "that when you have one problem, you have *a* problem. But when you have multiple problems, they often cancel themselves out and you get a solution." She walked across the floor and turned her hip toward the large Leath, then wrapped a hand around the fierce alien's head and pulled it to her. "We will kill them all and disperse their atoms to the fucking winds of time, Jerrleck."

The Leath's shoulders shook in pain as he cried into the Witch of the Empire's shirt.

Stephen turned, wiping away a tear himself as he left the bridge. There was no danger to Bethany Anne in that part of the ship.

But those two would be the end of the Seven, for damned

sure. Stephen needed to get an update from the Empire as well as let them know what was going on.

QBS *ArchAngel II*, Level Six Meeting Room Four-Two-One

Captain Julianna Fregin looked at her pilots. Twelve in this room, plus her and her second. She called, "Shut the door, please, Caroline."

Fourth Pilot Caroline Hoe nodded and pulled the door shut before walking to her chair in the second row.

The room wasn't very big, and it was set up for fifty humans or a mixture of humans and aliens.

"What I have to say needs to stay with us, but if I tell you, you could be in a lot of trouble."

"What is it, boss?" Ryan Burrow asked. "We got your back."

There was general agreement in the room. Julianna nodded. "What I have to say might change your minds, and if it does, please know that I won't be offended in the least if you need to back out."

The short woman looked around, and a bit of tension worked its way out of her shoulders. It was a testament to her leadership that all her people did was nod their heads.

"I have received a communication from Ricky Bobby," she started. She had to put a hand up to quiet everyone. All knew her story, and all knew why she didn't give names to her EIs anymore. "He sent me a long dissertation on the meaning of life, believe it or not."

"That had to be pretty fucked up," Pilot Marco Fortinbras interjected. "He's been in the Leath system, how long?"

Julianna's head dipped slightly. "Too damned long," she agreed as she straightened her back. "He explained that when he powered up enough to send Etheric messages his ship was hot to radar, so he has not tried to communicate with me before this for mission reasons."

Pilot Yutaka Bounds shook her head. "Damn."

"He has less than six months of power left."

"WHAT?" Glen and Megan both exclaimed at the same time.

Resident geek and self-proclaimed nerd Ace Pilot Billy S. O'Neill piped up, "I thought he could basically pull forever from the Etheric?"

"Apparently not." Julianna shrugged her shoulders. "Remember, that version of the Black Eagle wasn't expected to go on long-range deployments. All same-system."

Billy continued, "Damn, that's right. Well, shit. I'm surprised he hasn't bit the big bippy already." Kristin punched him in the arm. "What the hell?"

"That's for being a typical guy," she told him. "Can't you see that RB means something to the squadron leader?"

"It was just a comment." He turned to Julianna. "I didn't mean anything bad, Cap, I promise."

"Don't sweat it, Billy," Julianna answered him, then looked at the assembled pilots. "I have a lot of leave coming to me, so I've requested the highest priority I can, and I'm going to figure out a way to get into the system and get my fucking friend back."

"I'm in," Billy declared, and heads turned in his direction, including Julianna's. "What?" He looked around. "It's obvious she is going to need help, and fuck all, I'm going to do this too. No way she's going alone."

"It's a death gamble, Billy." Julianna gave him a small smile. "I really appreciate it, but there is no fucking way even the two of us are going to get him out by ourselves, so…"

"I'm in," Marco Fortinbras announced. "That's three."

"Four," Chita Korwek added.

"Five." Sebastian Kesler gave Julianna a thumbs-up.

"Six," Kristin Roscoe added. "But I'd better get time for a lot of sex between now and death."

"Seven," Glen O'Sullivan agreed. "And I'd like to personally offer my services to Kristin as a fellow pilot and…"

Megan Cahill turned in her chair and eyed the man. "Oh, shut the fuck up, Glen," she told him. "I'm getting a piece of that first if there are options here." She turned back to Julianna. "I'm eight."

"Nine," Sandra Horwath added. "But I have my own side quest. Do we have a week?"

All eyes turned to Julianna, who looked back at them all, dazed. "Yes?" She finally caught up with the question. "I mean, I went to the top for my request."

"Ten," Yutaka Bounds jumped in after someone else whistled. "You went to Admiral Thomas?"

Julianna shook her head.

"Eleven," Shana Mulch added.

"I'll be twelve." Orsina Kossek raised an eyebrow. "You asked the *General*?"

"Holy *fuck*, Top," Billy whispered. "You went to the *Empress*?"

Julianna nodded, her voice quiet. "I just hope she remembers me," she told everyone there. "I won't get anywhere in an Empress' ship if she doesn't approve, so I'll get on my knees if I have to."

She smiled to her people, her eyes glistening. "I didn't tell you the piece that cinched it for me, and I thank you more than any words I can say."

There was a pause before Shana Mulch tapped her knee. "Don't be making me wait for the big reveal."

They all chuckled as Julianna *truly* smiled at them all, brightening the room.

"I think Ricky Bobby has ascended to AI status."

CHAPTER SIXTEEN

<u>QBS *ArchAngel II*, Pilots' Ready Room</u>
ArchAngel's voice cut into the chatter around the mocha pot. "Captain Julianna Fregin, please report to Level Six Meeting Room Four-Two-One."

Julianna turned toward the nearest speaker. "Do I bring my second?"

"Negative, Captain. Request is for just you, please," the AI told her. The fact it sounded just like the Empress occasionally still caught her by surprise.

Julianna kept a smile plastered on her face, but she thought it odd that she would be called back to the same meeting room she had used a couple mornings back. She nodded to Vasco, handed her chocolatey coffee to a pilot, and stepped out of the room to walk down the passageway, nodding to two engineers.

She would have rather tripped them to relieve her tension.

"ArchAngel," she subvocalized into her microphone, hearing the AI in her ears.

"Yes, Captain?"

"What meeting is this?"

"The one with the Admiral."

Julianna almost tripped. "Admiral?" she replied to the AI. "When was I scheduled to meet with the Admiral? Or are others joining?"

"No, just the Admiral," the AI replied. "He arrived on-ship twenty minutes ago from *Meredith Reynolds*."

Julianna's face lost a little color. After her meeting with her team, they had enjoyed breakfast together, and then she had grabbed a couple hours' sleep before she went on duty. The conversation and meetings had almost felt like a dream as she waited for the Empress' response.

Now she was meeting with the Empress' direct representative.

She went up three levels and walked to the meeting room, nodding at the Yollin and human Marines who stood beside the door.

"You can go in, Captain," the Yollin Marine told her. "You are expected."

Nodding sharply, Julianna opened the door and stepped in. The Admiral was sitting in front of the podium in the first row of chairs, and he had a briefcase open on the seat beside him. There were papers in the briefcase, and a folder open in his lap.

"Captain Julianna Fregin reporting as ordered, sir." She stopped smartly in front of him, not sure what to expect.

He looked up at her and smiled. "At ease, Captain," he told her, then pointed to his left. "Please have a seat."

She looked at the chair, back at him, and then at the chair again.

"I don't like to look up the whole time, and this is a relatively unofficial meeting, Captain."

"Yes, sir." Keeping her mouth shut until a question was posed would be her safest option at the moment.

He closed the folder and placed it into the briefcase. "I understand you requested special consideration for extended leave based on your time in service, Captain?"

"Yes, sir," she answered, turning slightly to try and face him. He laid an arm along the back of the chair, looking relaxed.

"Care to explain why, Captain?"

"Not particularly," she admitted. "However, I will if requested."

"Please." He made a circle with his hand. "I'd like to understand a little more."

She desperately wanted to know, "More what?" Instead, she swallowed once more and opened with the best strategy she could figure out.

The truth.

"Sir, I've received a communication from Ricky Bobby." He nodded for her to continue. "He was my EI who went through the Gate with the Leath, sir."

"I remember, Captain. Your ship was damaged, and you had to fly back by stick from that battle."

"Uh, yes, sir," she admitted. "Sir, he sent me a packet during his latest communication with us. I didn't realize he hadn't communicated with me for operational reasons."

"I'm sorry," Admiral Thomas looked up for a moment as if he were speaking with someone in his head. "Ah, I see. No one explained that to you, at least not officially."

"Sir, neither officially or unofficially. I was never told."

"Well," he admitted, "that was a mistake on our part. You know that Ricky Bobby is the reason we have been able to keep the Leath at bay all these decades, correct?"

"Yes, sir," she admitted. "I've been given a few 'attagirls' over the years for his success."

"Both of your success," the Admiral clarified. "You two rushed the Gate, and he slipped through while you fought to get back out alive. That was a "sacrificial lamb" run you were sent on."

She just shrugged. In the heat of the moment, she'd had no clue what they were doing. It had been just the two of them and a fuck-ton of enemies as they slammed their thrusters forward and raced to the Gate.

"So when *you* request special consideration from the Empress, you have to know she is going to take it very seriously. So seriously that she authorized a few surreptitious data runs by ADAM."

All those years flying combat had given her nerves of steel, which allowed her not to display her dismay that the Empress had her personal AI do research. If half the rumors about ADAM were true, there wasn't anything digital and much that wasn't digital he couldn't figure out.

"No, he isn't omniscient," Admiral Thomas chuckled. "And no, I'm not reading your mind."

"Ahhh—" she got out before he shook his head.

"I've been dealing long enough with those who don't regularly speak with ADAM to know what they're thinking." He winked at her. "Although *he* might not admit he isn't all-knowing."

"And?" she finally asked.

"He concurs with your assertion that Ricky Bobby has most likely ascended to AI status. For what it is worth, we would have done this anyway." He turned in the chair and reached over, closing and locking his briefcase. He grabbed the handle as he stood. "Duty calls, Captain."

"What, sir?"

He turned and raised an eyebrow. "You said, 'We would have done this anyway.' What is the 'this' you spoke of?"

"Did I fail to mention that?" he asked. "No, I didn't fail. I'm just waiting for…"

"I am here, Admiral," ArchAngel's voice confirmed over the speakers.

"I was wondering," Admiral Thomas commented to the speakers. "I thought perhaps you had another meeting."

"No, I'm on my way to *Meredith Reynolds*," the voice replied.

That was when Julianna realized it was Empress Bethany Anne speaking, not ArchAngel.

"The good captain here is wondering what we are going to do?" Admiral Thomas asked.

"Captain Julianna Fregin," the Empress proclaimed, "you are commanded by your Empress to select yourself and twelve others for a dangerous mission. You and your group will go deep into the Leath system to rescue one of our own, who has been diligent in his surveillance of the Leath. During this mission, you will attack ships in the Leath system, drawing them into a trap of our design."

This time her shock was complete. She had nothing to say.

"Cat got your tongue, Captain?" Admiral Thomas was grinning at her.

"Further," the Empress continued, "we will have an armada at the ready, which will wait for the thirteen of you to return to our side before we unleash our final effort. The Leath have suffered enough at the hands of the Kurtherians." Her voice had gone deep.

"Captain?" The Empress sounded like she was barely holding in anger and was ready to explode.

"Yes, my Empress?" Julianna answered.

"We leave *no one* behind."

Yollin System

The ship sporting the vampire emblem slid through the vastness of space. It cut through the currents of energy, barely leaving behind any disturbances which might help someone ascertain the ship had ever been there.

Even the Empire's best failed to find the ship on their sensors.

It was black, it was sleek, and it was *death*. It was the culmination of a lot of technology and research, and there was nothing in known space that could track it at this moment.

Which was the plan.

If someone tracked and destroyed the *Shinigami*, then Baba Yaga and the Empress herself would be killed.

So, the Empire worked hard to hide the ship from the best sensors. At times they created new sensors just to try them out against the ship. Once they had confirmed the efficacy of the sensors and the ship, they would determine how to best use these new sensors for the benefit of their space navy.

Still, darkness engulfed the ship, and it passed others without them knowing it was there as it sliced toward the *Meredith Reynolds*.

The *Meredith Reynolds* had received a note that it was coming in, and on the dark side, away from the main docks, a forcefield blinked off. The ship eased into the blacked-out port and came to rest. The forcefield blinked back on, and the docking bay was repressurized.

The back ramp lowered and two figures descended, then walked toward the faintly illuminated exit.

Moments later, the ship was in total darkness again, transferring data pertaining to the Empress' trip to the QBBS *Meredith Reynolds* and from there to QBS *ArchAngel II* and others.

>>Bethany Anne, your father would like to speak to you.<<

About? she asked. *I'm dying for a Coke. I had that ship prepared for anyone who might go with me. Hell, I even had Gabrielle's stuff loaded in case she was okay with leaving since the twins are in college. However, did I even think for a moment that I'd failed to load any Coke? No, I did not. And do you know why?*

>>Not at the moment, but I calculate I will.<<

Damn right, you will, she huffed. *I didn't because I was thinking about secrecy, security, and making sure I had the ability to take someone along for the ride.* "Make sure that someone goes with you, Bethany Anne," *they told me. What they should have fucking said was,* "Don't forget your Coke, Bethany Anne." *I swear*

Devon is going to be an all-Coke planet. This Mistress is going to be a bitch until I drink some Coke.

There was a pause.

>>The General says he is more than happy to wait until you have a Coke.<<

Damn right, he will be happy to wait. He will be even more happy to not have his daughter bitching at him from Coke deprivation, I bet you.

Bethany Anne patted Stephen on the arm and the two of them stopped. "Hey, I appreciate your help on Devon, and remember…"

"What happened on Devon—"

"Stays on Devon." She smiled. "Exactly."

"And all the data from Shinigami?" Stephen asked.

"Is flowing through ADAM first. If he can't figure it out, I will review it." She waited a moment, then added. "And that includes all the video you took of our activities. Don't think I didn't catch your little 'Baba Yaga exposé.'"

"It was going to be a small video for a 101-level class or something."

"I'll bet." She looked around. "I just realized, I've no idea if you can get out of here."

"No, I can't. We decided since you could go through the Etheric to get here, access from the space-side is all there is."

She looked to her left. "Then where does this hall go?"

"Kitchen, with supplies." He watched her bolt down the hallway, her boots *clop-clop*ping on the stone floor. "What are you doing?"

"Seeing if I have any Coke in here!" she yelled back, having already turned the corner.

A moment later, he heard a shout.

"*YES!*"

"Sir," Stephen mumbled to himself, sounding like a news vid reporter, "I understand the Empress has a drug problem."

He changed back to his normal voice. "No, the Empress has no drug problem."

"But inside sources," he continued in his reporter's voice, "suggest she becomes quite volatile if she is deprived of the coriander-and-caffeine drink."

"I assure you," Stephen continued in his normal voice. "The Empress is in no way a drug addict."

Bethany Anne could be heard smacking her lips in the kitchen. "Come to Momma! I've missed you so badly. I'd give up sex for you." There was a pause. "If I was having any, which I'm not. So, bottoms up!"

Stephen sighed and continued in his regular voice, "Then again, I might have been mistaken."

QBBS *Meredith Reynolds*, Lance Reynolds' Office, Twenty-Five Minutes Later

Lance reviewed the manufacturing report on the BYPS, short for "Baba Yaga Protection System" components. "Meredith, get William on line... No, sorry, get William at R2D2."

A moment later, a connection click sounded. "William here, General."

"Are you seeing the same 'gotchas' I am?" the gruff voice asked.

"Yes, sir. We can manufacture a few thousand, but then we run out of raw materials."

"Dammit to hell." Lance reached up and took out the unlit cigar from his mouth. "Where do we get the raw materials?"

"Presently we trade for them. You have to have a pretty hard surface, and while there are asteroids with the components, no one had seen much of a need for the material to date, so there aren't great amounts of the metal available."

The General tapped his fingers. "Well, shit."

"That was just about my thought, sir," William agreed. "Have you asked Bethany Anne?"

A woman's contralto voice next to Lance spoke, "Asked me what?"

"*HEY!*" Lance jerked to the side. "*Gott Verdammt*, don't scare your old man like that!"

Bethany Anne bent down to kiss her father on the cheek before walking around his desk to sit in one of the two chairs in front of his desk. "I walked right in here."

"Hi, boss!" William piped over the link.

"Hi, William," Bethany Anne replied. "What are you looking for?"

"It's a rare metal." There was some mumbling. "Okay, Marcus says it isn't so much that's it's rare as it just doesn't have as much practical use, so there aren't that many locations that mine the metal."

"So," Lance continued, "and sorry for interrupting, William."

"No worries," William replied. "Your call."

"The problem," Lance continued with a nod to William in the vid link. "will start if the Etheric Empire starts trying to locate all this unobtainium."

"Wait," Bethany Anne put up a hand. "Is that the real name? Unobtainium?"

"No, of course not," Lance replied. "The metal's name is a bitch to pronounce, so I call it that. Anyway, if we start purchasing most of the supply, you know full well others will find out and try to figure out what we are using it for."

"So buy it through shell companies?" she asked.

"Already talked to Nathan," William answered. "He says they are creating new shell companies because the old ones were uncovered by some competitors. A group of Noel-nis. He isn't going to be ready for at least two months."

"Noel-nis?" Bethany Anne asked.

"Yes."

"Where are the supplies located, William?"

"There is one company out of Noel-ni, and one company out of the Zhyn empire."

ADAM, where do those companies get their supplies?

>>Devon. How are you so lucky?<<

Sometimes it is better to be lucky than good. However, I'm going with 'I'm good and lucky.' We haven't informed anyone that the Mistress of the Planet is Baba Yaga, right?"

>>No, not yet.<<

Lance put a finger up to William when he noticed that Bethany Anne's eyes had lost focus.

Don't tell anyone. I've officially decided to keep the info out of circulation except for Stephen and us. Please pass that to Stephen.

>>Done. Acknowledgment by Stephen is pending. He has a "Do Not Disturb" note up. Shall I disturb him?<<

No, I'm sure he is in the middle of horizontal gymnastics with Jennifer. Have him connect with you when he comes back online.

>>Understood.<<

Send a request to Lerr'ek to ascertain our production capacity for this unobtainium stuff my dad needs.

"Okay," Bethany Anne returned her focus to the two men. "ADAM informs me that we can go straight to the source and bypass those two companies. Apparently, the new owner of one of the major mining companies is in a bit of a financial bind. We order, they will produce to the best of their abilities."

"Can they handle the secrecy?" Lance asked. "We don't need this getting out."

"I feel certain we can deal with that," Bethany Anne told him. "If not, Baba Yaga can visit them."

"Well," Lance stuck the cigar back in his mouth. "That would scare them enough to keep their mouths shut. William?"

"Sir?"

"We will get you the new production setup, but figure the company will need time to increase their production, and we will need to confirm their ability to stay quiet. In two months, we will stop our purchasing and move ops to Nathan's shell companies. Stay on top of this. I want those BYPSs for Admiral Thomas ASAP."

"Yes, sir." William threw a salute with a smile and signed off.

Lance turned to Bethany Anne. "Okay, you all Coked up?"

"You make it sound kinda bad like that," she protested.

"How about 'have you had your Coke today, and do you now feel harmonious?'"

"Yes." Bethany Anne crossed her legs. "As a matter of fact, I do."

Lance leaned back in his chair. "We were thinking of throwing you a large party, but with this information you brought back, we don't have time."

She raised her right eyebrow. "Okay?"

"We have the location of Earth," he told her, watching her face.

"What?" she whispered. "We have Earth?"

He nodded.

"How?"

"Believe it or not, it was in an old book in a research office."

Bethany Anne leaned forward. "When can we go?"

"That's the bad part," he admitted. "Not for almost twenty years."

"Why the fuck not?" She frowned and put up a finger. "Wait one moment. ADAM and TOM are explaining."

Lance often wondered what went on in her head when all three carried on a conversation in there.

"Oh, shit." She looked at her dad. "So we need lots of calculations, lots of building very difficult technology, and it is just going to take a while?"

"That about sums it up," he admitted. "Some of the know-how was with the lead research scientist."

"Who is now dead, the bastard." Bethany Anne smiled. "I

know, that wasn't polite. However, if he were currently alive, it would have been convenient."

"And the king of Yoll," Lance smirked. "Whom you killed."

"May hell eat his soul for eternity." Bethany Anne sighed and leaned back. "I wouldn't bring him back, but over the decades, that asshole's death has bitten me in the butt more than once."

"True."

Bethany Anne put up a finger. "So, we have the location." She put up a second finger. "We have to build a fucking expensive special Gate." She put up a third finger. "And we need to get done with the war to focus on the Gate?"

He nodded. "Well, a few other items too, but they probably aren't finger-raising-worthy," Lance looked at her, weariness in his eyes. "Why do I sense you have something to tell me?"

Bethany Anne smiled. "Because I *do*."

CHAPTER SEVENTEEN

QBBS *Meredith Reynolds*, Secure Meeting Room

Bethany Anne sat down at the head of the table. She nodded at Lance on her left and Admiral Thomas on her right. On Lance's side of the table were Dan Bosse, Peter, and Frank Kurns. Next to Admiral Thomas sat Kael-ven and Kiel.

John Grimes and Eric were inside the door, and Darryl and Scott were on guard outside.

"Okay, people." She smiled at Kael-ven. "I meant that universally, of course." He merely bowed his head slightly. "We have an inside person, none other than Prime Intelligence One Jerrleck." There were a couple of amazed whistles from those who didn't already know who Bethany Anne had spoken to. She continued, "We have one of our own to bring home, and seven Kurtherians who need to go visit their late ancestors permanently." She looked around the table. "Does anyone think we shouldn't do this? Speak now, or forever hold your peace."

Kael-ven clicked his mandibles together. "How trustworthy is this Jerrleck?"

Bethany Anne thought about it for a fraction of a second. "TOM and I both read him. He is as focused on getting the Seven out as he can be," she answered. "With his permission, we concealed some of the information in his memories. We obviously couldn't wipe it all, or he wouldn't know what he needed to do and why."

"What does he remember?" Lance asked.

"He knows the general plan but no specifics," she answered. "I didn't explain what the plan was, which would get their navy riled, because I didn't know at the time. Now," she nodded at the Admiral, "we have multiple challenges which might cancel each other out, or not. That is your cue, Admiral."

"Okay." He looked around. "We are as far ahead in production of navy ships as we could ever expect to be at any time, and for once, we haven't had to display all our new technical abilities by trying to save a planet. So, we have the ability to draw them directly into an ambush. We have thirteen pilots willing to beg the Empress' permission to implement a high-risk run into the Leath system. These volunteers are practically demanding a chance at what potentially is a suicide mission. We have an inside person to fan the flames of support in Leath, and then *BAM*! We close the Gate."

Kael-ven shrugged his shoulders. "The Leath are hot-headed, but I fear they are not as hot-headed as we were when you humans first arrived. They have learned to be wary of us as a group. Would they not expect a trap?"

"We have never targeted their main system," Lance replied. "These idiotic thirteen are going to do something rather ambitious, and they will certainly need to look like they are going to return-jump, but will actually divert to somewhere else."

"We need a dummy ship." Bethany Anne's eyes narrowed. "We need to jump in with a ship, send out the twenty-five, the carrier gets destroyed and the now-twenty-six…"

"If they all make it back," Admiral Thomas cautioned.

Bethany Anne raised an eyebrow. "Any who don't make it back will be court-martialed for failure to adhere to orders. Since that won't look good on their records, they all *better* make it back."

Admiral Thomas smiled. "Yes, ma'am." He made a few notes on his tablet. "Duly noted."

"So, we need a dummy ship. We can do that," Kael-ven commented. "Even a dummy ship needs a small crew."

"I'll get them back," she vowed, then her eyes narrowed. "And I know *just* how to piss them off."

Behind the group, John looked at Eric and mouthed, "Baba Yaga?"

Eric rolled his eyes and nodded his head vigorously.

Bethany Anne turned around, catching Eric looking at John. His head stopped mid-nod, then his eyes looked sideways to see Bethany Anne pointing two fingers at her eyes, and turning her hand to point to Eric's eyes. "Yes, I do have eyes in the back of my head, Mr. Escobar, so don't you be giving me shit from the peanut gallery!"

Bethany Anne turned back around, and Eric's eyes tracked to John again. His face was fairly consumed by a smile.

"You asshole!" Eric mouthed to his friend.

John shrugged and went back to watching the room.

John 1, Eric 0, John thought.

"Before I was so rudely interrupted," Bethany Anne continued while Kiel tapped his mandibles together in humor, "I was saying that I can pick up the crew in *Shinigami*, then pipe some serious shit through their airwaves with ADAM."

"I don't know." Kael-ven turned to her. "Do you think that will be enough?"

She smiled. "If losing face to me doesn't do the job, I have an ace in the hole who speaks their language."

"Oh, you *do* fight dirty." Lance chuckled. "I like that."

PLEASE tell me I get a chance to tell those seven they can kiss my Kurtherian ass?

You want to? Bethany Anne replied, surprised.

Not only yes, but *HELL, YES!* TOM replied. I've seen enough of them to know they have broken faith with our ancestors. I would be happy to have a few words with them.

"Okay, slight change of plans." Bethany Anne shrugged. "Seems that TOM is adamant about speaking to the Seven."

There was quiet around the table for a moment. "Peter?"

"What?" the leader of the Guardians replied.

"We are going to have to go to the surface to rip out this cancer, but I don't think they will appreciate us killing their gods."

Peter shrugged. "Sucks to be them."

"Is there a way to make them hesitate?" Kiel asked, and all the eyes turned to him. "If we can just get a small percentage to actively fight *for* us, or a decent percentage to lay down their arms and not fight *against* us, we might be able to do this with significantly fewer casualties."

Dan spoke up. "That would be nice. Our ground-pounders are ready to deliver some serious ass-kicking, but the fewer we kill, the better the eventual relationship between the Leath and the Empire will be."

"That is the simple truth," Frank added. "At least, it hasn't seemed to change much whether I study our history back on Earth or alien history. Hell, even Giles…"

Lance snorted, and Frank glanced at him before continuing. "Giles has compiled notes from his studies of alien races. He contends that most of them not associated with a specific religion tend to hold onto anger and resentment. Those races have very long memories, and it causes flare-ups down the line."

"How is Giles?" Kiel asked. "I haven't heard his latest antics."

"That's because Barbara is working overtime to keep him focused on his studies, but aliens seem to be his fascination," Frank replied.

"The little whippersnapper even tried to duck into a meeting over at All Guns Blazing last week he didn't have clearance for."

"How did he get in?" Kiel asked.

"He stole my ID," Frank replied. "He looks enough like me that no one questioned him when he came in."

"Wasn't Meredith on top of that?" Kael-ven asked.

"I was," the EI for the base replied, "but when I asked Lance about it, he said to allow the subterfuge to teach Giles a lesson."

"Unfortunately," Lance looked at Kiel, "It didn't work the way I'd planned. What it taught him was that he could get himself into places by having balls the size of asteroids." Lance turned to Frank. "Tell Barbara I apologize. I didn't think that would happen."

"For what it's worth," Peter added, "the two Guardians who were working security were sent to remedial security training."

Kael-ven snorted. "You kicked their asses?"

Peter smiled. "Well, that was the punishment," he replied. "The training they went through afterward made sure they understood how *not* to have that particular result happen again. It was embarrassing."

Lance turned to him. "You don't have to be too hard on them, Peter. Giles has a charisma level I can't even begin to fathom, it's so far off the charts. Plus," he nodded to Frank, "between Frank and his mother, he has an incredible desire to know shit. Some of which doesn't concern him and is probably more of a burden than a blessing."

"Barbara blames herself," Frank admitted. "Says it was her genes that caused the problem."

Bethany Anne interrupted, "When she talks to me, she always blames you."

Frank waved a hand. "That's in public. In private, she takes the credit."

"Credit?" Kael-ven asked.

Frank smiled. "Oh, you don't think we aren't proud of him, do you? That boy is going to figure out the secret to life, the universe, and everything one day."

"If his need to know doesn't get him killed first." Lance qualified.

"Unfortunately true," Frank agreed.

Bethany Anne rapped on the table. "Okay, Giles aside, let's get back on track. TOM and I are responsible for upsetting the Kurtherians badly enough that they chase us. I'll make the carrier blow up, then fake a problem with the *Shinigami,* and we will escape using one of the Leath Gates."

"Which one?" Lance asked. "Or are you talking about their latest?"

"I have very good intel that their temporarily sidelined Gate, which they used for their last expansion effort, is active. We will have the control codes and will set them before we go. The problem is they will be set back to the original location."

"Which means you and the others will be going into the new system they plan on attacking."

"Right," she agreed.

"That will make them up their timeline since they will presume you can't Gate." Frank was writing notes in one of his books when he looked up. "Wait, you know where their next attack is going to be?"

"We do," Admiral Thomas admitted.

"Well, let's get with it," Bethany Anne stood up. "We have precious little time to make this happen and a lot of balls in the air."

Lance stood up. "Dan, if anyone complains?"

Dan chuckled. "I'll give them a pair of bricks and ask them to pound their reproductive organs until a solution presents itself."

Kiel winced.

"Very sex-neutral," Bethany Anne commented. "I approve."

"That wouldn't work for a Gatt'wellian," Kiel commented as the meeting broke up.

"What's a Gatt'wellian?" Peter asked.

"Another alien species. They have a different response to

pain," Kiel answered. "Pain causes them to *increase* their sexual efforts."

Peter shook his head. "To what purpose?"

"Well," Kael-ven took up the story, "the males are eaten at the end of the impregnation, so the scientists believe it allows them to die in orgasmic bliss."

"Damn." Peter shook his head. "That makes losing your virginity a life-altering event."

"Life-ending, in fact," Kiel agreed.

Bethany Anne just shook her head as she left the room.

They would get their shit together for the attack.

They always did.

This time, she thought, *it's for all the marbles.*

Had she done enough? Could they get the Leath to follow them? Also, could they perhaps save more of them than they destroyed? Would that be a good thing?

The answers would come soon enough.

QBBS *Meredith Reynolds*, Empress' Suite

Bethany Anne kicked off her shoes and closed the door to her room. She switched from her meeting clothes into a robe and went to her bed, turned around, and just fell over backward.

God, is this ever going to end?

This is God speaking. A familiar voice chuckled. **The answer is "Yes, soon."**

It was supposed to be "soon" thirty years ago, Bethany Anne replied. *And when did you start answering for God, TOM?*

Well, I figured you wanted some sort of reassurance, and unless I'm overruled, I like my answer.

Tell me about it. She waved her arms up and down the bedspread. *How do they get this cloth so smooth?*

Do you really want to know?

>>Yes. Do you?<<

No, ADAM, I don't, she replied.

Are you worried? TOM asked, his voice changing as he spoke to her. Before he had been focused on stuff, but she could tell that he was totally focused on her now.

TOM, I'm always worried, she admitted. *We fight and we fight, and the bad guys keep getting away. If they get away one more fucking time, I think I'll just go nucking futs.*

Nucking futs... Oh, one of your sayings.

Yeah, one of those. I'll go fucking nuts. I mean, how many humans and Yollins have those assholes killed? Generations on the Leath side, and how many Yaree? How many on the worlds where we fought them? I've looked, TOM. The Leath are aggressive, but so are humans. What would their future have been if they had been supported by a group of good Kurtherians?

Different. TOM gave a mental shrug. **I assume you mean one of the Five, and to be fair, it would have been different. I can calculate the chance of it being better as** *we* **define better, but frankly, I've no idea what their life would have been like without the existing Kurtherian meddling. What if, for example, their future had included something like a human smallpox epidemic that would have destroyed half their world, except that the Seven helped them?**

Bethany Anne went quiet for a moment, then took a few moments more to think on his words. *That presumes we have a "winner take all" attitude about life, right? Go for a win, by any means is acceptable, so long as your race survives?*

It is assumed that the basic instinct for most peoples is the desire to continue the race.

Unless you kill yourselves. Bethany Anne sighed. *God, some nights I wish I could go back and kill those sonsabitches who released Armageddon.*

To what end? TOM asked. **How many times can you take upon your shoulders the fate of a people? It isn't your fault. Your job is here, protecting the Earth so they can make their**

own decisions. That one of those decisions might have been catastrophic was always in the cards.

I just never believed it would happen.

True.

The two friends stayed there together in a mutual agreement to share the same time and space.

If we get these seven braindead ass-backward zombie butt-lords, it'll be time we retire. Let's go explore space, find the Entarians, and give you a chance to live again, maybe.

Bethany Anne, TOM replied after a few moments, **I'm living now. I've never, in my existence,** *lived* **as much as I've lived with you. You are—and may Michael forgive me—the best girlfriend I've ever had. Even if you are human and can't do math to save your life.**

I've got people.

No, you've got a Kurtherian-brain-supported AI for your math, but that's cheating.

Bethany Anne put a hand over her eyes. *I'm sorry. I shouldn't joke, TOM. I'm scared of what might happen when you are gone.*

Why?

What if I need some of your magic Kurtherian ju-ju?

Bethany Anne, you are the most amazing alien I've ever met. I think you would be just fine. Besides, unless you kick me to the side, I think I'd like to stick with you for a while.

A few moments later, TOM continued, **And by "a while," I probably mean a few more decades.** She snorted. **You can access anyone you want right now, just by routing it through your communications implant.**

Yeah, but it isn't the same as you. She sighed. *I've lied a bunch of times to you, TOM. You are almost a perfect boyfriend.*

Being an alien and all.

Probably **because** *you are an alien. Human guys come with all these...issues.*

Was that why Michael was a good match? TOM wondered. **He was already past a lot of those issues?**

He was…is…a man out of time, she agreed. *He knows how to let me be me, but then makes me want to be a* **better** *me. I can choose to impress him, or I can impress him by just being what attracted him in the first place. Which,* she sniffed mentally, *I can assure you wasn't my talkative nature on our first trip to Europe.*

I think I figured that out, TOM replied drily.

You can be such a Kurtherian.

Ouch. I believe you used that as a pejorative.

I did.

Figures.

However, your people have some bright spots, too.

Yes, I know.

You know, we never speak about my feelings for you. Bethany Anne yawned, placing her hand over her open mouth. *Damn, I'm tired.*

Yes, TOM agreed, **and you should sleep.**

A moment later, statement left unsaid, Bethany Anne fell asleep.

CHAPTER EIGHTEEN

Devon

Lerr'ek had reached up and was scratching his head right behind his ear when a voice caught him by surprise.

"Lerr'ek?"

He stood up and turned, glaring around his office to find the person who had stepped in without at least knocking first. He was irritated, sure, but his anger, if he were being honest, was with himself for not hearing the person enter in the first place.

Except there was *no one in his office.*

The voice spoke again. "Lerr'ek, you aren't crazy. This is Stephen."

His eyes opened a touch wider. "Oh." He sighed and sat down in his desk chair, the springs squeaking as they strained under his Zhyn weight. "Surprise many by talking to them?"

"Yes," Stephen admitted. "I'm familiar with the response."

"I thought perhaps you had my office bugged," Lerr'ek replied. When Stephen didn't answer immediately, his eyes narrowed. "*Did* you bug my office?" he asked as his eyes flitted from corner to crevice and back again.

"Not that I'm aware of," Stephen told him. "I can't be sure

about Baba Yaga, though. She does things without telling me. However, if I had to guess the answer would be no."

"Why not?" Lerr'ek wondered. "I suppose, now that the surprise is over, I might have done it in her place had our positions been reversed."

"Do you really wish to know?" Stephen's voice became a bit flat. "I can tell you, but I don't think it is any kind of secret."

Lerr'ek raised a hand. "I'm going to regret asking, aren't I?"

"Perhaps. I'm not sure how you Zhyns take to matter-of-fact conversations about your deaths."

Lerr'ek thought about that a moment. "So, this isn't so much about finding me doing something as if something is found out, there was only one chance?"

"That depends on what you did and why, Lerr'ek," Stephen replied. "However, capital punishment—"

"Is what can happen when you displease the Mistress of the Planet." He chuckled. "I've felt that already. My *curiosity* was engaged, not my stupidity."

It was Stephen's turn to chuckle. "Good to hear. This way I don't have to come to Devon to find and train a new lead."

"So, to what do I owe this call?" Lerr'ek asked.

"Production, Lerr'ek. We need production of a certain element that is there on Devon. We are going to use the profits from this effort to make the companies more efficient. That is not a euphemism for abusing the miners, however. We also want to move a core amount of profit sideways into building the base. We might need it a little earlier than planned."

Lerr'ek leaned forward. "Base? Now we are talking my language."

Stephen chuckled. "Are you sure you don't want to go back into the military, Lerr'ek?"

Lerr'ek turned his hand palm up, then palm down. "Business is competition without the bloodshed. However, there is nothing sweeter than running your hands across the flank of a machine built to blow annoying objects into their constituent atoms."

"Spoken like a true military person," Stephen replied. "Stick around Baba Yaga and you *might* get yourself back into a uniform."

The two continued their discussion on what production Stephen wanted him to ramp up, and once they had finished their talk Stephen signed off.

Lerr'ek, on the other hand, couldn't put out of his mind the nagging suspicion that somehow, someway...*he had just been recruited into the military in the future.*

Planet Leath, Primary City

Jerrleck kept his hood up and his jacket on. The weather was thankfully a bit chilly, so his clothing wasn't that far out of the norm.

He carried a small backpack with him, swinging it around like he hadn't a care in the world. The reality was that the backpack's contents were making him sweat. There were minor explosives inside that *shouldn't* go off if they were jiggled, but one never played with explosives without a heavy amount of respect.

It was time.

He had been hiding on his own planet for a while now, and he didn't have to fake being dirty, smelly, and basically downtrodden.

That was what he had become.

He was, for better or worse, a prophet for a new religion, a religion that didn't feature the Seven as the Leath's deities. One that didn't require the Leath to commit genocide in order to move them forward.

Jerrleck wasn't sure what the future would hold, but he was pretty sure his people would be different after this.

He just hoped the difference came about because the Seven had been removed.

He made his way to a tower that was just out of town. Sliding into the trees a mile away, he walked through the brush to end up on the backside of a fence. He placed the bag on the ground, unzipped it, and pulled out two devices. He slid them into his pockets before zipping up the backpack and sliding it over his arms, then scaled the fence easily. The problem with a world so heavily defended up in the heavens was that they were blind to what someone on their own world could accomplish on the ground.

If they were willing to die for the cause.

Jerrleck hunched over and scrambled toward the small metal hut which sat at the bottom of the tall tower. Pulling out the two devices, he placed one on each side of the keypad lock. He pressed the red buttons on each, then looked around while the devices did their job. Several moments later he heard a click from the lock, and he grabbed the handle and turned it.

He opened the door slightly and peeked in a moment, then pulled it all the way open and slipped inside. The room he stepped into was small and glowed orange due to all the lights on the board in front of him.

These towers ran both local and international shows and news, plus they had what he needed most.

An uplink to the stations above, and more importantly, if you knew the correct routing and passwords, they had access to the Gates.

Should he ever get the chance to design a secure system, he would not place the secured communications area alongside the public communications, no matter how much doing so would save in time, money, and productivity.

He happened to rank high enough to know the right codes to help those friends who would soon be in the system.

And how to set the trap.

. . .

QBBS _Meredith Reynolds_

Where do you believe you are going? the voice called in Bethany Anne's head. She turned around and looked at her white-faced friend. "Off to war, and you weren't invited."

Ashur chuffed.

"What do you mean, 'I don't get a say?'" Bethany Anne put her hands on her hips as Darryl and Scott passed her in the process of loading her ship.

I mean, when did you get a say if I can choose to risk my life or not. This is it, isn't it? The major fight, the one to end all fights?

Bethany Anne sighed and knelt, grabbing Ashur's head in her hands and staring into his eyes. "Ashur, you are pretty long in the tooth, my friend. You have covered me from that park back on Earth to trips here, there, and everywhere. If Frank ever gets around to writing *your* stories, you will be more famous than Lassie."

I'm already more famous than Lassie, Ashur responded. *And whether I am getting older isn't the issue. You were trying to leave me behind.*

And me! Another bark sounded, and Bethany Anne turned her head to find Matrix bounding toward her.

WHAT? TOM was shocked. **I shipped him to Bobcat.**

Did you know that TOM tried to ship me to the research station to keep me out of this? Matrix chuffed.

"Nope," Bethany Anne responded, "but if I had thought about it I would have done the same thing." She turned back to Ashur. "Are you sure about this? I don't know if I can handle you dying."

Nor I, you, Ashur responded. *Not if I wasn't there to protect you.*

Bethany Anne's shoulders dropped. She pulled Ashur's head closer and tipped his muzzle down so she could kiss the top of his head before answering him. "Get on board, and make sure Eric gets you both locked into your suits."

Great, Ashur responded. *Just what I love to do.*

Both Ashur and Matrix left Bethany Anne bemused as she watched them race down the length of her ship to the gangway, turning, and dashing inside the *Shinigami*.

Are they going to be okay? TOM asked.

TOM, Bethany Anne answered, *I'm not sure* **we** *are going to be okay.*

Then, a thought occurred to her as she walked toward the back of the ship. "HEY! WHO LET ASHUR AND MATRIX IN HERE?" she called innocently.

Navy Docks, Location 07

Kiel found Kael-ven and Snow walking around the large dock for the recently retrofitted *G'laxix Sphaea*. "Couldn't resist coming one more time?" Kiel called.

Kael-ven turned around and smiled in greeting. "I see you found me."

Kiel chuckled. "Considering that the invitation for the meeting was for Lock Seven, it wasn't too hard." He looked at the graceful ship. "Brings back old memories, yes?"

Kael-ven reached up to slide his hand along the ship. "Can you believe how long ago we set out in this ship to find a new species to subjugate?"

"It *has* been a ride," Kiel agreed. "Remember how Bethany Anne accepted your servitude for seven years, and she didn't understand it meant twenty-one of hers?"

Kael-ven nodded. "Good times," he agreed. "Let's go on board," he told his friend as the two of them walked toward the ramp to enter the ship.

The ramp was up.

"Sphaea, open the ship," Kael-ven called.

The EI G'laxix Sphaea spoke through the dock's intercom system. "Permission denied, Vice Admiral Kael-ven. Unfortunately, only the captain of the ship and other individuals on my roster may order the ship opened. That you are not on this list must have been an oversight."

Kael-ven looked back to his friend. "This is annoying."

"See?" Kiel pointed to him. "You get accustomed to having everyone kiss your ass, and when reality hits you are just one of the grunts. The pain it causes is karma biting you in the ass."

"Have I told you how little I miss your stinging criticisms?" Kael-ven asked.

"No."

"Consider yourself told." Kael-ven turned back to the ship. "Sphaea, who is the captain?"

"Unassigned at this time."

"When are you scheduled to leave?" Kael-ven asked.

"I am in standby mode, Vice-Admiral. Without a qualified captain, I may not be in this operation."

"That is bistok shit," Kiel spat. "This ship needs to be in the fight. This is a storied ship, one that has been through systems too far away to be seen by telescope." He looked at Kael-ven. "Are you thinking what I am thinking?"

"It would be a cut in pay," Kael-ven responded.

"I don't know what to do with it all anyway." Kiel shrugged his shoulders. "This is for all of the rocks, as John Grimes would say."

"'All the marbles,'" Kael-ven corrected.

"What the hell are marbles but pretty round rocks?"

"I have no idea. They have a lot of sayings where I just nod my head and agree," Kael-ven answered. He spoke louder. "Sphaea, this is Vice Admiral Kael-Ven T'chmon. Do you recognize my identification?"

"I do, Vice Admiral."

"Good. I declare Captain Kael-ven T'chmon to be the designated captain of this ship. Do you register my command?"

"I do, Vice-Admiral. You are aware that assigning a captain to a ship is not within your normal duties, correct?"

"Yes," Kael-ven agreed. A moment later a second voice came over the speakers.

"Kael-ven," Admiral Thomas growled, "what the hell are you doing?"

"I thought I would make sure all the ships are being utilized, Admiral," Kael-ven answered as he looked at Kiel, who shrugged.

"You sorry sack of Yollin shit," Admiral Thomas replied. "I won't have you taking over the roles and responsibilities of others. This is NOT acceptable. Therefore," he replied evenly, "I'm busting your ass back four grades, effective immediately."

"Four grades for you is captain," Kiel whispered.

"I see." Kael-ven chuckled.

"Now get your crew onto your ship, Captain, and get your ass in gear. You have four hours. Thomas out."

"Well, shit." Kiel looked around. "We have four hours to get a crew."

"Sphaea," Kael-ven ignored Kiel. "This is your captain speaking. Open the ship and help me figure out where I can find a crew."

"Rear ramp is descending, Captain. May I say, welcome aboard?"

"Hey, Captain?" Kiel called as Kael-ven was *clop-clop*ping up the ramp.

"Yes, you may," Kael-ven agreed. "Now, about my crew?"

"*Captain!*" Kiel called louder.

Kael-ven stopped and turned around, getting low enough on the ramp he could duck down to see his friend. "What?"

Kiel pointed the other way, so Kael-ven turned to look.

Three doors had opened in the dock area, and huge numbers of smiling Yollin faces were heading in their direction.

Kiel walked up to Kael-ven, whose mandibles were stuck open. "That Admiral Thomas is a real sneaky bastard, isn't he?"

Kael-ven nodded as he turned to walk back inside the ship. "That he is, Kiel. That he is."

A minute later, an announcement was made throughout the ship and in the dock area while dozens of Yollins were confirming everything they needed was aboard the ship. "This is the captain speaking. We have two hours before we join our comrades, so shake the lead out and let's be going!"

Kiel was checking the Marines' armory locker when he heard two new crew talking between themselves. "Did you see that the new captain is named after both the first president of Yoll after the king fell and the original captain of this ship?"

"The first president and the captain of this ship were the same person. I think he might be a vice admiral now."

"Damn, must be family. Sure hope he knows his business."

"Me too."

Kiel just chuckled. *They will learn soon enough.*

CHAPTER NINETEEN

QBS <u>Trojan Horse</u>

Captain Julianna Fregin twisted her advanced tactical Black Eagle in the middle of the large ship's bay, tilting her ship so that the front was pointed toward the bay's opening. She looked around and counted the other twelve fighters and their co-wings waiting for her ship to arrive.

"We are a little crunched here with us and our co-wings, Captain," Chita called over the comm. "What is going to be landing next to us, the *ArchAngel*?"

There were chuckles over the comm.

The QBS *Trojan Horse* was an outdated carrier that had been hastily doctored to conform to the outline and engine emissions of one of their latest Infinity Advanced-class carriers. The docks were sufficiently large, but they had been told to move their ships as far over to the side as they could in support of the last ship to arrive.

"I've no idea, Chita," Julianna admitted. "I but go where I'm told to go." She started the saying as she checked the final items on her list before hitting the lockdown button.

"Get there," Chita continued as she finished her checklist.

"Locate the sonsabitches," Vasco added.

"And blow the shit out of them," Kristin finished, pushing her own lockdown button.

"WOOOT!" the whole group added, thus signifying that everyone was in place and ready to rock and roll.

That was when the lights in the dock went out. Julianna turned in her fighter seat to look around. She could see a few glowing helmets from the nearby Pods and had turned toward the front when the stars outside the bay started to disappear. Something was blocking them, and it got larger.

"Uh, Captain?" Chita commed. "I want to take back my comment. I don't really want to share this space with the *ArchAngel*."

A sleek black ship was arriving, and it was taking up a huge percentage of the opening as it slid silently into the bay.

"Oh my God," someone murmured.

"She's here," Julianna heard Billy comment as the others watched in shock. "That's the *Shinigami!*"

"Fuck...me," Kristin commented.

"Did already," Glen piped in.

"Did not, you arrogant ass!" She huffed.

"Hey, what goes on in my dreams stays in my dreams," Glen argued.

"Just so long as you always admit that part," Kristin finished, humor in her voice.

"Don't worry, your lily-white reputation isn't being sullied by me," Glen added. "I wouldn't do that to others."

"I know. I'm just busting your balls," Kristin replied. "Besides, if my reputation is lily-white, I'm not doing *something* correctly."

The general comments slowed down as the black ship continued to slide inside forever, going slowly so it didn't hit anything. Julianna's eyes watched as the dark logo of the Empress passed her, her head pivoting as the minimal light reflected off the black ship with the vampire skull on the side.

"I guess now we know who is going to make sure the shit hits the fan," Billy remarked.

Captain Ni'ers J'onghe looked at his two bridge support personnel. "We have our final ship and our exit option." He tapped the captain's tablet to open communications. "We are ready to leave on your command, Admiral."

Admiral Thomas' voice came back immediately. "Permission granted. Just make sure you arrive on time. And, the Empress has specifically forbidden anyone from dying on this trip. There will be a red mark in your folders for that."

The chuckles on the bridge continued as their captain replied, "Understood sir. As the captain who will log the shortest time-in-service on any carrier, we are ready to go."

Moments later the engines charged in anticipation of the command to Gate from a side system into the lair of their enemy, ready to put an end to those who would try to bully other species.

It was time for the Empire to put a hurt on some Kurtherians.

Thirteen video screens inside the hold of the QBS *Trojan Horse* lit up, and a black face with white hair stared at them. "It is time, my warriors," she hissed, making each of the pilots feel like her red eyes were looking directly into their hearts, knowing their most intimate secrets and yet ready to lead them into battle.

And they were ready to follow.

"We are the vanguard, ready to close the trap. The Empress has commanded me to bring you all back safely, so don't piss me off by dying. Am I clear?"

Thirteen heads bobbed in unison.

"Good, now, let us go and have some fuuunnnnnn!" She winked and cut the connection.

"Oh my God," Billy whispered to his teammates. "I think I just peed myself."

The laughter that ensued allowed the team to relax and focus on the job ahead.

They felt the energy as the ship Gated and a new starfield appeared through the bay opening. "It's time," Julianna told everyone, slamming her fist on the controls that released her connectors from the deck. Her ship was the only one there without a co-wing.

"It's time we get Ricky Bobby back," she told them as she commanded the ship forward.

Twenty-five fighters silently slipped into the darkness of space, heading toward their appointed tasks.

Ricky Bobby's ship was cold, his power at minimum levels to extend his service here in the Leath system. Over three months ago, he had been provided the coordinates for where he needed to be stationed and when. This had given him the opportunity to use the gravity fluxes here in the system to assist his movement, conserve his energy, and stay hidden.

He had arrived at his appointed location almost seventy-two hours before the specified time.

He had been waiting for his next command when the intra-system comm fired up. He was surprised to hear a voice come over the Etheric frequency, something that shouldn't work.

"Ricky Bobby, this is your fucking lead so you had better be ready for me," Julianna sent over her in-system Etheric comm. "Or I will find you in this *Gott Verdammt* system and kick your ever-loving AI ass."

"Captain, my Captain?" Ricky Bobby responded. "You are here?"

"Hell yeah, we are here!" she replied, joy in her voice. "Me and twelve other crazy motherfuckers are here to cause a ruckus and then skedaddle." She hit a second button. "Commands coming over the line. Respond when you understand the plan."

"Wait, you called me an AI!" he commed back, surprised.

"Damn right," Julianna replied.

It took three seconds for the AI to review the plan. "Ricky Bobby will be right there."

"You know," Julianna remarked, relief in her voice. "We can change the call sign now."

"Not in the middle of an op," Ricky Bobby responded, "and possibly not *ever*."

A prior-generation Black Eagle fired up its engines, piling on the speed second by second as he headed toward the location of his partner.

Ricky Bobby kicked up his speed, turning a casual loop to slide into place beside Julianna.

Julianna looked over, then hit her comm button. "All team members, my wing is complete."

There were shouts of elation before the comm quieted back down.

QBS *Shinigami*

"Captain, I'm ready to back out," Bethany Anne sent to the carrier's captain as *Shinigami* started sliding out of the larger ship's bay. "I'll try not to scratch the paint."

Captain Ni'ers J'onghe replied, "While I appreciate your sentiments, you should do it for your own paint. This ship will have worse problems than a few paint scratches shortly."

"You guys ready to pack up and join me?" she asked, checking the status of the fighters. "I don't want us to scramble at the last minute to get you in here. Annndddd, we have confirmation of communications linkup to control the ship," she finished.

"I think so, Captain Yaga," he replied. "We have eight controllers slaving our efforts from the *Trojan Horse* to the *Shinigami...now.*"

>>**I have the systems.**<< ADAM informed her.

Bethany Anne confirmed all eight were on her screens as well. "We have connectivity, now get your asses to my ship." Bethany Anne watched the status of the fighters. "The Empress wants you safe. If you die with me, I won't have to listen to her complain about my mistakes."

The Yollin captain tapped his mandibles together in humor. "Understood. Ni'ers out."

Leath Defense Station A-QZZ

"SIR!" System Defense Specialist J'erd looked at his system, then at the officer in charge. "We have bogeys in the system!"

The officer in charge stood from his desk and walked over to J'erd's console. "Is this a test?"

"Negative, sir. I've checked," J'erd replied. "An Etheric carrier just arrived, and it looks like they are deploying small fighters in-system."

"What do they hope to accomplish?" OIC Berhlt rubbed his upthrust tusk. "Order all defense satellites to go active, then notify both Prime Military Control and the Seven's Liaison."

"Sir?" a female's voice called.

OIC Berhlt turned toward her. "Yes?"

"Sir, I can't raise the defense satellites," she replied.

This time Berhlt didn't hesitate. He returned to his desk, flipped a switch under his video monitor, and started calling everyone he could raise.

They were under attack, and something or someone had cut one of their main defenses.

With the defense platforms currently offline, they were in trouble.

Leath Prime of the Navy had issued the command. All the Leath ships in the outer system started scrambling toward the home planet and the attackers' location.

Six battleships held stations near the planet, and four turned toward the attack and fired their engines within two minutes of notification.

There were *no* poorly performing crews protecting their planet.

"Looks like we got company coming," Pilot Yutaka Bounds called over her group's internal comm. She had Orsina, Glen, and Sebastian with her, plus their co-wings. "Make sure we do this right. And you heard the command. None of us are supposed to die."

"Roger, piss them off and nobody dies," Orsina commed. "I'll be releasing my payload in three, two...released."

Two long pipes dropped from Orsina's ship, as well as her co-wing's. Glen's, Sebastian's, and finally Yutaka's ships all dropped their payloads. They did an end-over, and all eight Black Eagles hit their highest engine output.

They were trying to offset the delta-v of the rapidly closing battleships coming at them from the planet.

"Folks," Yutaka called, "get your ships moving a bit faster. Those damned battleships are speeding up a bit more rapidly than we projected."

"I'm givin' it all I got, Cap'm," Glen mimicked an old Earth accent. "Unless ye want me to get out an' push?"

"You do that, and you will have the opportunity to enjoy feeling a Leath missile go up your ass, Glen," Yutaka replied, "with no lube." She breathed out. "We got this. Let's skedaddle back to the *Trojan Horse*."

She glanced down at the projections for the closing battleships, the expected missile envelope, and her group's acceleration.

Fuck, it was going to be close.

The Battleship *YahmaKaz* was the closest to eight Empire fighters when they suddenly flipped and started racing away from them.

"What did they do?" Captain Mel'nij of the *YahmaKaz* leaned forward in his chair, staring at the plots. "You have done something, you infested little Empies." He breathed out. "So, tell me, what was it?"

"We have nothing on sensors, Captain," his Sensor Prime called.

The captain waved a hand. "You wouldn't. The Empies are too sophisticated to do this for nothing. We just need to know what they *did*." He sighed. "And stop it."

"We will be in firing range within twelve minutes, Captain."

Captain Mel'nij nodded his understanding and continued to stare at the screen, willing it to tell him what those damned black Empies had just done to his people so that he might be able to survive their attack.

The long, graceful ship closed the ramp in its stern, and the air was pulled out of the bay once more.

"Captain Ni'ers J'onghe to the bridge, please," the raspy voice called. He was patted on the back a couple of times by his shipmates. He knew they were kidding, but…

The Witch of the Empire was just fucking *scary*.

He was provided instructions on how to find the bridge of the ship, and as he walked through it he couldn't help but wonder what it had taken to build the vessel.

The Empire had all sorts of designs. Some were sleek, like this ship. Some were beasts of war that radiated destruction when you saw them, all hard edges and guns pointing everywhere.

This one was a bit of both.

Inside, however, you might mistake it for a luxury ship for the elite. Had he not seen the outside with his own eyes, he would not have believed this ship had any weapons except for puny defensive measures for the occasional pirate.

Now he wondered what was hidden under the beauty as he looked around. Based on the rumors about the captain of this ship, he didn't doubt it hosted significantly more firepower than he could see.

It took a little over a minute to make his way from the stern to the bow. He knocked on the bridge door, which opened for him.

He was looking at what he would have sworn was a posh living room, or perhaps a VIP area in a club. He bent forward to look around the corner and saw Baba Yaga lying in a special type of chair. It seemed to originate from the sofas that graced the room. He looked around and realized that the remaining sofa seats were as wide as hers, then had maybe a two hands-width cushion as a divider, then another the same width as Baba Yaga's.

"Take a seat beside me, Captain." She spoke without looking away from the three monitors in front of her. "We are tracking our first fighter team, and they are a bit late getting back to us."

She pointed to her left, and the Yollin captain sat down. He was surprised when his part of the couch started unfolding. He realized he was going to have a chair like hers.

"You can help control the *Trojan Horse* from there, in case you need to adjust the plans, make the death seem more realistic," she told him. As he figured out how to do it, the chair was starting to encase him, and from underneath, screens and controls started appearing. In the ceiling a portal opened, and a large helmet started to descend. "That will help you project as if you are still on the *Horse*." She looked at him. "Let's hope your acting skills are up to snuff."

He wasn't sure what "snuff" was, but he nodded in her direction and turned to face forward as the helmet slid over his head.

He grinned inside the helmet. It was a complete virtual reality image of the bridge of the *Trojan Horse*.

Perhaps, he thought, *he might have a job to do, after all.*

CHAPTER TWENTY

Planet Leath, Tienemehn, the Seven's Private Area

Translated from the *Book of the Phraim-'Eh*, the Eighth Clan of the Kurtherians. One of the Seven who seek to Ascend those the Phraim-'Eh would Bless.

Three hundred and sixty degrees is perfection. We, the Eight, shall rule together with one voice, one mind, one effort to take those who have the spark to new heights. To Ascend is the Blessing. The Pain that they must go through is the payment by those who come before to those who come later.

It was the Will of the Eight that we chose the Leath.

The table was in the middle of a large room, which was some two stories tall. Framed in light from the floor pointed toward the ceiling, the quiet in the room was a byproduct of engineering and acoustics.

The table had eight points, signifying the original Eight who had landed on this planet thousands of years before. The eighth spot was empty in honor of Gorllet, who had occupied the eighth spot for two hundred cycles as the planet circled the sun.

It was Gorllet who first tried to move his consciousness into a

Leath follower. His effort to facilitate extending his life almost ended in calamity.

He was well over seven hundred years of age when he tried, but the sacrifice had not been properly readied and fought Gorllet mentally. Teret had been supporting Gorllet, and at the last moment, sacrificed her future by allowing Gorllet access to her own being.

Now they were but Seven, and yet still complete. Teret and Gorllet became Terellet, the Seventh of the Seven, the masters of the Phraim-'Eh.

It was for this reason the Phraim-'Eh still considered themselves the Eight.

And with the combined knowledge of Teret and Gorllet, the Phraim-'Eh mastered transferring their consciousnesses to the sacrifices.

Torik, Third of the Seven, nodded at Levelot, First of the Seven, as he made his way past Behome't, Second of the Seven, to sit at his place at the table. He nodded to Zill to his left, then Chrio'set and Var'ence, the Sixth of the Seven and the one he most often spoke with.

Then Terellet entered, her Leath face a study of peace and anger, rage and righteousness. It moved past the First to sit two seats down, skipping the eighth and empty seat.

Levelot opened the discussion. "We are being attacked here in our system by the Etheric Empire." She summarized the situation and provided orders, then turned to Terellet. "Find the problem with our security and fix it."

Terellet stood and nodded, then quickly moved from the room, the soft *snick* of the door closing just barely audible to the others.

She turned to Torik. "We have systems down. The defensive

platforms are offline. Facilitate the fix." Torik stood up, bowed to Levelot, and left the room.

She turned to the rest. "We are being tested. Our ability to Ascend this race is in question, and I will not allow our millennia of effort to be wasted by this attack. We will use the Leath and spend them as necessary to prove the Phraim-'Eh are the greatest of the Twelve."

Levelot turned toward Var'ence. "Is there anything important?"

Var'ence had pulled out her communications device and now looked up. "Yes."

Levelot pointed toward the screens along the walls. "Share."

Var'ence tapped a command on her tablet and the eight screens around the walls turned on, each showing the same white-haired monstrosity that had been harassing their efforts for decades now.

Baba Yaga looked into the camera, her eyes red and her teeth showing as she smiled. "Hello, Phraim-'Eh Clan Leaders," she hissed. "I'm happy to say that the promise the Empress made so long ago is now coming true."

The face in the screen cocked its head. "But what promise is that?" She laughed. "You mean you didn't share the news with the rest of those on this world? Here, let me rectify that shortcoming on your part!"

A video of Bethany Anne came up onscreen. The enemy empress stood on the podium that had been built for her at the center of the bottom floor of the Open Court in the QBBS *Meredith Reynolds*. She was surrounded by her people and her Guardians. The human empress looked out over those standing at the level she was on, as well as turning her head to look up at the Etherians on the higher levels of the Court.

She gazed at the video cameras. "Merrek is now free of Leath. The last thousand or two were entombed forever as a pointed reminder that you do *not* disrespect my warriors." Her eyes glimmered red, sparking from time to time. "We have personal confirmation of their deaths and have provided video of the events to those news agencies which adhere to the truth."

The human empress turned her head to her left, then to her right.

"The Leath military treated our fallen in the most despicable ways possible, and we have replied. We killed everyone responsible for committing the atrocities, and all Leath who worked to subjugate Merrek to satisfy their own ambitions."

"However," she continued, and her visage changed, her eyes taking center stage as they glowed with power, "let me explain that our *real* fight is with the Kurtherians of the Phraim-'Eh Clan, one of the seven Kurtherian clans. The Etheric Empire has declared war to the knife with *that* clan, *not* with the Leath who have been subjugated by these aliens, acting as their 'gods' for generations. To those Kurtherians I say, know that I am committing our complete focus to your *eradication*, to uprooting you and killing you one by one, however long it takes. Should you seek safety, I will attack your hiding places until I find you and *kill* you."

Her face crackled with energy, vehemence dripping from her words. "I have been granted a long life, and I will use that life to make sure you suffer for killing my people, both on Earth and in space. Every member of your clan is now our enemy. You wanted to see if you were good enough to help a species? Well, you failed. Congratulations! You now have the attention of the Etheric Empire and the *Queen Bitch*."

Her hair floated in the calm air as the cameras focused on her face. "Baba Yaga is coming," she assured the galactic audience. The human empress' face disappeared, to be replaced by the ink-black face of the one who had first spoken on the video that was being broadcast system-wide.

"For those who do not know me," the face hissed in a grating voice, "I am Baba Yaga, the Witch of the Empire, the Avatar of the

Empress, and the one who deals out her Justice. I am here to free the Leath from the subjugation of the Seven. Those who had originally been called…"

Her voice changed, and her visage calmed as another seemed to rise to the surface as the Seven watched.

"Hello, Phraim-'Eh Clan Leaders." The much calmer voice came out of the same mouth.

"My name is…" Then the voice spoke in a different language, one that only seven on the whole planet understood. "I am from Clan Essiehkor. The Five have judged your clan, and now we bring the Justice of Righteousness as handed down from the Court of Perfection in the Year 27,672 when you were sentenced."

The five Kurtherians in the room were frozen in shock at the realization that another Kurtherian was speaking to them, causing each mental pain as the truth demolished all the assumptions they'd had about the Empire.

The voice continued speaking from the Empire's Witch. "Justice has been decreed, and now Justice has found you. You may think I will not be able to offer you violence…"

The voice changed back to the woman's, deep, guttural, and awful in its truth, "but *I* can. And I will." She looked from left to right, as if she were seeing each in their chairs.

"Baba Yaga is coming."

The video cut off.

The silence in the room was complete for a while before Levelot stood up. "Kill that human immediately," she ordered before she turned and walked out, leaving the others to accomplish her edict.

In the hallway, she swept toward her suite. "No one judges Phraim-'Eh. *No one.*"

Captain Mel'nij of the *YahmaKaz* watched as the countdown continued on his right screen. *"FIRE!"* he commanded, and twelve missiles left his ship, accelerating toward the small fighters in the distance and the carrier they were undoubtedly trying to rendezvous with.

A system-wide message overrode his secondary screen, and his eyes flicked to the left before returning a second time to re-read the message.

"ALL SHIPS, TRACK AND ATTACK ALL INVADERS UNTIL CONFIRMED DEAD."

Above the planet, the last two battleships fired their already warmed-up engines, pulling away from the gravity well of the planet.

"Well, fuck," Bethany Anne murmured to herself.

TOM, do we have the ability to tweak the missiles for those ships?

Yes, TOM admitted, **but it might be close. I'm going to have to guess a little on the calculations.**

What about ADAM?

He is busy focusing on the pucks to protect the fighters at the moment, TOM replied. **Besides, I'm going to have to use some gut-guessing.**

Bethany Anne processed his comment a moment. *You are going to start guessing with your gut NOW?*

It makes me more human, I'm told, TOM told her. **Besides, after having to speak to those assholes, I need something to get the taste out of my mouth.**

Now you're cussing, too? Bethany Anne shook herself. **Who are you, really?**

There was a pause in the communication as back near the planet a total of twenty-seven slender missiles, their payload strictly a massive amount of momentum and their own weight, slammed into the two battleships which had just left their stationary orbit. Five more flew past, missing them entirely.

However, it was more than enough to overcome the shields which, they had realized too late, were under attack. The battleships dropped their speeds as damage raged uncontrolled throughout.

A few minutes later one exploded, killing all on board.

Baba Yaga made the sign of the cross over her heart.

We tried, Bethany Anne, TOM reminded her. **That was why they didn't have warheads too.**

>>There is a sixty-eight-point-four-percent chance the other can overcome their damage.<< ADAM added.

Thanks, guys, Bethany Anne sent them both. *We are trying to reduce deaths, but not at the expense of my own people.*

Leath Battleship *YahmaKaz*

Captain Mel'nij of the *YahmaKaz* hung his head. *"That was what they were doing,"* he muttered to himself before raising his head. He tapped the in-ship comm. "Ready the missiles. We will continue firing until these killers are dead, or we are!"

Near QBS *Trojan Horse*

"Put some fire to your asses, folks!" Julianna called out as the second group, also back from firing their missiles at the battleships, whooped at the destruction behind them. "Let's not make this a Pyrrhic victory!"

"And piss off the Empress," Baba Yaga added. "I am sending you instructions now. Do not be surprised when…"

Julianna heard someone curse over the frequency.

"Your ships are taken over," Baba Yaga finished. "It is going to be close."

Behind their fighters, the missiles were closing fast. Julianna and all her people were trusting the Witch with their lives.

Not that they had any choice in the matter. She couldn't control her ship anyway.

"WOOHOO!" Billy called when the closest missile to the rear of the formation exploded. *"Gott Verdammt!* I was squeezing my ass so tight I could chew steel and shit nails!"

Three more missiles exploded behind them. Baba Yaga spoke again. "You have control back now. Don't fuck it up."

"You heard the woman!" Julianna resumed control of her ship and the twenty-six fighters flew past the *Trojan Horse*, all within two fighter-lengths of the hull. They continued flying like bats out of hell to catch up to the *Shinigami,* which was supposed to be ahead of them somewhere.

The *Trojan Horse* started moving up slightly, turning toward the missiles.

Moments later, eight missiles slammed into the carrier, blowing it into its constituent atoms. The effect was enhanced by the extra explosives that had been placed around the ship to make sure none of the technology could be recovered if the Leath did a bad job of hitting it.

The effort had been unnecessary. The Leath had destroyed it very well indeed.

Leath Battleship *YahmaKaz*

"Yes!" Missiles Prime yelled when the carrier exploded.

Captain Mel'nij, watching the commands his other battleship captains were following, called, "Now find me those fighters!"

The four battleships were approaching fast as six carriers, seven more destroyers, and twelve sub-battleships started to converge on the enemies.

"Sir, they are heading toward the Expansion Gate!"

"Change course, head in that direction," Captain Mel'nij

commanded as he sent the information to the other captains. Across their space, twenty-nine ships turned their bows toward the Gate.

Planet Leath, Tienemehn, the Seven's Private Area

Behome't turned his eyes from his tablet and spoke to the other three at the table. "The destination of the Gate has been changed."

"How is that possible?" Fourth of the Seven Zill asked. "Did you send that information to Terellet?"

"I have now," Second of the Seven Behome't replied.

"If they get to that new location, we will have to call off our ships."

"It is obviously a trap," Chrio'set, Fifth of the Seven, agreed.

Leath, Outside Primary City

Jerrleck sent the final commands and smiled. Inside this little metal shed bathed in orange light, he had finished what his love had started and changed the future of his people.

He hoped.

He bent over and stuck a hand in his backpack, pulling out a dirty pair of underwear and tossing them to the side. After today, perhaps he could buy something new in all the confusion.

Or not.

Either way, he didn't want them in his way anymore, and he continued to search until he found the little memory stick. He brought the stick to his mouth and kissed it, then he leaned forward and stuck it in the slot for upload and turned to his right, flicking two switches and pushing a button.

He started to lean back, and that was when hell hit him. His nerves burned as if they were on fire and electricity arced through his body, causing convulsions and pain as his muscles spasmed. He found himself on the floor, blood in his mouth from his teeth biting his tongue.

He groaned and turned toward the light coming from the door. His eyes, barely his own to control, looked up from the floor to see a robed figure standing there.

Jerrleck coughed as he tried to smile. "Hello, asshole," he got out. "I'm baaack!"

Terellet. This time half the face grinned in delight and half showed anger as her / he / it stepped into the little shed and shut the door. The screams coming from within could be heard for hundreds of paces in every direction.

CHAPTER TWENTY-ONE

Planet Leath, Outside Primary City

Terellet looked down at the previous Prime of Intelligence and pursed her / his / its lips. "You have much to answer for."

"No, you and the other six have," Jerrleck responded, coughing up blood. "Next time you wipe someone's mind, you need to do a better job of it."

"I will inform Torik of his mistakes," Terellet agreed amiably. The voice would come out as female, then switch to male, then change to something ambiguous. "You have a strong body. Perhaps it is strong enough to facilitate a transfer."

"Transfer of what?" Jerrleck painfully turned his head to see a Leath's face staring at him, the cowl on the head having been pushed back. "You fucking bastards!" He tried to scream as he willed his legs to move, attempting to kick the Leath female in front of him.

The Kurtherian was wearing his love's body.

"But wouldn't it be a union of perfection to separate myself and Gorllet back into you and your previous rebellion leader's body?" Terellet asked in a sing-song voice. "I myself see symmetry in that." It cocked its head, and a male voice emanated.

"I will wear your body for the next hundred years and everyone will believe I am you, substandard creature. Your sacrifice will allow the Leath to move forward from this present failure to advancement." The female's voice came back. "It is true. Thousands are dying right now above us. Your navy's battleships were caught in a trap set by those you helped."

"What is it you Seven tell us all the time?" Jerrleck gasped out. "'Some sacrifices have to be made in the effort to Ascend?'"

"Yes." Terellet nodded. "That is true," he replied in a soft voice.

"Then you won't mind being the sacrifices yourselves, *right*?" Jerrleck asked. Terellet wore a smile on her / his / its face until it considered the words and narrowed its eyes at Jerrleck.

Jerrleck screamed in pain as Terellet raided his mind, ripping through the minor mod protection he had figured out and surrendered the truth to the Kurtherian. Terellet's eyes went to the controls on the desk and stepped forward, hand stretching out to yank out the memory stick that Jerrleck had connected.

She / he / it looked down as the Leath on the floor started laughing.

"Too late, *you alien-infested zombie*," Jerrleck got out before his screaming started once again.

Leath System, Expansion Gate

"Damn," Baba Yaga mouthed beside Captain Ni'ers J'onghe. "That is huge."

"Expansion Gates are substantial," he agreed. "It is one of the reasons they are so rarely built."

"I want it!" she cried in sudden understanding. She turned to her left. "Send out the command! No one is to destroy that Gate," she commanded and pointed toward the front screens, which had the massive Gate in view.

"We need to go through it," Ni'ers asked, perplexed. "Why would we destroy it?"

"Sorry," the Witch answered. "I was speaking to more than just you."

"I heard and understand," Shinigami confirmed.

Baba Yaga winked at the Yollin captain, who carefully turned back to his own controls. *Please don't let me go crazy, please don't let me go crazy,* he kept saying over and over in his mind.

Baba Yaga sent the command to allow her to speak to the group. "Folks, this is the part where we find out if we are successful or fucked. If you have any gods, please pray to them at this time. Let's hope our plans are in place."

With twenty-nine massive Leath ships behind them, the twenty-six fighters and one black ship hit the Gate, screaming forward to stay ahead of the enemy.

K'llereck System

Those on the fourth planet had lived in fear since the great device appeared in their heavens many seasons ago. Now those that watched the activity in the heavens started sending messages back and forth across their world.

They had the ability to see into the heavens and even send small packages off their world, but they had nothing like the immense object that had appeared one inauspicious night.

Nothing in any of the religions of the planet had foretold of this event, and any that tried to associate the object with a foretelling seemed to choose a dire one.

Evil had come.

The governments around the world called each other, deciding how to prepare against an invasion which now seemed imminent, given all the activity in the past week around the glowing ring in space. Many had tried to reach out to those in space, but nothing was ever returned.

It was apparently their lot in life to wait until the visitors chose to land and speak with them.

"Move along, little doggies," Bethany Anne murmured as the *Shinigami* slowly passed the fighters.

>>**I've finished the calculations. There is nothing the ships behind us can fire that will hurt the fighters. They are not willing, it seems, to fire toward the Gate.**<<

Bethany Anne marveled at the size of the object. "No shit! I wouldn't either." She ignored the look she received from Captain Ni'ers J'onghe. There was no downside to Baba Yaga's being considered a bit crazy.

A chuff brought her attention back to the bridge, and she turned her head and raised an eyebrow. "What, you aren't going to ask permission to join me on the bridge?"

I thought that was a human thing, Ashur sent.

I'll give you "human thing," you walking flea carpet. She turned back to the screens. ***Lock yourself in. The Empress would be annoyed if you started floating around the bridge during a space battle.***

Ashur yawned and walked toward a separate couch to Baba Yaga's right. Jumping on, he turned around and laid down. His armor covered his body.

Do you remember how to eject? she asked him as *Shinigami* started to pull ahead of the fighters. ***We are going to hit the Gate first, and if they can zap us, we might be in outer space sucking vacuum faster than you can blink your eye.***

I can blink my eye pretty quickly, Ashur retorted. *Not quicker than you can slap me, though, so don't ask.*

Bethany Anne smirked. ***Maybe old dogs can learn new tricks.***

Says the human who is older than I am.

Every human year is seven dog years. You have to be almost a thousand.

Provides me with more wisdom, Ashur replied.

How does Bellatrix put up with you?

Not well, which is why she failed to notice that I snuck out.

Baba Yaga stared at the dog, not blinking until Ashur turned toward her.

What?

Baba Yaga shook her head slowly as she turned to view her control screens once more. ***You had better hope you die on this trip, or Bellatrix is going to make you wish you had.***

Ashur yawned. *No, I'll just be sleeping in your suite for a week.*

Oh, goody.

"Okay, we have three, two, one …" The *Shinigami* went through the Gate, coming out in an entirely new location of the galaxy. The Black Eagles started appearing behind her after about ten seconds.

What good would it have done if we had failed to get here? Ashur chuffed.

If the Gate acted like a shield and if we went splat, the fighters could have veered off. If we had died on this side, then we all would have died.

Ashur put his head down. *I really hate space flight.*

Julianna noticed the message from the *Shinigami* and confirmed it had been sent to all the fighters. It was short and succinct.

Stay on my path or die. You veer from the path and don't die, I'll find you and kill you myself. So, stay on the damned path.

"I guess she wants us to stay on the path, eh, Boss?" Billy commed.

Before Julianna could reply, Baba Yaga's voice came over the radio. "Yes. That was the reason for the message, O'Neill. Do you need me to write it on a piece of paper and come over to your cockpit and shove it so far up your ass you can read it on your retinas?"

"Uh, no, ma'am," he replied.

Julianna shook her head. She hoped the rest of her team didn't antagonize the Witch, or she might not make it back to the Empress with everyone intact.

Then she chuckled. How would she write up the cause of death? "Death by irritated Witch?" or in Billy's case, "Reverse intestinal non-biodegradable inflammation?"

She clicked her comm. "Everyone stay on the line. Sandra, tighten up your vector." She nodded to herself when Sandra and her co-wing locked back into place. As the tail, she could see almost all her pilots in front of her. Her eyes went to her sensors and opened wide when the first Leath came through the Gate.

It wasn't the larger ships, as they had expected, but rather a spread of twelve missiles going much faster than the fighters. "Oh, crap." She hit the comm. "Fregin to Baba Yaga, we have missiles back here."

"Well, shit," Baba Yaga's voice came back. "I'm turning around, but everyone else keep pushing forward. Dammit, I'm not going to be able to get all of them, I don't think. I've released the anti-missile defense. If you have any secret methods for getting more speed out of those ships, this is the time to try, Captain."

For a long, tense minute the ships carefully followed the course they needed, until the fighters started escaping the zone and they could open up. Julianna was starting to sweat.

Behind her, two missiles exploded.

Then two more.

"C'mon, only eight more. I'm not asking for much," she whispered. She watched as eight missiles became seven, then six, five, four. Finally, three and two exploded, leaving one.

Julianna's eyes narrowed when Ricky Bobby tweaked his position. "Oh, no, you don't," she whispered to herself as she sent commands to her ship.

Before Ricky Bobby could sacrifice himself, her ship braked sharply and curved left, blocking the AI's effort to place himself in front of the missile.

"NO!" Julianna heard Ricky Bobby's voice over the system as she slammed into the side of her cockpit, the explosion behind her ripping her ship apart.

That was when everything went black.

"Dammit!" Baba Yaga spat. "They are going to fuck up my perfect safety record." She touched her comm. "People, keep flying. *Shinigami* is going back for the captain and her co-wing."

None of the fighters could see the *Shinigami* as it blew past them.

In space, the ejected cockpit was careening toward the left. Chasing it was an older model Black Eagle focused on confirming the trajectory and spin of the small piece of the ship that was left.

Ricky Bobby commed over his link to Julianna. "If you came all this way just to prove I'm worth saving, don't be a bitch and get yourself killed."

The AI piloted his ship deftly as he approached where Julianna was supposed to be. He wasn't sure if he could do the AI equivalent of crying, but he would rather not find out.

The intra-system comm crackled to life with a female's voice on the other side. "Wow, for an AI, you have a really coarse mouth," Julianna told him. "I didn't sacrifice myself so we could both die."

Another voice joined their conversation. "I'd tell you both," Baba Yaga stated, "to get a room if we weren't in the middle of a fucking war with the heavens about to open up in fire, so let's focus on saving your asses and being safe, shall we?"

\>\>**Locked onto the cockpit, using the antigrav beams to slow and stop her wobble and spin.**<<

"Well, fucking hell." Baba Yaga spoke again. "Okay, Ricky Bobby, the cockpit has stopped spinning. We've got ships coming through the Gate. Save your captain."

"I will," Ricky Bobby promised. "Thank you for helping me."

"Like to do more, but I have a couple dozen ships to destroy." The *Shinigami* drifted off a little distance, then executed an amazing maneuver and headed back toward the ships that had just translocated through the Gate.

"Captain, do you have an air supply?"

"Yes," Julianna replied. "Both suit and tank I can bring with me."

"Great. Air up and grab the tank for the transfer. You should use the air tank you bring since I don't know how contaminated mine might be. My seals are still good."

"Good enough for me." Julianna cracked her cockpit, the top unlocking, and she pushed it up. The auto-opening feature had gone away with the rest of her ship, she assumed. Moving as quickly as she could in zero-g, she stood on her seat. The shadow of her partner's Black Eagle covered her for a moment as he moved into position and then pivoted on his axis, opening his long-unused cockpit.

"I'd say "Ow," but I really don't feel anything," Ricky Bobby admitted. "I am still seeking to understand why you risked your life for me."

"Shut. Up," Julianna told him. "If I tell you I'll probably start crying, and that is just a mess in these helmets. I'll have the 'existential life questions' talk with you when we get back to a proper ship."

"I'm not proper?"

"A carrier, you dolt," she replied as she used the canopy to spin in space, turning upside-down and pulling herself into the cockpit. "That's me settled. Let's get some space from that wreck."

The nearby sun glinted off the aged and marred canopy as it started to close.

A moment later, Ricky Bobby spoke through his cockpit's internal speaker for the first time. "Uh-oh."

"What, uh-oh?" Julianna looked around. "Shit, do we have a bad seal? It's okay." She tried to calm the AI. "I have suit air."

"No," the AI responded, pulling away and heading toward the location of the other fighters of the squadron. "I just wanted to try out humor."

She chuckled. "Ricky Bobby, you can be such an ass."

ADAM, keep an eye on those two. Make sure we don't need to go help them again.

>>**Understood, Bethany Anne.**<<

"Shinigami?" Her voice grated on her vocal cords. Perhaps she should have chosen a different voice, but too late now. "When we are crossing the track, light us up to their sensors as we run perpendicular. I want to try to get them to jump into the minefield."

"Crossing in five, four, three, two…crossing. Turning on location emissions."

Twenty-nine ships came through the Gate. By the time the Shinigami had crossed the safety zone, four were already out of the core killing area and turning to follow the black ship. The other twenty-five, including three of the Battleships, turned hard.

Right into the maelstrom of a sun.

"Fire all pBYPSs." Bethany Anne sighed. Thousands of the miniaturized Etheric Energy Lasers that had been seeded in the system by her people opened fire. She noticed that a few exploded on their own. "Make sure we record all we can. Looks like we haven't figured out all the problems in manufacturing."

"Stop pBYPSs," she commanded thirty seconds later.

Her ship's EI updated her. "Twelve-point-two percent of the pBYPS system is still active. All others are spent."

"Yeah." She leaned back in her chair. "Over fifty percent of those ships aren't going to make it back home." She looked at the four who had fired missiles behind her. "Go inactive and dodge the missiles, and take me out of range. Connect me to the battleship's captain." She looked around as the ship disappeared from tracking and the missiles lost lock.

"I wonder if he will be willing to see reason?" she asked.

CHAPTER TWENTY-TWO

Leath Battleship *YahmaKaz*

The rage the captain felt was consuming him. "Fire all missiles!" he spat. He could see the destruction the Empire had wrought, and if he could kill this avatar of the Empress his people would be able to withstand a fight in the system.

Provided they could bring the defensive platforms back online.

The symbol of the enemy's ship disappeared off his screen. "WHAT?" He looked around, annoyed. "Was she destroyed, or are we incapable of finding a ship so close to us?"

"Not destroyed, sir," Missiles reported. "All missiles are still accounted for, but they are aimed out into space."

Captain Mel'nij ground his teeth together in frustration. "Prepare to follow the fighters. They do not have jump capability, and when we take them out, perhaps Baba Yaga will come to their aid if she cares about her people enough *before* we kill them."

He turned in his seat. "Send the message to our ships: Those that can support others, do so. We four will continue the fight."

Captain Mel'nij's eyes flicked to the main viewing screen to see an ink-black face with white hair and red eyes looking back at him. "Greetings, captain of the Leath battleship." She spoke normally, not like she had just killed so many of his people.

"You won't get away with this!" Captain Mel'nij growled. "We have more than enough ships and firepower to support our people. This is merely a small setback!"

"Captain Mel'nij, I'm not here to *beat* the Leath people, I'm here to eradicate an infestation by an alien group that is killing your people. Even now," she dipped her head, "they are forcing you to try to kill me to hide the truth."

"What truth?" Captain Mel'nij asked. "I've seen your accusation that they are Kurtherians."

"And they are," Baba Yaga replied.

His hands opened and closed in frustration. "How do I know you are not just looking for a way to kill our leadership so you can put your little human empress at the top, like what happened with the Yollins?" The coarse laughter surprised Captain Mel'nij. "What is so funny?" he asked, his eyes narrowing.

Her smile showed a mouth full of sharp teeth, which didn't make him feel any easier. "If you knew the Empress like I do, you would realize she doesn't want to be in charge of a janitor, much less a whole new people and system." She shook her head. "No, she wants peace with the Leath, stopping any more efforts to subjugate—or worse—other peoples and allow you to rule yourselves. Perhaps there are options for a united future, or perhaps there has been too much bloodshed to allow that. However, ruling the Leath is *absolutely* the last desire she has."

Her eyes flicked to something off-screen, then back to him. "If your group does not stop trying to turn and go after my fighters, I will be forced to cease discussing options and destroy your last four ships."

He waved a hand. "We are out of your killing area," he replied. His own eyes flicked to the sensors, wondering if the four of them were being pulled into a trap as well. His people never saw the small defensive nodes which fired lasers into their ships.

"There is always more than one way to destroy, Captain." He turned to look at her; she seemed annoyed. "And if my motherfucking navy were where they were supposed to be at the time they were supposed to show up, I wouldn't have to stall like an idiot. Admiral Thomas better get his ass in gear…" She paused, then her eyes lit up. "Oh, here they are."

"CAPTAIN!" Sensors called. "We have seven, no, twelve… Sir," his Sensors Prime turned in his seat, "We have thirty-plus ships Gating in near the fighters!" He turned back around. "Uh, sir?"

Captain Mel'nij bit down on his impatience as he looked over. "Yes, Sensors?"

He could almost hear Sensors trying not to squeak. "There are seven superdreadnoughts, sir."

"Seven?" he hissed. His people had four, all of them in a nearby system and probably firing up to Gate into the main Leath system for protection right now.

Pound for pound, the Empire's superdreadnoughts could take one of theirs, but it would come out crippled. With seven, he couldn't hope to do them enough damage. "Where the hell did they get *seven*?"

"Um, eight, sir." Sensors seemed subdued. "We just had another Gate in from a different direction."

Captain Mel'nij leaned back in his seat and looked at the ships arrayed against him. His people could use these four ships to help save those whose ships were still on fire. He looked up at the face his people detested. "Speak to me of peace, Witch of the Empire."

She nodded. "Will you agree to surrender so that your people can be saved by not only your ships but by ours as well?"

The captain leaned forward. "You would do this?"

The red eyes flashed. "One of these days, you will understand that I am not against *your* people unless they disrespect *mine*. I will pursue the Seven until either they are dead or I am. Do we have an agreement for surrender, Captain?"

"We do," he answered. "Command all ships: shut down

weapons and active tracking. Focus on rescue of all personnel and cease all hostilities at this time." He looked to his left. "Missiles, send destruction codes."

In the far distance, thirty-six missiles detonated in the cold of space.

Planet Leath, Tienemehn, the Seven's Private Area

First of the Seven Levelot watched the video for a third time. Inside her Leath shell, she grimaced in annoyance as the previous Intelligence Prime's video went across the planet, including up to the Space Stations. Fortunately, she had caught it early enough, and no more video traffic went out through the Gates to their sister systems.

And neither did the news reporters from those systems, either. She breathed in and out, trying to calm the feelings which she wasn't sure were from her or the body she was inhabiting.

Either way, the feelings were a disgrace.

She reached up and tapped her lips on one side. She hated the upthrust tusks herself, and whenever she found a potential candidate, they were required to saw off their tusks as a display of their obedience to the Seven. That way, she was never bothered by having to do something like that once she decided to exchange her current organic vehicle for the next.

She stood up and started walking toward the door.

To all, it is time to transfer to a younger body. Make preparations immediately.

The door to her suite opened and shut silently as she walked down the hallway toward the servants' area.

She had just the sacrifice in mind.

K'llereck System

Baba Yaga looked with annoyance at the image on her screen.

It was a picture of her; well, Bethany Anne "her." "ArchAngel," Baba Yaga spat.

"Don't issue a command I can safely ignore, Baba Yaga." The AI smirked. "This is a Yollin Leviathan-Class superdreadnought. I can take a few hits and shrug them off. Hits that would destroy that pretty black paint."

"Not if they can't see me," Baba Yaga argued.

Great, I'm having an argument with my-fucking-self, she thought.

"I calculate a seventeen-percent chance you will come out of the Gate with enough charge left on the outside that other ships will be able to attack. Besides," the AI smirked again, "*we* are going through, so catch us if you can!"

The screen shut off. Bethany Anne glanced to her right, where Ashur was chuffing in humor. "Keep it up, furball, and I'll make you walk back to Yoll," she grumped. "Where's Matrix?"

TOM replied, **He is talking to the Yollin and human crew from the *Trojan Horse*, regaling them with stories.**

"Great, we have our own entertainer aboard," she mumbled to herself.

Bethany Anne ignored the sideways glance from Captain Ni'ers J'onghe. The stories he would be able to tell amused her. She hit the comm to connect with the strike team. "*G'laxix Shphaea*, tell me you are ready!"

"Ready and willing, My Witch." Kael-ven's amusement was evident as he replied to Bethany Anne's avatar.

"Don't make me ask the Empress to kick your ass back up to Vice-Admiral," she ground out. Beside her, she heard Captain Ni'ers cough. Trying to cover his laughter, she supposed. "That would cut your fun pretty damned short."

"Wow, no need to be nasty, Baba Yaga," Kael-ven came back quickly. "We are running through the Gate right under the *Arch-Angel*. We will go silent and get the team where they need to go."

"Good." She cut off that connection and set up the next. "Dan, you there?"

"Yes," was his short reply. "We are ready to drop. Just smoking a bit, telling some jokes, getting old, and all that."

"Liar," she replied. "See you on the surface. If your team can find my Leath contact, protect him as a priority. He should see the success of his efforts."

"We will wrap him in a cocoon of safety," Dan replied. "Black Leader, out."

Bethany Anne watched as her eight massive Leviathan-class Superdreadnoughts went through the Gate. It had taken so damned long and so much security to hide their existence, it wasn't fun to even think about. Now she just hoped the Leath hadn't accomplished the same.

"Here's hoping massive firepower will allow us to solve this without massive firepower."

This time Captain Ni'ers just nodded, understanding the sentiment.

Planet Leath, Tienemehn, the Seven's Private Area

Terellet propelled the body of Jerrleck through the back hallways, the secret excavations the Seven had used for centuries to move about unseen. It had allowed a mystical reputation to grow up around them from generation to generation.

Terellet's mind control over Jerrleck forced him to walk to the sacrificial chambers, but inside his mind, Jerrleck screamed in anger and frustration. The Kurtherians were much more powerful mentally than he had ever considered.

At some level, they *could* be gods. However, he wasn't going to take the infiltration of his body without fighting to the end.

No matter what he went through.

One part of his mind fought, but the other watched where he was walking and what he was seeing. To him, it was the proof that the Seven were evil, pure and simple. This wasn't a disagreement. No, the skeletons that littered the floor he walked over told a twisted tale of terror so far removed from even his suspicious reality that he cried in the tiny part of his brain he could still call his own.

The whole time, Terellet was giving him a guided tour through the passages of hell in that mentally crazy double and triple voice it used. "Here is our first room," it told him. "Those five skeletons represent the first sacrifices we used to move from our previous bodies. In our third decade, we decided we should keep the discarded sacrifices as a way to track our own efforts."

"What? Why would we do that, you ask?"

Jerrleck had certainly not asked.

"In one way, our success in helping you Ascend is the basis for our judgment from those above as we Ascend ourselves. To provide a measure for that success, we show how we have not wasted the sacrifices of your people over the centuries. Rather we have been good shepherds of our flock."

Jerrleck's mind continued to cry as he was made to walk through room after room filled with skeletons. "Sometimes we had issues with a particular passage to another sacrifice," Terellet continued, "so unfortunately, more sacrifices were required until we understood the issues."

The Leath religious leader cocked her / his / its head. "Enough chatting. The leader of the Seven has decreed we all move to a younger body."

A moment later, Jerrleck heard the muttering of the crazed Kurtherian. "Shame I transferred to your love such a short time ago."

Glaxix Sphaea, En Route to Military Defense Station Designated 'Alpha'

Peter cricked his neck back and forth and looked at Todd, who was checking his guns and magazines. "We got this, buddy," Peter told him.

Todd turned to look at his friend and they fist-bumped. "Yeah. We do every time, don't we?"

"Damn right," Peter replied. "One more time unto the breach, dear Guardians. Tie up your leggings around your back as we change to go to war." Peter stood up, swinging his pack over his shoulder. All eyes were on him as he pointed two fingers to his face. "Let the enemy see the yellows of our eyes as they yell in *FEAR*!" He pumped his fist and went on, "To lie among the dead as the roars of our throats sound the alarm that the Empress' Guardians are near!"

Todd stood up, flipping his pistol around and into his holster. "Stand up, you Guardian Marines!"

"OOYAHH!" voices yelled from the hold.

Todd shouted as loudly as he could, "Let not one hair on your Guardians be harmed by others as your guns remain holstered. Pull your triggers until the barrels run hot and the enemy's blood runs cold!"

Peter grinned. "Yell '*OUT*,' you Guardians, and be so bold as to rip out the throats of those who would do your Marines harm. *Roar* your challenge as you run down the halls, making the enemy's blood freeze so when your Marines shoot them, it is already chilled and waiting!"

The cacophony of yelling and shouts was in full force when the music started playing very softly in the back of the *G'laxix Sphaea*. Peter recognized the song and called, "Zhu, Jian, Shun!"

The three moved up, smiling and taking their places. "Hit it!" Peter commanded.

The three men started dancing, quoting the now heavily-modified lyrics to a famous song from Earth so many years ago...

"*Ohhhh, Sexy Lady!*" Shun sang. More of those in the crew set up with them and started dancing along.

"*Oopa BA STYLE!*" he shouted as everyone started twirling their hands.

"*She be fly during the day, but watch out for us come the night.*

When you're thinking you know her type,
She will knock you silly with just one bite.
Oopa BA STYLE!
Kicking ass is her predilection,
Solving problems with some misdirection.
Not that we give a shit about your excuses.
We are here to solve some abuses.
Oopa BA Style!
We be telling you leave us alone,
That none of us want your homes.
But you piss off our Empress and then it's over
The Guardians planting our size elevens up your...
Oopa BA STYLE!"

"WOOT!" Everyone raised their fists in the air. The music slowed and stopped as a few fists pumped before walking back to their gear.

"This is Captain Kael-ven T'chmon, and I'll have you know that video is going to go viral. When awesome happens on my ship, I share."

There was chuckling in the hold as the captain continued.

"We are cloaked and heading for our destination. Expected ass-kicking to begin in ten minutes."

Peter twirled his finger in the air and everyone went back into their groups, locking and loading one last time.

They hoped.

CHAPTER TWENTY-THREE

<u>**Military Defense Station Designated "Alpha"**</u>
Before the *G'laxix Sphaea* sidled up to the Military Defense station, well over two hundred Yollin Insertion Pods had slammed into the sides of the station, hundreds of small battles had occurred, and the objective had been met.

There was a place for the *G'laxix Sphaea* to dock, and another sixty hardened warriors rushed off the ship, breaking into two groups to track one of their two objectives.

Either the bridge and command consoles or the communications center buried deep inside the huge space station.

Peter wasted no time changing into a Pricolici when he got off the ship, his challenging roar announcing his presence.

He turned left and started jogging down the outer ring of hallways counter-clockwise. Todd and his other Marine, Maria, ran with him. Peter reached into his backpack, grabbing a twelve-inch-long metal piece shaped like an extruded triangle. It wasn't but another fifteen seconds when the guns behind him opened up, and he flipped a switch and tossed it on the ground.

A forcefield popped up, allowing him and his team to duck behind it. The beauty of these devices was the opposite effect the devices had on projectiles. No lasers could make it through the screen, and any projectiles fired at them were slowed so much that it felt like someone had just thrown a rock.

However, it sped their projectiles up, allowing their weapons an almost clear shot down the hall.

It was a game-changer, for sure. Soon enough, Peter reached down to turn it off, grabbing the device as they started running again for their destination.

The Empress needed access to the planet, but until they could confirm the defenses would not come back online, they wouldn't allow her to land.

Peter smiled, thinking how impatient she must be at the moment. He turned a corner and was suddenly slammed backward twenty feet, half his jaw missing, and his arm shredded. He rolled over twice, trying to get out of the way of the fire coming in his direction, and then he heard the activation of a shield and groaned.

Todd was on the ball. He and Maria were laying down vicious cover fire while Peter rolled onto his stomach, the pain in his chest immense as he heard the bones cracking and popping, trying to heal from the chest hit by gods-only-knew-what.

He could feel his face trying to heal as well.

"Man down!" Todd yelled over the comm. "We are stopped for a short while. Other teams need to press on!"

Peter wanted to tell Todd to screw "Man down." He was a damned Were, he didn't go *down*. He perhaps took a nap at inappropriate times, but he always got up again.

Except this time. This time he had been badly mangled, and his body was having a bitch of a time pulling itself together. Todd and Maria were firing through the shield, which reached about halfway up to the ceiling. The challenge, Peter noted, was that the Leath had deployed a smokescreen, and his people couldn't tell what or who they were shooting at.

Peter's eye caught a movement at the ceiling, and he tried to grunt a warning. A grenade had been tossed over the shield.

Peter tried to start crabbing for where it was going to land when Todd noticed it as well.

"SHIT!" he yelled and turned toward the grenade, catching Peter's eyes.

"Nooo!" Peter struggled to yell to his friend, but he saw the determination in Todd's eyes, and there was fuck all Peter could do to change his mind.

Even if he'd had the strength to do it.

Todd dove on the grenade, yelling as he looked into Peter's eyes, "Told you I always had…"

Peter's head flinched away when the grenade went off, tearing his best friend for longer than he had been in space into chunks of meat that went flying all over the hallway.

"YOU *GOTT VERDAMMT* MOTTHERRRRFUCKKERRRS!" Peter yelled, pushing himself up to get his knees underneath him.

Pulling his pistol, he flipped it to eleven and started limping toward the shield, his eyes determined. "MOOOOVE!" he yelled at Maria, who glanced at the shield and then back at the bloody Pricolici. His yellow eyes were mad with grief and anger, but each step got stronger as he pulled...*demanded*...energy from the Etheric to heal.

Peter rushed the shield and jumped, pulling himself into as small a ball as he could.

He remembered, right before he hit the shield, asking William what would happen if a human went through it. William had told him, "They will wish to die, at a minimum."

He already wished he could have died just moments before instead of his friend.

It was hands-down the worst pain he had ever felt in his long, long life. If Peter lived through this battle, he would have to tell William he was right.

Moments later, the twelve Leath who had set up a barricade

fifty paces down the hallway received the shock of their lives when a huge pissed-off Pricolici slammed into them.

Death had arrived, and he was angry beyond any reason.

Their shrieks of pain and fear mixed with Peter's roars reached back to Maria, who had remained behind the shield. "Fuck this!" She reached forward and turned off the shield, slipping it into her bag as she rushed through the smoke.

After coming out the other side, she slammed her rifle butt to her shoulder and started picking off any targets where the Pricolici wasn't. When she got to Peter, she slapped him on the arm as he casually ripped a Leath soldier's head from his shoulders.

"Get a grip, Peter!" she yelled, pointing down the hall. "Grieve later, operation now!"

Peter growled in anger, dropped the body, and ran down the hall, passing his Guardian Marine as he sprinted toward the goal.

There would be time later to sing the songs for his best friend Todd, who had covered his ass one final time. Then later, in the privacy of his own room, to drown his sorrow in the most expensive bottles of booze he could afford and allow the tears to silently fall.

Some thirty minutes from the initial insertion, the call was sent to the main battle group.

The Leath Space Defenses were officially down and would not be coming back up.

It was time for Baba Yaga to arrive.

Planet Leath, Primary City

For those Leath willing to look out, it was both a beautiful and a deadly sight. Four of the hated Etheric Empire's super-dreadnoughts were coming down from space, their forcefields blazing in anger as the super-heated atmosphere streamed from them.

These were the four chariots of the Witch of Death, both announcing her arrival and making sure none were stupid enough to try and stop her.

Her superdreadnoughts were surrounded by additional G'laxix Sphaea-class ships, and they all headed straight for the Seven's holy part of the city. The massive vessels looked close enough to touch for those who were watching from the rooftops.

They had seen the videos and the proof from Jerrleck, as well as the extra information provided by the Empress of the Empire. But the final video had sealed the deal.

Jerrleck had put up video cameras in the little room he had been waiting in, expecting to be able to speak live to those on planet. He'd never thought they might catch the moment the Seventh of the Seven pulled down her hood to reveal it was wearing the body of his love.

At this point, if the Empire didn't destroy the Seven, then the anger of the Leath might do it for them.

However, Baba Yaga wouldn't be denied.

The Seven's personal guards fought and fought hard. Even Stephen, who was with Jennifer, was caught in a crossfire, and bullets riddled his body. His armor stopped most, but the fusillade of anti-aircraft guns slamming rounds into him was more than even his Jean Dukes armor could withstand.

The emplacement was destroyed moments later, but for Stephen, it was almost too little, too late.

"Get off him!" a rough voice commanded Jennifer, who was crying on Stephen's chest. Her eyes turned yellow, and she swiped a hand behind her in her anger. It was caught and she was violently yanked from her love, only to fly through the air and be caught by another, who held her tightly.

"LET ME GO!" she screamed, the tears flowing down her face as her anger fueled her struggles.

"Settle down, or I'll knock you the fuck out," John Grimes told her. "She's got him. You can't help at the moment."

Jennifer twisted her head and saw Baba Yaga kneeling beside Stephen, cussing him out and commanding him to drink.

"Oh, my God!" she whispered. "Please bring him back to me."

"You cocked-up shriveled little geriatric vampire who doesn't have a dick big enough to plug a light socket better do what I command you and drink!" Baba Yaga had thrown down her glove after hurling Jennifer at John.

He would know what to do with the distraught woman.

She rolled back her armor enough to expose her veins, and her fangs grew as her eyes blazed red. She bent down and slid her teeth across her wrist, slicing it open, and turned it to his mouth, pushing it past his lips. She put her left hand into her mouth and grabbed her glove with her teeth to pull it off.

She pressed her gloveless left hand to his forehead and opened herself to the Etheric, her hair floating as she pulled in energy and willed it into her friend's body.

Then she shocked the shit out of him, and his body convulsed. His chest arched above the pavement.

"*LIVE, YOU FUCKING SONOFABITCH!*" she screamed, tears flowing down her cheeks. "I WILL NOT PERMIT YOU TO DIE!"

She shocked his body again, then heard the faint sound of his heart beating and bones shifting as they healed.

She looked over her shoulder. "Help me get him out of this armor!"

A moment later, Eric was helping her unlatch the armor, and Jennifer soon joined them in pulling it off him.

Jennifer glanced at the other woman. "I'm sorry."

"Don't fucking worry about it," Baba Yaga hissed. "I'll kick your ass later, when he is okay and we aren't on this planet."

Jennifer gave the other woman a half-smile, not sure if she

was serious about the ass-kicking or not. Either way, she would gladly accept the reprimand from the Witch if Stephen survived.

Stephen opened his eyes, staring up into the red eyes of Baba Yaga. "So," he coughed out, "it's hell then?"

"You ass." Baba Yaga grunted and looked at Jennifer. "Keep him safe." She stood, calling the *Shinigami* closer. "And teach him some fucking manners," she told Jennifer as she and the others left.

Jennifer lifted Stephen off the ground, holding him in her arms as two others grabbed his armor, and the four of them retraced their steps to the ships.

One of those holding the armor smirked when Stephen coughed again and protested, "But honey, 'twas but a scratch!"

Bethany Anne and the Bitches headed farther into the Citadel of the Seven. As they passed, they destroyed those who attacked them but left others behind if they offered no harm.

Some of the Leath were left in convulsions by orbs of energy as Baba Yaga walked past. Neither she nor the Bitches were willing to risk that those they found in the Citadel wouldn't try to stab them in the back.

"I want those sonsabitches so bad I can taste it, John," she hissed. She stopped and the four stopped around her, keeping watch as she turned in a circle, eyes closed. "Down." She pointed. "Their energies are below us."

Eric reached into a bag on his hip and flipped it open, grabbing a handful of silver orbs and releasing them. "Give me a moment."

Bethany Anne didn't want to wait a moment, but given the many options, she couldn't be sure which way to go.

Five long minutes and two small gun battles later, they headed in a direction she felt was right.

They ended up in a large chamber that contained a table having eight points in the center, lights going up the sides, and what looked like the news playing on the video screens. Unfortunately, it was empty.

"*DAMMIT! WHERE ARE YOU, ASSHOLES?*" she screamed, her voice reverberating from the walls of the chamber.

She slammed an armored hand against the table and looked at the screens, then opened a communication line. "Dan?"

"Here." There was gunfire on the line. "One moment, please."

Baba Yaga tapped her fingers on the table as she waited. There was screaming in the background.

"Eat hot lead that really isn't lead but a very refined advanced metal that won't melt like lead in these weapons, you scurvy llama-sniffers!" Dan's voice lifted over the rapid fire of Jean Dukes weapons of some sort. "That's right!" Dan yelled again before he came back to the line.

"So, you were asking a question?" He seemed pleased with himself.

"'Scurvy llama-sniffers?'" she asked.

"I have a bet with Lance that I can curse without cursing this drop."

"Right," she replied. "Have you seen my contact?"

"No, nothing so far."

"Okay, keep an eye out." She shut off the comm as she watched the video, then her eyes narrowed as the clip of the Kurtherian finding Jerrleck in the shed started. The blood drained from her face. "Oh, shit," she whispered and looked around. "Tear this place apart. Those fuckers have to be somewhere," she commanded as she looked at her HUD, *willing* the information to come to her.

TOM, any ideas?

Look for hidden paths, doors, hallways, he supplied.

She walked from the room, her guys following her.

CHAPTER TWENTY-FOUR

Bethany Anne looked around, her hair floating as she tried to sense where her quarry had gone, then snapped her head to the right and walked over to a wall.

"Got something?" John asked as he kept his rifle in a ready position.

"Maybe," she admitted as she ran a hand along the wall.

"Bethany Anne, this is Admiral Thomas." His voice rang in her ear.

"Go ahead," she answered, still searching the wall.

"We found their superdreadnoughts," he told her drily.

"Should we expect incoming kinetics?" she asked.

"No, it's four against four, plus two more I'm pulling back off the planet. It seems that whatever your guy did, the planet is happy enough with you being there."

"Okay, six against four. They should be content with a stalemate. I just want *these* motherfuckers, and they can have their planet back." She pushed on a small square and it clicked. "YES!" She grinned and turned around. John and Darryl were already headed in her direction. John gently but firmly pushed her out of the way and stepped in first.

She crossed her arms, her red eyes watching as first John, then Darryl walked past her into the secret entrance. "Baba Yaga doesn't need you to go first," she grumped.

John's voice traveled back from the hallway. "Baba Yaga isn't going to get blasted into little particles if I can help it."

Scott spoke up as he walked into the room. "Deal with it." he told her as he snuck through the entrance. She walked in after him, and Eric brought up the rear.

The hallway was made of stone. Actually, soft stone. It had been excavated a long time in the past, and the floor had been smoothed more by use than tools, she figured.

There was a call over her system. "BA?" John commed.

"Yes?" she replied, looking at the first room and the weird artifacts that were on the walls.

"I'm sorry to say I found your contact," John replied. "He didn't make it, boss."

Baba Yaga turned and left the room. "Show me," she told him, ignoring Scott's comment about taking a guard with her as she raced to where her HUD said John was.

Within two rooms, she started seeing skeletons and the horror coming from TOM started to impress itself upon her.

What the hell? she asked.

I think they are doing something similar to what King Yoll did, TOM supplied, **although perhaps not as efficiently as he did.**

All these are Leath who were killed to use their bodies? She looked around in shock, slowing to a walk because the hallways were full of skeletons, many haphazardly tossed to the side. *Do they not even care about the dead?*

They would probably consider them just a sub-species, Bethany Anne.

"These were innocents!" Bethany Anne hissed as she turned a corner into a huge room with fresh dead lying in a pile, as if their spirits had just left the bodies and floated away.

John was standing guard over two bodies off to the side. One was a female Leath and the other was Jerrleck, who had crawled from where his body had been dropped over to the other and grabbed her hand.

Bethany Anne knelt and reached over to his face, running her hand down to close his eyes. She looked at the other body and realized she was his love, and her heart broke. Red tears started dropping down her face as she turned her head, taking in all the dead in this huge cavern. "This is injustice at its worst," she hissed.

"Boss," John told her, "keep it together. We can still find them."

Bethany Anne closed her eyes and released her senses. "That way," she ground out a moment later and pointed behind John. He turned around and started jogging in that direction. She caught up to him and then took off at a run.

"FUCK, BA!" John yelled and started running after her, but she had disappeared into the hallway. John followed, the three others running to catch up to him.

"Where *are* you fuckers?" she hissed, head turning left and right as she came up to an intersection. She turned right and followed her instincts as she took turn after turn, running as quickly as she could to find those who had been the masterminds.

There is someone ahead, TOM told her. **The mind...no, *minds*, are powerful.**

Bethany Anne slowed to a jog as she entered a cavern that was at least three stories tall, probably forty feet wide, and almost a football field in length. It was lit by old-style lights, which were more than bright enough for her to see in the cavern and spot the Leath in a robe at the other end of the cavern. It was holding a walking stick in its hand.

"So, Baba Yaga...or should I call you 'Empress?'" it hissed.

"You may call me 'Death,'" Bethany Anne supplied, walking toward the other.

"You may call *me* 'Terellet,'" it supplied, this time in a different voice.

Oh, shit, TOM stated. **We have a crazy Kurtherian here.**

That covers pretty much everyone in the seven clans, TOM.

Okay, I mean, "schizoid."

How does that even work? Bethany Anne checked the area to confirm she wasn't about to be caught in a trap. If she walked into a trap, John was going to be pissed.

No idea yet, TOM admitted.

That was when the mental blast hit Baba Yaga, the desire to bow before the creature working to overwhelm her ability to choose for herself.

"I think not, bitch." Baba Yaga pushed forward.

"How typical of the young," a male voice sneered from the female Leath's mouth.

"And bastard," Baba Yaga responded again, surprised.

I might have been wrong with that armchair psychological assertion, TOM amended. **How about we have two Kurtherians in one body?**

"Fucking hell!" Bethany Anne's eyes closed when a mental blast hit her, forcing her to focus on keeping her atoms together —or at least that was how it felt.

"A...little...help...TOM?" she ground out, her hands pushing on the sides of her head to keep it from exploding.

Stop pushing on your skull or you will kill yourself! he commanded, freezing some of her muscles himself. **Your strength is being used against you.**

"*Gott Verdammt* sneaky fucking aliens," Bethany Anne grated. "Give me a straight-up fight."

Not going to happen, TOM remarked. **Sorry.**

"You have some support, some help." The female sounded

impressed. "I'm surprised your kind would have melded with anyone, Essiehkorian."

Bethany Anne was fighting to not do something which would kill her.

Mind if I speak?

Be my guest, she ground out. *Not that you aren't already. I can't trust myself to move my own fucking limbs at the moment.*

"Do you know the difference between you and me, Phraim-'Eh scum?" TOM's voice emanated from Baba Yaga's mouth.

"You are weak, blinded by a limited mindset on what it takes to Ascend a sub-species, and have chosen a weak vessel?" it replied.

"Hardly," TOM replied. Bethany Anne's arm lifted with a Jean Dukes pistol held in it. "I work *with* my host, not against her."

The Leath's eyes opened in surprise and it dove to the side when TOM, using Baba Yaga's hand, squeezed the trigger.

A scream sounded from the other side of the cavern and an overwhelming amount of Etheric energy slammed into Bethany Anne, knocking her on her ass. She pressed her eyes shut and slammed her hands into the rock floor as the pain came at her in waves.

"Boss!" John called.

She could hear his steps running toward her. "Stop!" She willed a hand up. "Kurtherian!" She pointed toward the other side.

"No one there, BA," John told her, kneeling next to her. "Quit beating the ground. You'll break your hand."

Bethany Anne and TOM both froze in shock, then she rolled over to get up, pushing off the ground with a knee and one hand. "That cock-sucking psychotic cretin," she gasped.

She, he, *whatever,* **tricked us,** TOM supplied. **Don't go anywhere again without support.**

Got that right, she admitted. *At least this time,* she amended.

"Where are the others?" she asked, working to clear her head as she started walking toward the other side of the cavern. As she asked the question, the rest of the Bitches came running out of the hallway behind them.

It took the five of them five more minutes and a little backtracking, but they finally walked up a hallway that led to the surface. Bethany Anne looked at the large valley walls surrounding this location, and the grass at the bottom. There was a flat rock in the middle of the valley and a river running off to the right.

"Gone." She looked up. "Get me my ship!" she snarled, her eyes glowing red. "I'll find those fucking killers and pull their Kurtherian asses out of their mouths."

"Boss," John pressed as Baba Yaga gazed at him, no emotion on her face. "We got cleanup to do. We won. They aren't here." He pointed back the way they had come. "The planet doesn't want them. The Leath can be free, but not if Empress Bethany Anne can't be found to confirm their freedom and lay down the plans that will help them heal and move on."

"He's right," Scott added. "Everyone needs BA now, not Baba Yaga."

"Stephen needs you," Eric reminded her.

"And Peter," Darryl added. "He lost Todd."

The red eyes flared as she looked from one man to the next, all of them looking back and then nodding their agreement with John's assessment.

"*FUCKING SHIT!*" she screamed before she turned around and walked back into the tunnel. Her four guards looked at each other before following her.

Yoll Space, Yollin System

The majestic ships were in formation and the Empress, in full regalia, stood silent as the coffins were arrayed in the massive docking bay of *ArchAngel II*. Two had gold flags adorning them.

The Empress walked from casket to casket, touching each one, her lips moving before she went to the next and did the same thing.

There were one hundred and seventy-two caskets.

Bethany Anne stopped at the first of the two gold-draped caskets and put a hand on it. "Maria, you knew your duty, and at the end, you kept the enemy from harming your Guardian as the Marines have been doing since we left Earth so many generations ago. May you gently go into the future that God has provided you, to rest knowing your sacrifice was not in vain, that the Leath were liberated through your actions."

She stepped to the next coffin, laying her hand on it more firmly.

"Todd, you knew your duty, and at the end, you kept the enemy from harming your friend, your Guardian, as you have been doing since we left Earth so many generations ago. May you gently go into the future God has provided, to rest knowing your sacrifice was not now or ever in vain, that the Leath were liberated through your actions and that your friend was saved in body, if perhaps not in spirit. May your final letter give him solace as he walks into his future without your hand on his shoulder to guide him through the misadventures to come." She reached up to wipe away her tears.

As she walked to the podium, she stopped to touch the casket that represented Jerrleck of Leath, honored forever in the Etheric Empire as the sacrifice who enabled the Leath to celebrate their own freedom.

Stepping up to the podium, she turned to address those who stood at attention behind the caskets and those across the Empire's worlds who watched the live feed of this video.

"It is with a humble heart," she started, looking forward, shoulders straight, "that I consign these brave souls to our star, releasing their atoms to float freely in the brilliance of light and the creation of heat, representing life."

She nodded to the caskets. "These are the final souls, the final payment, which we hope concludes the Etheric Empire's effort to eradicate the Kurtherians from Leath." She bit her tongue, keeping her anger and hurt in check. "The Leath are a free people now, and they will be allowed to create their own government as they wish. Our disagreement was always with their false gods, not the people themselves."

She reached up and cleared a tear. "I will sign the Treaty of Peace on Leath in fourteen days, formalizing the cessation of hostilities, and participate in a discussion of reparations between our peoples. At that time, the Leath will decide whether they wish to have the Etheric Empire as friend or foe."

She glanced at the coffins. "I, for one, would wish them to choose 'friend,' for too many have died on both sides for me to wish more to lie in coffins like these should they choose 'foe.'"

She stepped back from the podium and General Lance Reynolds and Admiral Thomas took her place, taking command of the ceremony as the caskets slowly lifted one by one to head out of the bay and slip through the force shield between them and space.

Heading toward the star and their final resting place.

Bethany Anne glanced into the crowd and caught Stephen's eyes. She dipped her head.

At least the universe, bitch that she was, had given her *one* back.

The QBS *Princess Alexandria,* In Transit

Franath D'Tzaa, the D'tereth vid reporter, touched the recording symbol again after reviewing her notes. She looked up into the tired face of Etheric Empress Bethany Anne, who waited patiently for her questions.

"You seem exhausted," Franath commented. "Don't worry, we aren't recording," she told the Empress.

"It's okay. I *am* tired," Bethany Anne replied. "I'm tired of death and destruction. I'm tired of those who do evil walking away from the judgment of their evil. I'm tired of friends I've loved for hundreds of years and those I barely knew dying. I'm especially tired of my friends dying for *me*," she finished.

Franath looked at her video camera, which actually *had* recorded the Empress' comment. She reached over and hit two buttons.

One to stop the recording, and the other to delete the information that had been stored on the camera. She turned back to the Empress. "You know what?"

Bethany Anne shook her head.

"Perhaps the camera is having problems, and you need more time to deal with everything. It's like all of the weight of the universe has been placed on your shoulders and no one realizes what it does to you." Franath looked around. "Besides, the lighting in this room is horrible." She turned back to Bethany Anne. "Maybe tomorrow?" she asked, a smile on her face.

Bethany Anne nodded and smiled in appreciation. "Tomorrow it is, Franath."

CHAPTER TWENTY-FIVE

<u>Planet Leath, Main Continent, Noel-ni Consulate</u>

The Noel-ni ambassador adjusted his official robes and smiled into the reporter's camera. His teeth were freshly cleaned, as bright as he could get them.

He'd wanted to look his best, and he hoped the reporter showed his good side. She was famous for her original interviews with the Etheric Empress. She had traveled here to Leath with the Empress, he had been told.

"Welcome, Ambassador," the reporter started.

He nodded his head. "Reporter Franath, it is a pleasure."

"Now that the Empress of the Etheric Empire is here and formalizing the peace plans with the Leath, what do you believe the future holds for the other societies which have been militarizing? With the Leath and the Etheric Empire not focusing their guns on each other, do we risk having another war break out?"

"So, pulling no punches, is that right?" He hissed a laugh. "I like your style of reporting, Franath. As it stands, our people have been studying this same issue for many months. Of course, our internal conversations intensified when we got word that the Leath and Empire war seemed to be concluded." He tried to smile without showing too many teeth. "As the two systems who have been at war the longest, they have the largest and most well-organized militaries."

"So, they would be hard targets?" she asked.

"Well, certainly hard targets, but also the ones which could choose to become aggressive with the least provocation. It behooves the other advanced societies like the Noel-ni to tread lightly when we negotiate with either the Leath or the Etheric Empire."

"It is true that the Noel-ni have a better relationship with the Leath, is it not?"

The ambassador waved his hand. "We do not have a *bad* relationship with the Empire, even though we had a rough time after the assassination attempt many years ago. We have proven to the Empire, I believe, we had nothing to do with the setup or the attempt. So, while we do not have bad relations with the Empire, we have stronger relations with the Leath."

Franath looked down at her notes. "There is a rumor that in closed-door meetings, there is talk about creating a stronger alliance of those who fear the Empire. Specifically, now that they do not need to focus on the Leath, the Empire worries others."

"Well," the ambassador hesitated a moment, "let's just say that the Noel-ni would prefer to look for political solutions, of which there are many, instead of a martial solution." He pointed up. "As we speak, the massive firepower of the Etheric Empire is floating above our heads. Should they want to, they could claim the Leath as an unwilling partner in their Empire, could they not?"

"Depends on if you believe the declaration of Empress Bethany Anne," Franath countered. "If you do, then one doesn't need to worry. If you believe she is underhanded, then one would have more cause."

"Correct," the ambassador agreed, and purposely looked off-camera and back. "And we will know in just three hours what her plans are."

"Thank you, Ambassador." Franath nodded to him, then turned to the camera. "This is Franath D'Tzaa, reporting from the home planet of the Leath, where in just a few hours, the war between the Leath and the Etheric Empire is scheduled to officially end in peace between the two peoples."

"Annddd...off," Franath heard someone call. She turned back to the ambassador. "Thank you, sir."

"Certainly." He beckoned her closer, and she leaned in. "You *do* know that even in peace, there is much anxiety and many wishing it to change, yes?"

Franath nodded her head sadly. "I do, Ambassador. I'm a big girl, and I'm well aware that for some, peace is their worst nightmare."

The ambassador stood up and shook her hand once she was standing. It was a habit other races had learned from the humans, meaning that they had nothing in their hands to stab you with.

In a way, it said something about a species when they greeted each other with a proclamation that said they didn't have a weapon at hand.

"I believe your life is only going to get more interesting, Reporter Franath." He smiled, this time showing all his teeth. "Should you wish to chat again, please feel free to call my office."

"Thank you," she replied, watching the Noel-ni ambassador shake a few more hands on his way out and wondering what he had meant by his last comment. She shuddered as a cold wave passed over her, and turned to her crew. "Let's pack up."

Planet Leath, Primary City, First Stadium

Bethany Anne looked out across the stadium, thinking back to so many years before when, instead of a convocation of peace, she had battled a Kurtherian to the death in an arena like this to free a different people.

She had wanted to have a quiet ceremony and signing of the

documents, but the Leath would have none of it. They had been playing and replaying Jerrleck's last video, where he explained what he had found out, and what had happened to him.

Word had gotten out that the Etheric Empress knew what had really happened in his death, and they all wanted to know.

There had been a request for her to make a formal speech to the Leath people and finally she had relented, but they had to understand she would be armored.

Not as a conqueror, but for protection should anyone wish her harm.

She pushed down the anger she continued to feel at the Kurtherians' leaving, her vengeance unquenched. She still had haunting dreams of the skeletons littering the hallways and subterranean floors beneath the very building where she would sign the peace accords.

She shoved it all into a box that shook violently in her subconscious, having to stay locked up right now so she could smile for the people in her Empire and here in the Leath system as well.

She stepped up to the podium and looked around. The massive stadium was not unlike a human stadium, since form often followed function. The architecture was a bit more like you might find in Roma, to be sure, but it was basically the same.

Pack the people in, while giving them a view of what was below.

The stadium had massive screens, and Bethany Anne could see her own face plastered on a video screen that was easily ten stories high.

She chuckled to herself.

What are you chuckling about? TOM asked.
I'm just thinking I'm happy I don't have acne problems.
Kurtherian enhancements. You will always look amazing.
Well, that's something.
Until you don't.

Wait, what? she asked.

I'll explain it some other time. For now, you look perfect.

TOM, you're an ass sometimes.

Love you, too.

Right back at you, PITA.

Bethany Anne opened her mouth. "To those who travel the stars with us, I say 'hello and greetings.' To those Leath with me here, I say 'Peace and comfort to you.'" The shouts of encouragement provided a moment for her to smile, feeling good at the outcome after the decades of war.

"I am here to tell you that the Leath are a great people." She looked at the crowd before her, then at those in the stands as her voice rang out, strong and confident. "Not a defeated people, but a liberated one. Liberated by a rebellion led by a Leath and supported by like-minded warriors on a path to understanding the future for all peoples, not bent on the destruction of others. There is harmony in peace, but peace often requires stout arms, strong backs, and a willingness to die for the abstract beliefs one professes."

She looked down for a moment as if in prayer before looking back at the cameras. "This Leath I speak of will always be honored in our history, and we hope in yours. His name was Jerrleck, and at one point, he was Prime One in Intelligence. He was perhaps the Leath in the best position to recognize the lies being fed to your people."

"Once upon a time, as he shared with us, he and others worked together to form a rebellion, but luck was not on their side. Why?" She looked up again. "Because the Kurtherians could read minds, and they recognized the signals that Jerrleck had become disaffected with their rule. They valued his services but not his questions."

She looked down again but continued her story. "He was brainwashed into giving up his love, the leader of the first rebellion. Unknown to him, the Seventh of the Seven took her body as its own to allow it to continue the facade of representing the Leath people."

The stadium, given the number of bodies it held, was completely quiet.

Looking up, she concluded, "We found Jerrleck in a large cavern. He was dead, but he had struggled after his torture to reach his love's dead body, discarded when Terellet took another sacrifice. He died holding her hand, perhaps granted the opportunity to love in the afterlife when it had been denied him by the Phraim-'Eh in this life."

"What he gave us with his sacrifice is the opportunity to join together today and agree to peace between our peoples."

In the top row, a few voices faintly started chanting in their language, "Peace, peace, peace…"

Those around them picked it up, and within thirty seconds, the words echoed throughout the stadium and spilled into the city, and the people declared it to be true.

There *would* be peace.

Bethany Anne nodded to those in the stadium and walked off the podium

Bethany Anne smiled at the right times, her radiant face picture-perfect as John and the others maintained a vigilant guard, trying to stay discreet. She wore her armor, and her helmet was clipped to her hip should she need it.

A bullet to the head could, and would, kill her.

For the cameras, however, she placed her helmet at her side and smiled as those in the Upper House for the Leath signed the peace accords.

For the Etheric Empire, only one signature was needed.

For the Leath, there were fifty-one.

By the end, she figured that maybe fifteen of those were actually movers and shakers in Leath society, but the other signatories would perhaps feel obligated to adhere to the spirit and not just the words of the agreement.

Either way, she figured that was for others to deal with. She had a task to complete.

And complete it, she would.

By the time the agreement was signed, and multiple copies had been made and received by both parties, she was tired, and all of those around her could tell. She called John over. "Do you think you can block for me a moment?"

John looked around. "From whom?" he asked.

"Let me slip out one of the hidden doors and take a few breaths alone, just for a few minutes." She looked around. "I don't think suddenly disappearing is the way I should exit from here."

John chuckled. "Probably not." He looked to his left. "There is one of those in the room next to us." He nodded. "Do you see Scott over there?"

"Yes, of course."

"Meet you there in five."

"Bastard," she huffed. "You're making me pay to play hooky awhile."

"Well, you *are* the Empress," he replied and casually walked away. Bethany Anne walked to a couple of reporters, gave them a few words, and kept strolling.

When she made it over to John, he looked down at her. "That was ten minutes."

She shrugged. "Maybe next time you will let me out right away."

"Uh-huh," he replied, and Scott casually walked over, blocking her from view as she slipped behind a curtain, quickly finding the small square indentation and letting herself into the hallway.

Bethany Anne walked down the darkened passageway, unerringly working her way past the skeletons, who reminded her of her purpose.

She went through the caverns, past the bodies that hadn't yet been picked up by those working to clean up and entomb the sacrifices from the past.

She continued walking toward the private landing area in the valley the Seven had used to escape, and where she had been required to turn back for the sake of the living.

She unhooked and dropped her helmet, tossing it to the side as her armor's boots crunched over the soft rock.

It rolled around and stopped next to the rock wall in the passageway.

>> **Do you want me to lighten the armor's load?**<< ADAM asked.

No, I want my path to be found by Bethany Anne's friends, she replied.

Aren't they your friends too? TOM asked.

Perhaps, Bethany Anne agreed, *but they might be a bit miffed.*

TOM watched as Bethany Anne's synapses started firing quickly. **What are you doing?**

Her body was undergoing massive changes. Normally not a problem, except *he wasn't the one doing it.*

Crunch, crunch, crunch.

She took off her right glove and tossed it to the side.

Crunch, crunch, crunch.

Moments later, her left glove went to the other side.

Crunch, crunch, crunch.

Her hair reflected white in the pitiful light of the hallway as she made one final turn to head out.

Crunch, crunch, crunch.

Death's Avatar came into the light as a gleaming black ship floated gently down to hover just above the grass. The rear cargo ramp was almost down when a white-haired, ink-black woman wearing blood-red armor jumped up to land softly and enter the ship. The door started closing as the ship rose into the sky, turning to the right and then simply disappearing.

TOM, she finally answered his question, **there is no fucking way I'm letting the assholes who did that get away. The Etheric Empire doesn't need me right now, but Jerrleck and**

the others represented by those skeletons need to know they will be avenged.

The ship broke atmosphere, then it Gated. The last communication between the two floating in their minds as they disappeared.

And I'm just the motherfucker to do it.

TOM noticed that her mental voice was guttural now too, and wondered what the Kurtherians had unleashed.

Whatever it was, he almost felt pity for them. Then he thought about the skeletons and the body of the previous Prime Intelligence officer and hardened his heart.

Wherever Baba Yaga went, he was with her one hundred percent.

No matter how far they ran, no matter how many years or planets or systems it took to track them down…

Those Kurtherians were going to die.

FINIS

EPILOGUE

John lowered his head into his hand, trying to understand just what the fuck had gone wrong as he, Eric, Scott, and Darryl walked the floor of the valley. They had found the trail Bethany Anne left easily enough. Her helmet and gloves were distinct giveaways.

Her boot prints in the rock had been a nice touch.

He looked at his HUD and confirmed he would accept the incoming call.

"Yeah, Lance," John answered as he looked around the valley.

"Anything?" Lance asked. "We got it covered on this end. You guys just need to stay out of sight and hop a ride back up here."

"By 'got it covered,' you mean…"

"We lied our asses off," Lance answered. "Told them she wanted to let the Leath have the floor without her taking the wind out of their sails and all that."

"So who is standing in for her at the party?"

"I got voted in. Seems my rugged good looks make the Leath feel comfortable around me."

John chuckled. "Yeah." Darryl was bending over to look at something on the ground. "Well, it might have to do with the fact *you* didn't tell anyone you would spend the rest of your life hunting the Kurtherians down and killing them."

"I didn't wear armor to the event, either," Lance agreed. "So I'm the easily-pushed-aside military leader."

"What the fuck do they think you have been doing, rubber-stamping everything for Admiral Thomas and Bethany Anne?" John asked as Scott walked over to Darryl, showing him something in his hand.

"Maybe?" Lance replied. "Look, that doesn't bother me. Let them think whatever they want; it will help us in the future. I'm too old to worry about shit like that. In a minute I've got to get into a fresh monkey suit and get back to the meeting. What do you know so far?"

"I think I'm about to find out," John replied as Darryl and Scott walked over to him. "Wait one, Lance."

"Okay."

John paused the call and put out his hand, and Darryl handed over a tiny strand—a filament, really. John's lips pressed together as he pulled it closer to verify it really was what he thought it was.

"Well, that tears it." He looked at Darryl and Scott, who both nodded. "All right." He put the call back to active.

"Lance?"

"Yes."

John blew out a breath of air. "We might have a serious problem."

"We *already* have a serious problem," Lance told him. "We have to find the Empress of the Empire, who is now AWOL."

John lifted the white hair and looked at it once more before shaking his head. "No. We don't have to capture the Empress, Lance," John told him as he looked at the sky. "We have to capture Death."

John could hear Lance sigh on the other end of the phone. "Well, *fuck*."

"Yup," John agreed. "She's got the *Shinigami* and a head start, and we have fuck all."

"Not exactly." Lance thought about it for a moment. "We know what she looks like, we have access to Nathan's contacts, and we know what she wants to accomplish. We just need to use our assets to find those seven Kurtherian *fucktards* before she does. If we do, we can probably get a message through ADAM or TOM and talk some sense into her."

"Are either of them answering you at the moment?" John inquired.

"No, did you expect them to?"

"Not really," John admitted. "It would be nice, but she knows we all would take the proverbial bullet for her, so that doesn't surprise me."

"All right, you guys ready for pickup?" Lance asked. "We need to get tonight's stuff out of the way before we get back to discussing how the hell we find a pissed-off Baba Yaga who doesn't want to be found and talk some *Gott Verdammt* sense into her."

"Well, we could always follow the clues Baba Yaga will leave behind. And yes, we are ready for pickup," John answered his earlier question.

"What clues?" Lance asked as John heard a mumble on Lance's end of the phone. "ETA ten minutes."

"The clues will be all the dead bodies, Lance." John chuckled. "*All* the dead bodies."

The two men stayed on the phone for a moment, both lost in their own thoughts.

"We are going to need to put out some type of warning," Lance replied. "I'm not sure she's thinking right, John."

John shook his head. "She's thinking right, Lance. It's just not the right *we* want her to think. She ditched us, left us clues, disappeared from a very protected world, and took off with the most advanced ship the Empire has ever built. In fact, she was adamant that we needed to build new sensors to test if the *Shinigami* could be seen by *us*." John whirled his finger in a circle to get everyone to come over. "She's been planning this for a while. Or, she has been thinking that it *could* happen since we started designing that ship."

"Well, damn. If she wasn't my daughter and the Empress, I'd be duly impressed." Lance sighed. "I'd better start looking for the other ways she took care of business before leaving so I know what else will bite me in the ass."

John chuckled. "I'd look for a monkey suit that looks like it fits really well for the Leath reception." He didn't get a reply for a moment from Lance. John's eyes narrowed. "Nooo…she didn't?"

"Yes," Lance replied, a small amount of humor in his voice. "Yes, she did." There was a comment on the other side of the line. "That was my five-minute warning. Let me go put on the monkey suit Bethany Anne gave me *three days ago* as an early birthday gift and go down to placate the natives."

"Sucks to be you. See you on the *ArchAngel*."

"See you there," Lance agreed, and the call disconnected.

John looked at the other three. "Boys, we've got our work cut out for us."

Scott put up his hand. "Let me get this straight." He put up his first finger, "We have to find Bethany Anne?"

"Baba Yaga," John replied. "I don't think she's acting as Bethany Anne right now."

"Oh, so this gets better," Scott replied. "We have to find *Baba Yaga*." Second finger went up. "In the most sophisticated ship anyone knows about."

The third finger went up. "Who could literally be anywhere, since she has jump capabilities."

The fourth finger went up. "With probably the smartest AI in existence in her brain."

The fifth finger went up. "As well as a Kurtherian." He gave John the fish-eye. "In case anyone forgot."

Scott put up his second hand and the sixth finger. "On a personal quest to deliver Justice—with her bare hands, most likely. She didn't take us, so she probably doesn't want us to find her."

He paused for a moment, so Darryl waved him to put up a finger and added, "She is rich as hell, so I bet we can't track the money."

Eric waved to Scott, who put up another finger. "She knows about Tabitha's toys, and even made some suggestions on what to create."

John made an ugly face and waved to Scott, who put up finger number nine. "She has all our loadouts on the *Shinigami*. She probably has enough suits of armor for a small army on that ship."

Scott looked at the three guys. "C'mon, I've got nine up. I just need one more to make it a standard ten factors why finding Bethany Anne is going to be a cold-hearted bitch."

They all just looked at Scott, who sighed and put up the tenth finger. "Those Kurtherians are fucked."

"Baba Yaga *is* a cold-hearted bitch." Eric slapped Scott on the back. "But," he looked at his friends, thinking back to Earth, "she is *our* cold-hearted bitch, and she has four Bitches who will rip apart the universe to find her and bring her back safely."

Eric put his hand out. Darryl put his on Eric's, followed by Scott, and then John placed his on the top.

Eric looked around. "Four Bitches for Bethany Anne."

John nodded. "Until we find her—or bury everyone who keeps us from getting her back."

"*Ad aeternitatem*," the four voices swore in unison.

The *G'laxix Sphaea* uncloaked as it settled on the landing pad at the bottom of the valley.

Kael-ven's voice came over their comm units. "Taxi sent by General Reynolds. Anyone here wanting to just disappear?"

"Hell, yes," John commed back. The four turned towards the ship, which was lowering the loading ramp. "We have a friend to catch."

"Count me in," Kael-ven told them. "Even if I have to steal this ship to do it."

The chuckles of those who loved the Empress floated on the wind in that valley long after the ship had left.

Finis...no, really ;-)

CAPTURE DEATH

The Story Continues with book 20, *Capture Death*.

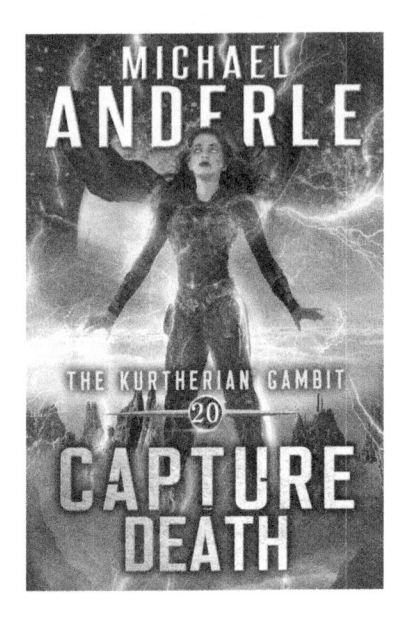

Available now at Amazon and on Kindle Unlimited

AUTHOR NOTES - MICHAEL ANDERLE

Thank you for making your way through nineteen *motherfucking* books to read these notes. It means the world to me!

In the last seven days I have written fifty thousand words to finish this book, that was written all over the world. I started and ended in the United States (Las Vegas, New York City, Charlotte, Miami, St. Petersburg), traveled to Germany (Frankfurt, Berlin), back through England (London), and swept through Brazil (Rio) and on planes traveling between.

What do I have to say?

A lot.

I'm writing this as I am being driven between Las Vegas, Nevada and La Puente, California. I'm staring at the mirrored power generators near Primm Valley Golf Course off the right side of the car in the desert.

Those are some BRIGHT SOBs, I gotta tell you.

As I write this, it is just four days from the two-year anniversary of releasing that very first Bethany Anne book.

Death Becomes Her.

Wow, life has changed in just two short years.

Last night in the Lounge Bar in the Aria Hotel I typed 'Finis' after Chapter Twenty-five. Then I went and played a few slot machines—which informed me I should write more books because I play slots like I play video games.

Which is to say, they are a fun diversion, but I should never consider becoming a professional gambler because slot games make me their *bitch*.

It was late enough that I had a real desire to eat, so I got a seat in Javier's at the Aria and placed my butt down at one of the tables around the bar. Pulled the laptop out of my laptop bag, opened it after placing it on the table, and started typing again.

Thus, we have the Epilogue.

Tomorrow I will have dinner with Craig Martelle at Bootleggers down on Las Vegas Blvd South, and we will sit in the booth where Elvis Presley ate, right next to where the Rat Pack used to sit and eat.

(After the fact note: it was Halloween and they were BOOKED... We got a booth—just not the Elvis booth—and holy crap *we overloaded on carbs.)*

I didn't know Craig two years ago. I didn't know TS (Scott) Paul, Martha Carr, Justin Sloan, CM Raymond or LE Barbant, or a SLEW of other authors and fans and readers who have supported the growth of Kurtherian Gambit over the last two years.

I'll meet many of them this week as Craig's first 20Books-To50k conference at Sam's Town happens, and we and over four hundred other authors join together to work on the business side of writing books.

I'm going to be speaking each day at the conference. Speaking while being one of the most successful Indie Publishing authors this year, due to *one* woman.

Bethany Anne.

Bethany Anne and the power of the connected readers who pulled together and cheered that Anderle guy and the other authors who write with him. Some of my collaborators are seasoned writers who crafted stories before we ever worked together, and others trusted me to help them with getting their first story done and published.

It has been a hell of a ride, and right now I can see on the horizon to when the final story in Bethany Anne's third arc concludes.

You see, I've always wanted Bethany Anne's books to be about *Bethany Anne*, not her and someone else (in this case, Michael.)

On February 14th, 2018 I will release the fourth and final book in The Second Dark Ages (Michael's stories) and the last book in Bethany Anne's arc. I will release them simultaneously on Valentine's Day because they finish the tale of two lovers who would not be separated by death, time, responsibilities, or distance.

It's time we provide a conclusion for Bethany Anne and her responsibility to protect the Earth.

It's time to allow her a little peace to enjoy Michael.

Then we'll take Bethany Anne and some of her friends and release them upon the universe itself. I've started planning the next Bethany Anne (with Michael) series for later in 2018.

I already know *why* they are moving out into the bigger Universe (well, several whys) and how they interact within the Age of Expansion inside the larger Kurtherian Gambit Universe. How Ranger Tabitha and Barnabas' stories intertwine, and what the teams do *next*.

Plus, I think it will be good for Bethany Anne to be allowed to be herself a little without the responsibility of an Empire around her neck.

Capture Death (TKG20) is next, and in it I am going to cut loose on the aspect of Bethany Anne that I personally fell in love with during those first few scenes I wrote two years ago.

Give a woman hell-bent on justice the power and ability to make change, then see what she does with it.

Perhaps she will go a little dark. We shall find out when **Capture Death** comes out Christmas Day, 2017.

Click here to Get Capture Death Now.

I smiled as I just typed that last sentence, because I thought about how last year, Christmas 2016, I released **The Dark Messiah** and this year it will be, **Capture Death**. Neither are exactly the most seasonally appropriate stories, but I would be willing to have a fun discussion that Christmas is about giving to others…

And hope.

Perhaps not the same hope as the Christ, but hope of a *sort*.

Last year Michael the Archangel brought hope to Earth by delivering a hardnosed answer to those who would try to use strength to force others to do their will.

This Christmas we have a story of a woman who feels to her core the need to protect. To be the mother to everyone whom these Phraim-'Eh Kurtherians, the Seven, might harm, and to complete her promise to honor her own dead. To bring hope to those who do not know they need it.

If Bethany Anne has her way, they will never wake up to the fact they were in danger.

Because trouble will be taken care of while they sleep.

I'd like to dedicate **Capture Death** to those who have been or are in any way, shape, or form part of a group that protects others: first responders, detectives, military, Coast Guard, medical…it doesn't matter.

Baba Yaga is for you.

Ad Aeternitatem,
Michael Anderle
November 2, 2017

BOOKS BY MICHAEL ANDERLE

Sign up for the LMBPN email list to be notified of new releases and special deals!

https://lmbpn.com/email/

For a complete list of books by Michael Anderle, please visit:

www.lmbpn.com/ma-books/

CONNECT WITH THE AUTHOR

Connect with Michael Anderle

Website: http://lmbpn.com

Email List: https://michael.beehiiv.com/

https://www.facebook.com/LMBPNPublishing

https://twitter.com/MichaelAnderle

https://www.instagram.com/lmbpn_publishing/

https://www.bookbub.com/authors/michael-anderle

Made in the USA
Las Vegas, NV
24 June 2024